Midnight Escape

Rebecca Deel

DEDICATION

To my amazing husband.

ACKNOWLEDGMENTS

Cover design by Melody Simmons.

CHAPTER ONE

Brenna Mason jammed her key in the lock and shoved open the door. "Dana?" The knob banged against the wall and bounced back, slamming her suitcase against her knees. She scowled, shouldered past the door, and dragged her luggage into the living room.

She set her laptop case by her feet. The blinds were drawn, the room gloomy. The cream- colored couch glowed in the dimness. Her throat tightened. Maybe she had overreacted and nothing was wrong. Her sister could be mad at her since their last conversation ended on a sour note. Brenna had told her sister the truth, even if it was unpleasant to hear.

Dana's bedroom door remained closed. Had she been out late last night? If so, she was dead to the world. Brenna shivered. Bad choice of words, no doubt a result of her chosen occupation. Usually her sister woke at the slightest sound. "Dana?"

Brenna opened the bedroom door and peered inside the darkened interior of her sister's room. The room was empty, bed made. As usual, nothing out of place.

Could Dana have forgotten Brenna was supposed to fly in this morning? Her lips curved. Better chance her sister left her waiting at the airport to find her own way to the apartment as a way of making her point. She didn't need or want her big sister meddling in her life.

Brenna noticed the message light flashing on the answering machine and pressed the playback button. All ten messages were from her.

Her stomach knotted.

Where was Dana?

Eli Wolfe shifted the camera, pressed a button and zoomed in on the woman giving Marcos Sartelli a piece of her mind. He would love to hear the words spilling from her gorgeous pink lips. The whiskey-colored eyes sparked, a scowl dominating what would have otherwise been a cover model's face.

"Well, Marcos," Eli muttered, "What did you do to tick her off?" He snapped another series of pictures, captured the woman's image for later identification. If she wasn't the type of woman who operated in Marcos's world, he'd track her down and warn her off. She didn't want to play in the Sartelli sandbox. This one was a step up from his usual arm candy.

Sweat trickled down Eli's forehead. He wiped his face with the bottom of his untucked shirt and flexed his cramping arm muscles. The spunky brunette reappeared in his camera lens, her cheeks flushed from more than the killer mid-July heat in downtown Nashville.

Yet again, Eli wished he'd learned to read lips. Movement to his left snagged his attention and, shifting the camera, he sucked in a silent, steamy breath. Great. "Nice going, beautiful. Marcos's guard dog is on your six." His favorite guard dog, too. Juan Mendoza lumbered into Eli's line of sight, 300 pounds of muscle and mean on a six-foot body topped by a cue-ball head.

Mendoza stepped closer to the woman, his hand slipping into a drooping pocket. Oh, this wasn't going to be good. Eli scowled in the woman's direction. Did she realize the danger she was in? The guard probably had his favorite weapon of choice, a .357 silver-plated magnum, secreted in that pocket, a gun which could blow a hole a mile wide in that gorgeous body.

Eli hadn't wanted Sartelli to know he'd returned to town just yet, but he couldn't stand to see the brunette's furious expression dissolve into one of terror. Mendoza crowded into her personal space enough she stepped closer to the black limo waiting at the curb for Sartelli.

"Not that way, beautiful," Eli said. He sighed. No help for it but to distract the construction magnate and his two-legged canine and hustle the woman out of the line of fire.

He slipped around the corner of the building, tossed his camera into the glove box of his black Camaro and locked the car. He tugged on his Nashville Sounds baseball cap, retraced his steps and sauntered up the sidewalk toward his quarry, whistling "You Ain't Nothin' But a Hound Dog." Who didn't love Elvis?

He drew within a few feet of the trio, and the woman's words drifted on the humid breeze to Eli. "The last time anybody saw her, she was in your company, Mr. Sartelli. I will find her, even if I have to go through your yard ape to do it."

Yard ape? Eli whistled louder. Yep, perfect description of the leg breaker five feet in front of him. The men swiveled in his direction. The woman's attention shifted to Eli, curiosity etched on her face.

"Wolfe." Sartelli sneered. "Didn't realize you were back in town."

"Miss me, Marcos?"

"About as much as I miss my mother-in-law."

"Oh, that hurts, man." Sartelli hated the 85-year-old Sicilian native. If he didn't need the old woman's money, Eli doubted the owner of Sartelli Construction would still be married to the old lady's daughter.

Sartelli eyed Mendoza and inclined his head toward the waiting vehicle. "Escort Ms. Mason to the car. We will continue this discussion in cooler surroundings."

Eli stepped up beside the lady and slid his arm around her waist, pressing his fingers into her side. He hoped she understood his silent message to play along with his charade. "Now, Marcos, you can't take off with my girl. You already have a wife and a woman on the side. Go poach on someone else's territory."

Ms. Mason drew in a startled breath. "But . . ."

Oh, man. So much for understanding his telepathic message to keep quiet. Must be out of practice. Yeah, he'd get right on that as soon as he rescued the gorgeous brunette from Sartelli and Mendoza. Time for Plan B. Though turning his back on the two went against all his training and made the nape of his neck itch, Eli swung around and gathered the woman into his arms. "Don't worry, sugar. Marcos won't mind talking to us later. Right now, I want someplace quiet and private. I missed you." His hands tightened on her arms as his lips brushed her ear. If she fought, Eli would have a much harder time pulling off the scam. Might work anyway if he begged her to forgive him for their fight before he left town. He could plead stupidity which he figured Marcos would buy into in a heartbeat.

Always assuming, of course, the lady didn't expose the game by claiming he was crazy. Silent laughter rolled through his mind. Some nights he'd agree with the assessment, afraid of losing his mind to the ghosts walking in his dreams. At least they no longer haunted his days. Progress of sorts, he supposed.

A city bus pulled to a stop beside the limo. Under cover of the engine's roar, Eli whispered in the woman's ear. "Play along, sugar, or we'll leave this street in matching body bags."

As he hoped, his warning shocked the woman into silence.

"She's your woman?" Marcos's voice was ripe with suspicion.

The lady in question stiffened in his arms. Probably objected to the tone and terminology unless she objected to being manhandled by a stranger, even one known for his charm with the ladies. Eli tossed a grin over his shoulder at Sartelli and turned back to the woman in his arms and kissed her tempting pink lips. Despite the danger making his skin crawl, the Mason woman's sweetness captured his attention. He lingered longer than he'd intended for the effect. Even if she slugged him later, the pain would be worth the taste of pure, warm honey.

Eli lifted his head. He smiled at her stunned expression. Hand cupping the back of her head, he gently pressed her face into his neck to hide any telling expressions. A quarter of a turn and his gun hand was hidden by their bodies which were still plastered together. A perfect fit, too, although this was a lousy time to notice that fact. "She's incredible, isn't she?"

Sartelli's eyes narrowed. "You are lying."

"Lying?" He grinned, though the muscles in his body tensed. What if Sartelli didn't buy his story? Eli calculated the odds and decided he'd better convince the man of his sincerity, fast. Marcos was sure to have at least one weapon and his yard ape more than likely had two on him with more stashed in the car. Mendoza might be dumb as dirt, but the man liked hurting people and carried weapons to enable his hobby. "I'm hurt, Marcos. Do you think a woman as gorgeous as Ms. Mason would allow a total stranger to kiss her on the street in broad daylight?"

"Ms. Mason?"

The light changed and the bus engine revved as it pulled away.

The woman shifted her head so her mouth rested just below his ear. "My name is Brenna," she whispered.

Sartelli's tone sharpened. "Why do you call her Ms. Mason? You don't use her first name? You wouldn't be lying to me, would you, Mr. Wolfe?"

Eli relaxed a tad. The lady was gorgeous and smart. "I call her a lot of things. Sweetheart, sugar, honey, beautiful, but her name is Brenna." His voice hardened. "And she's mine, Marcos."

"So you're looking into her sister's disappearance?"

Her sister's disappearance? "You are going to help us find her, I'm sure. So like you to show civil responsibility."

Sartelli laughed, his reptilian eyes cold. "I wouldn't help you find your own grave, Wolfe."

Eli shook his head. He didn't believe that for a minute. Sartelli would like nothing better than to see him and his teammate six feet under. "You sure about that, Marcos? I have a lot of friends on the force. Would only take one phone call to make your life a whole lot harder than it is right now."

Mendoza eased forward a few steps and dug deeper in that pocket.

Eli visualized that beefy hand curling around the weapon's grip, his finger stroking the trigger. Nothing appealed to the Texas native more than playing with his favorite toy. He maneuvered Brenna behind him, keeping his hand on her wrist. He checked out her shoes with his peripheral vision. Satisfaction curled through him. Flats. Good. Shoes she could run in if she had to. And that might turn out to be the case if he couldn't bluff the construction tycoon and his guard dog.

"Juan." Sartelli nodded toward the limo. "Ms. Mason has delayed us long enough. I'm sure our paths will cross again soon, Wolfe." He got in the back seat and slammed the door.

Mendoza glared at the two a moment longer before he slid behind the wheel and pulled away from the curb in a cloud of exhaust.

Brenna yanked her wrist free. "Okay, buddy. Who are you?"

He turned her toward his car and, hand on her lower back, urged her along the sidewalk. "My name is Eli Wolfe. I'm a private investigator. Do you have a car close by?"

"I hired a cab." She slowed her steps. "Where are we going? I still need to talk to Sartelli and now I'll have to track him down all over again."

"We can't talk on the street, Ms. Mason."

"Ms. Mason? Kind of formal, isn't it, since you told Sartelli I'm your girlfriend."

"All right. Brenna, then. We still can't talk on the street." He scanned the pedestrians passing by on either side of them as they approached his Camaro. He clicked the remote and hustled her into the passenger seat. None of Sartelli's usual goons appeared to be hanging around, but then again Eli and his partner had been out of town for a few weeks. Maybe his thugs had come up the evolutionary scale a few notches.

Eli sank into the driver's seat and cranked the engine, air conditioner going full blast.

Brenna moaned. "Oh, that feels so good. I'm not used to this heat." She adjusted the vent so that the air blew her black curls all around her head.

"Where do you live?"

"Virginia, a little place called Pound. Look, Mr. Wolfe, I don't know you. Why should I trust you enough to let you drive me anywhere in an unfamiliar city? You could be a serial killer or something."

"Sugar, the killer just pulled away from the curb in a stretch limo. You're lucky I happened along when I did and rescued you."

Brenna's head jerked away from the air vent and turned in his direction, her eyes narrowed. "Rescued me? Like I'm some helpless little female who doesn't have enough sense not to get into cars with strangers?"

Eli's eyebrow rose.

She sighed. "Okay, point taken. No rides with strangers aside from this car and some guy claiming to be a PI. I had no intention of going anywhere with Sartelli. I only wanted information."

"He wasn't giving you an option, Brenna. I know Sartelli and his goon. You were seconds away from a ride to nowhere." Eli dug into his pocket and grasped his cell phone. "Here."

"A cell phone? What's this for? I have my own."

"Yeah? Bet yours doesn't have Metro police homicide detective Cal Taylor on speed dial. He'll vouch for me." He punched the number to his friend's personal cell and handed the instrument to Brenna.

His friend answered on the second ring. "Homicide. Taylor."

"Detective Taylor, this is Brenna Mason. I'm sitting in a car with an Eli Wolfe. He says he's a private investigator and that you will vouch for him."

The rumble of Cal's baritone voice carried across the car's interior. Eli checked for traffic in his mirrors and pulled out. If the lady still didn't trust him after talking to Cal, he'd pull into a restaurant and talk to her in a public setting. But standing on the street where Sartelli's thugs had another chance to snatch her? Not going to happen. No one deserved what he suspected Sartelli was involved in. Brenna's side of the conversation consisted of "Uh huh" and "I see" for several minutes. What was taking so long? Cal must be giving Brenna his life story. Ticked him off and made him uncomfortable.

"Thank you, Detective Taylor. Here he is." Brenna handed him the phone.

He pressed the phone against his ear. "Hey, Cal."

"What's going on, Eli? New client doesn't trust you?"

"Not exactly. I stumbled into something while tailing Sartelli."

The teasing note dropped from Cal's voice. "Anything I should know?"

"I'll let you know as soon as I figure it out."

"You better. Watch your back, Eli. Sartelli's painted a target on it. Later, man."

Eli slid the phone back into his pocket. "Are we okay now, Brenna?"

"Dream on. Where are we going?"

"My office."

Eli shoved open the frosted-glass door with Wolfe Investigations stenciled across the middle. The first thing he noticed was the receptionist desk. Empty. Again. Eli rolled his eyes. What did his partner do this time?

He stepped aside and motioned Brenna to the office on the left. Behind the closed door on the right, the sound of the computer keyboard clicking at high speed clued him in to the mood of his cantankerous partner. Wondered if he should look for a body. "I'll be with you in a minute. Why don't you take a seat in my office. Can I get you anything? Water, Coke?"

"Water, if it's cold."

"Coming right up." He detoured to the small kitchen at the back of the office suite, grabbed three bottles of refrigerated water, and pounded on his partner's door.

"What?" a deep voice snarled. "I thought you left. And good riddance, too."

Eli threw open the door and leaned against the frame, arms folded across his chest. "Not the way to get a date, Jon."

Jon Smith glared at Eli, his face red. "If you're offering, forget it. You aren't my type."

"Not me, man. You're too scary."

His partner snorted. "What are you doing back here? Thought you were tailing Sartelli. Lose him?"

"Nope. Got distracted."

A sardonic look crossed Jon's face. "What's her name?"

Huh. Been friends with Jon too long. He grinned. His teammate knew him well. "Brenna Mason." Eli inclined his head toward his office. "Come meet her."

"Better not be another receptionist. I've had enough of the air heads on stilts."

Eli gave a mock sigh. "Jon, what am I going to do with you? Can't keep good help in the office. You chase them off before noon every time we try out a new one."

After a few more keystrokes, Jon rose. Eli tossed a bottle of water his way. His partner snagged it in mid-air. "Good help? The last receptionist, Candy or Cindy or some other C name, had to sing the Alphabet song every time she filed anything. Drove me insane after the first ten minutes."

"Is that all?" He glanced at his partner. "Not like you to toss a poor young lady out of the office for just one flaw." Couldn't resist needling his partner. Too much fun to watch Jon's temper spike even further. "How long did she last?" When Eli had left the office at 9:00 this morning, Cissy was sitting happily at the front desk, a wide smile on her lips.

"I was patient with her."

Eli's brows rose. "How long?" He had a meal riding on the outcome. If the girl lasted until 10:00, his mother owed him a home-cooked meal of his choice. She had guessed Cissy, the daughter of her best friend, would at least make it until noon. Fat chance. Jon hated incompetence and he ate incompetent people for breakfast. Or at least they claimed he did.

Jon scowled, his brows beetling. "10:30."

Eli laughed. His mouth watered at the thought of his mother's lasagna with thick slice of chocolate cake topped with French vanilla ice cream for dessert. Since Jon had made the upcoming meal possible, he might invite him along. Maybe. "You are so predictable, dude." He pushed away from the door frame and walked to his office. Brenna had seated herself in one of the director's chairs in front of his beat up desk.

He swallowed hard. The lady made even his yard sale reject furniture look good.

She turned around and eyed his frowning partner, wariness in her gaze.

Eli smiled, hoped to reassure her his grumpy partner was all bark. If she knew the truth about either of them, Brenna might run screaming into the street. Unless she had a spine of steel. "Brenna Mason, this is my partner, Jon Smith."

She remained silent a moment. "You're kidding, right? Jon Smith?"

"Afraid not. He's got a birth certificate to prove it."

"One worn ragged from repeated showings." Jon extended his hand. "Nice to meet you, Ms. Mason."

She withdrew her hand from Jon's and smiled. "Oh, call me Brenna. No need to stand on formality since Eli and I are practically engaged."

Jon smirked. "Well, pretty fast work, Eli. Didn't know you had it in you or that you had such good taste."

"Do I tell you about the kiss now or later?" Brenna asked and waggled her brows.

Jon's mouth quirked up on the ends. "Now. Is that how you met lover boy here?"

Brenna laughed. "Yes. He claims he saved me from a killer. Is he telling the truth or just putting me on?"

His partner straightened and sobered, attention shifting to Eli. "Sartelli?"

Eli nodded. "Brenna was talking to Sartelli in front of the Bat building. His guard dog, Mendoza, had at least one piece on him."

"Probably the .45 he loves so much."

"That's what I figured. Brenna stepped on Sartelli's feelings."

"Woman after my own heart."

Eli frowned. "Hands off, Smith. I already told Sartelli she was my girl and kissed her to prove it."

His partner sat in the second director's chair. "What business do you have with Sartelli and his goon squad?"

Brenna settled back in the chair, accepted the water Eli handed her and twisted off the cap. "I'm looking for my stepsister, Dana."

Jon stiffened, darted a look at Eli who set his water bottle down on the desk with an abrupt thunk. "Dana Cole?"

Brenna's eyes narrowed. "You know her." A statement, not a question. She recognized that look. Question is, how well did Eli and his partner know her sister?

"We met." He shared a long look with Jon. "How long has it been since you heard from her?"

"You're not getting by with that lame answer, Wolfe." She studied the two men over the water bottle as she drank. Dana never mentioned either of these two men when she called. She never talked about men, period. "How do you know my sister?"

"Working another case," Jon said, his expression guarded.

"And, of course, you can't talk about it."

"Sorry."

No, he wasn't. This was probably a waste of her time. No one had ever cared enough about Dana to get involved. Why should she expect a different reaction now? She squashed the guilt, mentally forcing it aside to deal with later, as she had for years. No amount of guilt would help her find her kid sister. Couldn't really call her a kid anymore. Dana was 25, five years her junior.

Eli leaned against his desk, hands cupped around the edge. "When did you last hear from Dana?"

"Two weeks ago."

"It's not possible she went on vacation?"

Brenna shook her head. "We call each other three or four times a week. I would know if she were going on vacation. She would have told me."

"People change, Brenna. They grow apart, particularly when they're in different states."

People did change. In Dana's case, it was for the better. She'd grown stronger since she left Pound, since she escaped the confines of the past. "She would have told me. We don't have anyone else but the two of us. Dana wouldn't want me to worry."

"How did she sound when you spoke the last time?" Jon asked.

"Upset. She's been having problems at work."

"Do you know who she worked for?"

"Why do you think I confronted Sartelli? Dana is his administrative assistant. The night she disappeared, Dana had a late dinner with Sartelli. She was supposed to call me at 11:00 so we could talk about what was bugging her." The cold knot in Brenna's stomach grew. "She never called."

#

Eli turned his head to look at his partner. He raised his brow, a silent question to see if Jon wanted to get involved in the search for Dana Cole, since they were already neck deep in a murder investigation. Jon gave a minute nod. Just as he'd thought. Eli focused on Brenna. "Do you have a dollar?"

She frowned. "Yes. Why?"

"Hand it to me."

Brenna bent over, grabbed her purse and pulled a dollar bill from her wallet. Her hand shook as she extended her arm, the bill clutched in her fingers.

He took the money and tossed it onto his desk. "You just hired Wolfe Investigations to look into your sister's disappearance."

Brenna stiffened. "But I don't have the money to pay your expenses right now."

"We'll work something out later."

She stood, shook her head. "I'm sorry for wasting your time, Mr. Wolfe."

"Aw, come on, Brenna. You can't go back to acting as if we're strangers. You'll dent my reputation with the ladies."

A slight smile curved her lips. "I can't hire you, Eli. I'll find Dana myself. Somehow."

Eli straightened from the desk and laid a restraining hand on her arm. "You can't do this alone, Brenna. If you do, you'll end up dead."

CHAPTER TWO

Eli glanced at the silent woman seated beside him in the Camaro, her face framed by the passenger window. He could almost see the millions of thoughts flying through her mind. She was worried about Dana. She should be worried. Sartelli played for keeps and he played dirty as Eli well knew from experience.

He turned right at the intersection of Bell Road and Zelida and made another quick right into the Hickory Place apartment complex where Dana lived.

"Apartment 631." Brenna pointed to the left. "She's on the top floor."

Eli nodded and, spotting an empty space, parked the car. He opened the door. "Will we need to find the complex manager for a key?"

Brenna shook her head. "Dana gave me a key."

They climbed two flights of stairs and walked a dim hallway to the last apartment. Eli held out his hand. "Let me unlock the door and go in first." Just in case there was a problem. He doubted it, but you never knew in his line of work. Some surprises were deadly. As messed up as his life was, he preferred it to the alternative.

"I've already been here this morning. It's empty."

Rebecca Deel

"Yeah? That was before you made Sartelli's acquaintance." Eli wiggled his fingers and waited.

"Fine." She slapped the silver key on his palm and stepped to the side.

Eli unlocked the door and stepped inside the darkened apartment. The place had the stale smell of en empty, lifeless dwelling. Dana hadn't been here for a while. A trace of vanilla scented the air.

He turned and whispered to Brenna. "Stay here. Let me make sure the apartment's empty."

She nodded. Eli searched the bathrooms, bedrooms and kitchen plus the closets. No hidden occupants waited to jump them. He retraced his steps down the hall to the front door. "All clear. Come see if anything is missing or out of place."

"Like her place was searched?"

"That's right. Have you contacted the police about Dana's disappearance?"

"Two days after she went missing. They told me the same thing Sartelli did, that it appeared Dana went on vacation. But it's not true, Eli. I know Dana's in trouble."

"Let's get to work." Eli headed for the living room, his gut churning. Dana might be in more trouble than her sister realized.

The first place Brenna headed was the kitchen. Her sister was a yogurt fanatic, always stocking multiple flavors. If she had been here recently, her yogurt stash would tell how long ago she'd been home. That should have been the first place she checked when she arrived earlier in the day.

She yanked open the appliance door and counted. Four containers. Only a two-day supply and Dana shopped for groceries early on Saturday mornings. She loved to shop when most people were in bed. Claimed she got the best deals and selection that way. The yogurt count meant Dana

16

had disappeared the Thursday night she was supposed to call her.

Tears misted her vision. She blinked them away and noted the date on the milk carton. She wrinkled her nose. Two weeks past due. Yet another indication of her sister disappearing two weeks ago.

"Well?" Eli asked.

"She disappeared the night she was supposed to call me."

Eli looked skeptical. "How can you tell that from a peak in the refrigerator?"

"My sister eats two containers of yogurt every day. One in the morning, one at night. She didn't eat one Thursday night, Friday or Saturday morning of the week she disappeared."

"She couldn't have just skipped a few? Maybe she got tired of them. I know I would." He shuddered.

Brenna eyed him. Typical male comment. "You don't understand, Eli. My sister is a chronic list maker. She does everything the same way, eats particular foods each day of the week. Nothing can be out of place. Drives her crazy."

"She's OCD?"

"I don't know about that. Dana likes things to be under her control, especially the space around her and her life. She hates clutter and disorganization."

A pounding on the door interrupted them. "Dana! Thank God you're back. Open up."

Brenna stiffened and headed toward the door.

Eli tugged her back. "Let me. We don't know who this is."

Maybe not for sure, but Brenna could guess.

The detective pulled a gun from under his shirt, held it at his side, and yanked open the door.

Brenna's eyes widened. He was armed. Logical, given his profession, but disturbing. The thing was black and big and looked like a perfect fit in the hand of the man who wielded it with competency. Was Eli Wolfe as comfortable with violence as he was with the tools of violence? A question for consideration later.

A man in blue-jean shorts and a white muscle shirt stood in the doorway, his fist raised for another round of pounding on the wooden door. He scowled, his arm dropping, hand still clenched. "Who are you? What are you doing in Dana's apartment?" Then he noticed Brenna standing behind Eli. "Brenna. I didn't know you were coming today. I can't believe Dana didn't tell me."

"Are you a friend of Dana's?" Eli asked.

"Tim Russell. I live across the hall."

Brenna moved up beside Eli. "Do you know where she is, Tim?" If anyone would know, it might be Tim. He wanted to be so much more than a friend, but Dana hadn't been interested.

Tim's gaze jumped from Brenna to Eli to Eli's gun. He paled. "You don't know? She didn't tell you?"

"Would I be asking you if I did?" Brenna frowned.

"She's on vacation."

Brenna's mouth curled downward. "That's not possible. She doesn't have any money." She ought to know. Dana still needed her help to pay the rent. Brenna wondered how much longer she could dole out money. Not much longer, if her own career didn't turn around soon.

Tim shrugged, irritation flickering in his eyes. "Maybe not, but she's on a cruise to the Bahamas. I've been getting postcards in the mail every day from her telling me how much fun she's having."

No way. Brenna's heart thudded against the wall of her chest. No way on earth Dana was on a cruise. Tim was lying, hiding something. Had he hurt Dana? She opened her mouth to accuse him of just that, but Eli's hand tapped her back. A signal to keep quiet? She closed her lips.

"How long has she been planning the cruise?" Eli asked.

A muscle ticked in Tim's jaw. "It was a spur of the moment thing. I didn't even know she was thinking about it before she was just gone. Who are you, anyway? A cop?"

"Take anyone with her? A friend, a boyfriend?"

A frown in response. "Not that I know of." His tone implied great displeasure at the idea of her taking another man.

"Have you talked to her since she left?"

Tim scowled. "She doesn't answer her cell phone. Maybe there's no cell service on the boat."

Amusement twinkled in Eli's eyes as he put away his gun. "Probably not since there are no cell towers out there unless she has a satellite phone."

Brenna knew that couldn't be the case. Dana had a pre-paid phone that she used for emergencies and calls to her.

"Why didn't she ask you to go with her?"

Brenna's gaze darted to Eli. He must be fishing for information. If he knew Dana well, he had to know about her issues with men.

"How should I know?" Tim swung toward the door. "I was going to ask her that when I knocked on the door."

"Did you two have a fight before she left?"

Tim's eyes narrowed. "What business is that of yours? Who are you anyway?"

"Eli Wolfe." He handed the other man a card. "I'm a private investigator. Ms. Mason hired me to look into her sister's disappearance."

"Disappearance?" Tim eyed Brenna. "You're wasting your money. Pay him off and give Mr. Wolfe his walking papers. Dana just needed some time away. I'll see him out for you and make sure he doesn't bother again." He puffed out his chest and flexed his hands.

Brenna shook her head. "I want to see the postcards from Dana."

An odd look crossed his face. He shrugged. "Come to my place. I'll get them for you."

Brenna walked across the hall, Eli trailing a step behind. Tim's apartment was the mirror opposite of Dana's home. He led them to the kitchen where a pile of postcards lay on the table along with old pizza boxes stacked on one end. She wrinkled her nose. Neighbor Tim couldn't make a trip to the nearby trash bin? Ick.

Tim handed the postcards to Brenna. Each one depicted a different scene from island paradises. Palm trees, aquamarine ocean, bikini-clad women.

She turned each card over and read the inscriptions before passing them to Eli. Most of the messages mentioned Dana having a great time. One brought up her deepening tan and a new red bikini that she was sure Tim would appreciate when she returned. Brenna licked her dry lips, fighting back a surge of nausea.

Eli must have noticed her distress because he cupped one hand under her elbow. "Mind if I keep these? I'd like to read them again later. Might be important."

Again, Tim shrugged. "I guess. Not like there's anything personal on them."

And Brenna detected a hint of anger over that as well. Jerk. Dana had better taste in men than Tim Russell. "Thanks, Tim. Call me if you hear from Dana." She pulled a business card from her pocket with her cell phone listed.

"Sure thing." He saw them out and slammed the door behind them.

Eli led Brenna into the kitchen and guided her to the picnic-style bench. "Sit down before you fall down. What happened? What did you notice, Brenna?"

"The cards. The cruise. It's all wrong, Eli."

He sat across from her and pulled a small notebook from his pocket. "Tell me." So far, all the evidence pointed to a young woman taking a spur-of-the-moment vacation.

"There is no way Dana went on a cruise." Brenna folded her arms around her middle. "She's terrified of water, won't get in a pool, much less a bottomless ocean."

"Ocean liners are like floating cities. You hardly even know you're on a ship." He ought to know. He'd spent enough time on carriers during his years as a SEAL.

Brenna shook her head. "She had a near-drowning experience as a kid. This is more than a mild fear, Eli. It's a phobia. She won't even take a bath, only showers."

Eli thought about that a minute. If this was a phobia, it would be a stretch to imagine Dana on a cruise liner by her own choice. He'd buy a seaside vacation with a gorgeous beach to walk at sunrise or sunset, but not a cruise. "What else?"

Brenna leaned against the table, her gaze focused on the pine knot in the wood grain. "The handwriting on the back of the postcards isn't Dana's." She lifted her purse from the floor, dug through the contents of the mini-suitcase and pulled out a card. "Dana sent this to me a month ago for my birthday. Check the handwriting against the postcards. It's not the same."

Eli opened the card and examined the handwriting, compared it to the postcard inscriptions. Though untrained in the art of handwriting analysis, he noticed the difference in the swirls and loops.

An invisible band tightened around his chest. He wanted to believe she was safe somewhere, enjoying some well deserved time off. But the facts weren't supporting his desperate wish.

Brenna pulled one postcard from the stack in front of him. She pointed at the bikini babes on the front. "She mentioned wearing a new red bikini on this one. Dana would never wear a bikini."

Eli blinked at the absolute conviction in her voice. "Why not?" He studied Brenna's downcast head. He didn't know any reason why Dana wouldn't look great in a two-piece swimsuit. She had a body most women would kill to attain. Curves in all the right places and a body designed to fill such swimwear. Not that he'd spent much time thinking about Dana that way. He'd have to be dead not to notice her beauty, though.

Brenna lifted her gaze to his. "How well do you know my sister? You never answered my question earlier."

And he didn't intend to spill everything right now either. If it did turn out that Dana was missing, their relationship might have led to her disappearance. Man, Eli hoped not. More guilt might really send him into a tail spin he couldn't pull out of. He swallowed around the knot in his throat. "We share a love of the same restaurant."

"Qdoba."

"Ah, you know the place." He smiled. "She took you there?"

A small curving of her lips. "Dana won't con me into taking her anywhere else. She loves Mexican food. We both do."

Eli made a mental note of Brenna's food preference. Might come in handy later. If she didn't hate his guts when she learned the truth.

"Did you know Dana well, Eli?"

"We're friends." He shrugged. "She seemed to need one."

Brenna sighed. "More than you know."

"So what's up with the red bikini? Obviously we aren't close friends or I would already know."

"Our mother died when Dana was 16 years old. Ross Harrison, our stepfather, agreed to take custody and help her pay for college." Her jaw tightened. "Said he loved her like she was his own daughter. I was in college at the time, out of state. When I returned for summer break, I noticed a change in Dana. The bubbly baby sister was gone, replaced by a quiet young woman. A stranger, really."

Oh, man. Eli's heart sank. He could guess where this was going and it explained so much about Dana. The reservation in her interaction with him. Smiles but no touching. Never treating their association as anything more than pure friendship, brother and sister stuff. Always meeting him at Qdoba rather than let him pick her up.

A bleak expression grew on Brenna's face. "I thought the change came because she missed Mom. They grew so close after I left for college. Anyway, even though I probed throughout the summer, Dana never opened up. And, at the end of the summer, I went back to college for my senior year. After I graduated, I got a job at a newspaper as a reporter and never came back home. Dana encouraged me to go out on my own, to do something I loved. Besides, it wasn't home anymore without Mom."

"What happened to Dana?" He dreaded hearing the truth, but knew it was necessary. Besides, if Dana lived the experience, Eli could man up and listen to it.

Tears trickled down Brenna's cheeks. She didn't seem aware of them. "Mom died from cancer in the summer between my junior and senior years. Dana and I went shopping before I left for school. The swimsuits were on sale. I bought her a red bikini as a gift, a suit she'd been wanting for weeks. After I left, Ross saw Dana laying out by the pool in that red bikini. He decided then he had to have her."

Eli dragged his hand down his face. Dana deserved better than that. He wanted to track down the sleaze and kill him. "He molested her?" His raspy voice gave only the small hint of the violence simmering in his gut at that moment.

She nodded. "Ross convinced Dana that he controlled all the money Mom had left to us. He said if she told anyone about what was going on, he would cut off all the money for my college education and that she and I would be living on the street. Dana believed him. My sweet baby sister did exactly what Ross the Rat said in order to protect me and keep a roof over our heads."

Eli fought the urge to throttle somebody, preferably Ross Harrison. Dana had been a kid at the time, vulnerable because of the death of her mother. So susceptible to a predator who should have represented security in a time of chaos and heartbreak. "How were they found out?"

"One of Ross's friends walked in on them a week before her high school graduation and called the police." Brenna brushed the tears from her face. "The police called me because Dana was still a minor and told me what had been happening. Eli, Ross made over the red bikini so much that my sister associated the color and suit with him. When Dana's psychologist helped her realize what Ross had done to her and that it wasn't her fault, Dana shredded that swimsuit with a pair of scissors. She doesn't wear anything red and refuses to buy any swimsuit, let alone a bikini."

She tossed the postcard across the table. "My sister did not write those messages. Something has happened to her."

CHAPTER THREE

Rage boiled inside Eli. If Ross Harrison had been in the room at the moment, he would gladly help the man on to his eternal judgment. "When you were here earlier, did you take time to look around?"

Brenna shook her head. "After I realized she wasn't here, I called her office. I thought maybe she forgot I was coming today. The receptionist told me she was on vacation, just like Tim claims."

Eli rose from the table. "I need to talk with Dana's neighbor again. Why don't you look around, see if anything else seems out of place or weird. Check her closet and dresser drawers. If she did leave on vacation, she would have taken her suitcases, clothes, shoes, makeup." He smiled. "Dana never appears in public without every hair in place, clothes wrinkle free, and matching shoes."

Brenna appeared pleased to have a job with a purpose. "I'll let you know what I find when you return."

He crossed the hall and knocked on Tim's door. Within seconds, the slender blond neighbor opened the door. "Got a few minutes, Tim? I have questions I need answered."

Tim peered past Eli's shoulder. "Where's Brenna? Is she with Dana?"

"Dana's not home yet." And if his suspicions were correct, she wouldn't be unless he and Jon found her soon. His gut clenched at the thought they might already be too late to help her. He pushed through the doorway into Tim's living room and waited for him to close the door.

The other man waved him in the direction of the kitchen. "I was just making myself lunch. We can talk in the kitchen."

Eli trailed the neighbor, took advantage of the opportunity to glance around. The living room was filled with Miami Dolphin memorabilia. Their dolphin symbol covered every available surface including pillows and a framed Dan Marino jersey hanging on the wall over the couch.

"You're a Dolphins fan."

Tim chuckled. "You noticed, huh? Dana complains about all the football stuff."

After the story he just heard from Brenna, he doubted Dana had spent much time in Old Tim's place. "You from Miami?"

"Tallahassee. I've been in Nashville for the last ten years, but never learned to like the Titans. What about you? Any particular team you favor?"

"New Orleans Saints. It's almost 5 o'clock. Kind of late for lunch, isn't it?"

Tim opened a package of hoagie bread. "I manage The Watering Hole so I eat dinner around 11:00." He waved some bread at Eli. "You want one? I've got ham and white Vermont cheddar cheese."

"No, thanks." Eli sat on a bar stool. So Tim managed The Watering Hole on Old Hickory Boulevard. Interesting coincidence. "When did you last see Dana?"

"Couple weeks ago." Tim piled ham on his bread.

"Can you be more specific? What day? What time?"

Tim scowled. "What difference does it make? She's on vacation."

"I don't know about that, Tim. Brenna thinks something happened to Dana. I'm afraid she's right."

"You just want a paycheck."

Heat burned Eli's cheeks. "This isn't about money. Dana's a friend."

Tim gave him a sharp look, suspicion brimming in his eyes. "She never mentioned you to me, Wolfe. And Dana and I are close. Very close."

He doubted the nightclub manager had as much of a claim on Dana as he insinuated. Given her history, Eli doubted she trusted men much beyond friendship. Explained why she kept both him and Jon at a distance, much to his partner's dismay. Although, thinking back on their interactions, her attention mostly centered on Jon. Could his partner have missed the signs? "If you care about Dana as much as you say, you should be concerned that she's disappeared on a spur-of-the-moment vacation without telling anyone and without planning. That's not like her and Brenna's worried. What's the harm in giving her peace of mind until I find her sister getting a tan on some cruise ship?"

"Yeah, okay." Tim slathered on mayonnaise and deli mustard. "So, Dana and I had a date Wednesday night two weeks ago. I left her at her door around midnight."

A date? Fat chance. Wishful thinking on Tim's part. "Did you talk to her that Thursday?"

"Nope." Tim took a big bite from his sandwich and chewed. "I don't see Dana or talk to her until she comes home from work. I get home around 4 or 5 in the morning and sleep until about 1:00 in the afternoon."

"What about the Thursday she disappeared? Where were you?"

"Asleep until 1:00. I expected Dana to arrive home about 6:00. I planned to take her to dinner, but she never came home from work before I had to leave. Figured her boss gave her a late assignment or something which delayed her."

"So you worked at the bar that night."

"Yep and about 250 people can verify my presence behind the bar. Our bartender quit just as the evening rush began." He grinned.

"Do you know anyone who would want to hurt Dana?"

That chased the smile off his mug. "You think I hurt her?" Outrage filled Tim's voice.

"Did I say that?"

"I would never do anything to hurt Dana. You better not be spreading lies about me, Wolfe. I'll sue you into oblivion. I have friends with powerful lawyers."

"If I find out you had anything to do with Dana's disappearance, lawyers won't be able to help you."

"You threatening me?"

"Nope. It's a promise." Eli stood. "Thanks for your help, Tim. I'll see myself out."

Tim Russell swallowed the last bite of his hoagie and swigged half a bottle of Bud Light to wash it down. Stupid private eye. Who did he think he was? He dropped his plate in the dishwasher and snatched up the phone. When a voice answered, Tim said, "A private investigator just left my place. He's looking for Dana."

"What's the investigator's name?"

"Wolfe."

"Eli Wolfe?"

"You know him?"

"Unfortunately, I know a lot about Mr. Wolfe. None of it good for our business. What did you tell him?"

"Exactly what we agreed to tell the cops if they asked, that she's on vacation. Even showed Wolfe the postcards."

"Did he buy the explanation?"

Tim leaned back against the counter, a knot forming in his stomach. "Not really." The silence on the phone grew to an uncomfortable length. "It's Brenna's fault. I did what I was supposed to do."

"Brenna? Do you mean Brenna Mason?"

"Yeah, Dana's sister." His speech gained speed as he hastened to extricate himself from a very dangerous conversation without accepting any blame. In this business, being blamed for something was a death sentence. "She didn't believe the story about the cruise and insists something happened to Dana. She's the one who hired Wolfe."

A sigh echoed across the phone line. "I am very unhappy with your performance, Tim."

A chill seeped into his bones. Beads of sweat rolled down his temple. "I'll take care of it. I swear."

"You will do nothing. If Wolfe continues to probe into Dana's disappearance, I'll take care of him and the sister permanently."

A dial tone buzzed in his ear. Tim threw the phone onto the white counter and rubbed the knotted muscle in his neck. A wave of hatred rolled through him. This was all Dana's fault. If she had minded her own business, he wouldn't be in this mess. The gig was too good, a lot of money flowing into his Cayman bank account. He wasn't giving it up without a fight, no matter what it cost Dana.

Dana opened her eyes to a dark room with lousy peeling paint and the rank scent of mold and mildew assaulting her nose. Using a sliver of light glowing from under the locked door, she glanced around the walls of cement block, prayed this time to spot an avenue of escape. Same 10 x 10 cell. Same cot with a thin green scratchy blanket tossed over her body.

She ran her tongue over her dry lips. Dana grimaced. She needed to drink more water today. Still didn't want to.

Hated to use the facilities in front of Ape man, a leering grin plastered on his face. He never turned his back, no matter how hard she pleaded for just one minute of privacy.

Dana rolled to her side and eased to a sitting position, experience having taught her fast that nausea awaited if she rose too quick. The room still swam in her vision as if she'd stepped off the merry-go-round at the park. Another minute and the feeling passed. She breathed a sigh of relief. Dana stood, hugged the wall until slimy wetness registered under her fingers. She shuddered. Yuck.

Leaky roof on top of high-level stink. She shuffled to the door and turned the knob. Still locked from the other side. Dana leaned against the door, her strength already gone. What was she going to do? She had lost count of how many days Ape man kept her a prisoner in this cold, dank dungeon. With no windows, she had no way of knowing if it was daylight or dark outside. The days and nights ran together in an undistinguished circle.

Voices on the other side of the door caught her attention.

"How long do we have to keep her here? Did the boss say?"

Dana shuddered, recognizing Ape man's slimy tone.

"Until we're told to do something different. The boss has something special in mind for the Cole woman, but all the details haven't been worked out yet."

Dana pressed her ear closer to the crack between the door and the frame. Something special? What did that mean? And did she really want to know?

"She's a looker, that one." Ape man's laugh sent a shiver of disgust racing down Dana's spine. "Wouldn't mind some time with her, one-on-one. Maybe I'll ask for that privilege."

Bile rushed up Dana's throat, gagging her. She clamped a hand over her mouth. No, not again. Just thinking of that lecherous thug laying his hands on her made her want to puke.

"Forget it. No one touches her. The boss wants the woman to arrive untouched."

Arrive? Blood drained from Dana's face. They were sending her someplace else? She quelled the panic which threatened to swamp her hard-won composure. If the boss sent her somewhere else, how would she get back home? For that matter, where was she? For all Dana knew, she might be in the heart of Africa instead of the sweltering heat of Tennessee.

The sound of a key in the lock vaulted her into movement away from the door. She put as much room between herself and the door as she could before Ape man shoved the door open.

"You're awake." The grin appearing on his mouth did nothing to soothe her uneasiness. "Good. The boss will be pleased."

Dana blinked at the bright light pouring in from the hall. More bland paint and cinder block walls. Reinforced the dungeon persona. Her gaze jumped from Ape man's broad face to the skyscraper tall man dressed all in black behind him. Was he the boss? The glare kept most of his features in a haze of light, but highlighted the tray in his hands.

She focused on the bottle of water. Dana could almost taste the clear, life-giving liquid. Although she hadn't paid attention to the food, her stomach had because when the smell of quesadillas reached her nose, the emptiness took precedence over everything else.

Weakness caught up with her. Dana stiffened her knees, determined not to lean against the wall for support until these bozos were out of sight.

She eyed the tray once more. The food looked so good. An unpleasant thought occurred to her. What if the food was drugged? Dana almost snorted. So what if it was?

Couldn't be any worse than what she'd already suffered. She had to keep up her strength. That meant eating when possible and drinking fluids. The possibility of being weak and helpless because she'd refused food and water almost brought on a panic attack. Never again. Not if it was in her power to prevent. She wasn't that scared 16-year-old kid anymore. She was stronger than that now. And these cretins weren't Ross Harrison, her own personal nightmare.

Skyscraper placed the tray on the cot and backed away, watching her. "I'll return for the tray later, Miss Cole. You must eat. If you don't we'll have to resort to other less pleasant methods of giving you nutrients. It's up to you, of course. Intravenous or forced feeding are options, though not preferable."

Dana blinked.. Miss Cole? A thug with manners? She remained silent, not trusting her voice to come out anything but a frog's croak since her throat was so dry.

Ape man leered at her, slowly allowed his gaze to drift down her body. Dana hid trembling hands in the pockets of her black pants. She prayed Skyscraper didn't go far. And wasn't that a laugh. He was as much her captor as Ape man, but he gave no indication he saw her as anything other than a prisoner. Small comfort.

Finished with his disgusting perusal, Ape man closed the door with a thud and slid the lock home.

As soon as the two men's footsteps faded, Dana hurried to the cot and scooped up a wedge of quesadilla. Cheese oozed into her mouth, the salty cheddar flavor exploding on her tongue. Whether it was drugged or not, it tasted amazing. While she chewed and swallowed, Dana twisted the bottle cap. She drank, savored the liquid.

Minutes later, the key rattled in the lock and the door swung open. Skyscraper's gaze swept the empty tray. He nodded. "Very good, Miss Cole. Reggie speculated that you wouldn't eat again. I'm pleased to see he was wrong.

Wouldn't want you to lose weight. The boss would not be happy about that. Please, come with me."

Reggie? She preferred the name she'd dubbed the thug. Strengthened by the simple meal, Dana rose. "Where are you taking me?"

He retrieved the tray and nodded toward the door, indicating she should go out ahead of him. "The restroom, of course."

The meal in her stomach threatened to make an appearance. Another peep show, this time with Skyscraper joining the audience. She lifted her head, tilted her chin at what she hoped was a defiant angle. She had to stay healthy if she stood any chance of escaping these Neanderthals. She could handle it. No choice if she had a shot of returning to Brenna alive. Had Jon missed her?

Her eyes watered as she stepped out of the room. Ape man lounged against the wall, waiting, watching. Dana passed him without comment and walked down the hallway to the bathroom. She heard his footsteps echoing behind her.

She reached the bathroom, flipped on the light and walked inside, locked her jaw against begging again for them to leave her in there alone. Her cheeks burned. If Ape man and his companion got a thrill out of watching, she guessed she'd make their afternoon.

"Leave the door unlocked." The door closed behind her with a soft snick.

She steeled herself for the leering gazes and lascivious grins and turned. She was alone. Her jaw dropped. Grateful, almost in tears, Dana hurried and completed her business in privacy for the first time in days.

The door opened as she dried her hands. Skyscraper indicated she should follow him. He gripped her arm and led her back to the room. "Lie down, Miss Cole."

He didn't say that, did he? "Excuse me?"

"Lie down. Now."

His eyes chilled her. Whatever warmth she noticed earlier had now been replaced by a coldness that seeped into her bones. Had she been handed off to Skyscraper for his entertainment? "What if I refuse?" How lame was that? She couldn't think of anything stronger than that?

He laughed, the sound unpleasant to her ears. "You'll get hurt, Miss Cole. I'll force you to comply." An unpleasant grin curved his mouth. "I'm sure Reggie is more than willing to help if I need him. I don't, but he's been begging to get his hands on you. Refuse my request and I might walk away and let him have you." The grin disappeared. "Choose. Now."

What happened to no one being allowed to touch her? Dana fisted her hands. Could she find a way to hurt him? Sure, but she better make it good the first time. No second chances with this guy. If she couldn't knock him out, Skyscraper might kill her for refusing him. Her resolve stiffened her spine. So be it. At least she would go down fighting.

Impatient, Skyscraper shoved her toward the cot. Dana steadied herself on the edge of the cot and sat. His eyes narrowed. "Last chance, Miss Cole. I will hurt you and enjoy every minute of it. There are many lessons in pain I can teach you."

Dana looked around, desperate for anything to use as a weapon, but the Neanderthals had made sure nothing left in this room could be used against them. Not that she had much chance against two men this size, but she would give it all she had before Skyscraper or Ape man knocked her out or killed her.

Skyscraper reached into his pocket and pulled out a hypodermic needle. Dana's eyes widened. She drew back as far as she could. "No." She hated needles and she didn't know what was in that hypo but it couldn't be good. Every time she woke up after the drugs wore off, her brain felt like it was wrapped in three inches of cotton.

He slid his other hand into another pocket and hauled out a picture. "Look."

She refused. Skyscraper grasped her hair in a painful grip and forced her head around. "Look at her, Miss Cole. Recognize this woman?"

Eyes watering from the pain, Dana glanced at the picture and froze. Brenna. She raised her gaze to the ice-blue eyes. "Leave her alone. She's no good to you. She doesn't know anything."

"Maybe you told her about your activities. She can get me what I want."

She shook her head. "I haven't seen her in months. Please. Leave her alone." Her gaze absorbed her sister's smiling image. She recognized the publicity shot from the back of Brenna's latest book. Tears welled in her eyes. Would she ever see her sister again?

"If you fight me, Miss Cole, I will kill you and take your sister as a replacement. Her fate is in your hands."

Tears trickled down her cheeks. She couldn't let these monsters at Brenna. She didn't live in the real world. She buried herself in her books, lived through the characters who came to life on the page.

Dana bit down on her lower lip and sighed. She offered Skyscraper her arm without any comment or resistance. He uncapped the needle and plunged it into her muscle. She winced. Within minutes, her terror began to fade. Her brain slowed to snail speed. As her vision faded to black, Skyscraper laid her back on the cot.

CHAPTER FOUR

Eli shut the door on Tim's cursing and returned to Dana's apartment.

He found Brenna standing in the middle of her sister's bedroom with her hands planted on her hips, frowning. "What is it? Find something?"

"Nothing is missing. All her clothes are on the hangers except for what she was wearing the day she disappeared."

Eli eyed the closet. "You sure?"

"See for yourself."

He moved closer and examined the contents of her closet. Skirts, blouses, dresses and pants all hung together in order of color and type. Only two empty hangers remained in the closet. From the looks of it, Dana was wearing a shirt and pants when she disappeared. "She was wearing a blue shirt and black pants?"

"That's what it looks like to me. Knowing my sister, she was probably wearing black flats as well."

Eli turned to stare at Brenna. "How can you tell that?"

Brenna nodded to the shoe rack hanging on the back of the closet. "Dana doesn't wear heels. She says they hurt her feet."

Sure enough, all the million pairs of shoes in different colors in the rack were flats. Obsessive, but practical. "What about her suitcases? Maybe she took jeans and t-shirts if she went on vacation."

"If Dana went on vacation, she headed to a nudist camp. I already checked in her dresser. Nothing is missing in there either." Brenna closed the closet door. "Did you learn anything from Tim that might help us?"

"He's very territorial about Dana."

Brenna frowned. "But he was only a neighbor, a friend. Dana told me he wanted to change their relationship to something more, but she turned him down, told him she didn't feel that way about him."

Any man or just Tim? For Jon's sake, Eli hoped Dana's negative feelings about men stopped at Tim's door. "Wonder if she convinced Tim." If she didn't, maybe the bar manager took exception to her turning him down. Maybe he wanted to make her pay for the rejection.

"Dana didn't mention problems with him after their talk."

"When was this conversation with lover boy?"

"About a month ago, right around the time my latest book hit the shelves."

Book? Dana hadn't mentioned her sister was a writer. "What's the title? Is it something I might have read?"

Brenna smiled. "Doubt it. The book is a Medieval romance, not something you'd notice at the bookstore unless you shop in the romance section."

"Can't say that's on my reading list these days. I might pick up some copies for my mother and sisters."

"If you want, I'll sign them for you."

"Great." Eli followed Brenna back to the kitchen. He gathered the postcards and slid them into his pocket. "I think we're finished here. I'll go back to the office and show these to Jon. Maybe he can dig something up on the computer from these cards. He's a top flight technogeek. I'll call you if we get anything useful."

"Forget it, Eli." Brenna grabbed her bag and laptop. "You work for me, even if your rate of pay is about half a cent an hour. Where you go, I go."

"Within reason, Brenna. If Jon or I feel the situation is too dangerous for you, you stay home or at the office. Deal?"

"We're wasting time, super sleuth. Let's go."

Eli rolled his eyes. "Smooth, Mason, real smooth. I'll let that slide, for now. Don't make me regret it."

Jon's fingers flew over the keyboard. The computer beeped at him, elicited a scowl from Jon. "Come on, you can do it, baby."

A slamming door from the reception area clued him in to the return of his partner.

"Jon?"

"Yeah." He coaxed the screen to change with a few more keystrokes. A satisfied grin curved his mouth. Oh, yeah. That's what he wanted to see. Screen after screen of financial records flooded the working space. Jon saved the information in Sartelli's file for later study and turned as Eli strode into the office with Brenna Mason two steps behind.

Eli slid colorful cards across his otherwise clean desk. "Take a look at these. Dana's neighbor says she's been sending one to him every day."

He stiffened. Postcards. Jon scanned the picture on the front of each card. Ships, bikini babes, ocean scenes with the proverbial palm tree. If Dana had been sending one a day, he counted that she'd been gone for ten days. Maybe that was why she hadn't returned his phone calls. He hoped that was the case. He should have followed up before this. She never ignored his phone calls. Same on his side, too. Not about to admit his heart skipped a beat whenever her name appeared on his cell screen. "Could have picked these up anywhere."

"Neighbor Tim says she's on a cruise to the Bahamas. Think you can find her?"

"She's not on a ship," Brenna said. "I told you that."

Eli swiveled to face their client. "I remember, Brenna. But we have to prove she didn't board a ship like Tim claims. To do that, we need to check the passenger manifests aboard the cruise ships headed to that area and check the hotel guest registry. Maybe Tim got the venue wrong. Maybe Dana flew."

Brenna snorted. "With what money? She couldn't even pay the rent on her own with the salary Sartelli paid her."

Jaw clenched, Jon swung around and faced his computer screen again. With a few keystrokes, he tapped into his favorite search engine and called up the cruise lines that sailed in the waters of the Caribbean. Yeah, so he had random facts floating around in his head. He'd booked tickets for his mother and her best friend a few years back. The information stuck.

He sifted through the postcards, reading the inscriptions on the back of each. "This isn't Dana's handwriting." His gut clenched. That didn't bode well for his beautiful friend. He hoped he was wrong.

Eli frowned. "How did you know that? Brenna had to tell me that bit of information. Thought I finally picked up info you didn't know first."

Jon shrugged. "It's not important." He wasn't going to tell either of them about the notes they had been sending to each other. Ever since Dana had agreed to be an informant for Eli, Jon had made it a point to stay in touch with the sad-eyed beauty. The pretense was to keep an eye on her. Sartelli was dangerous and Jon didn't intend for an innocent woman to become a victim of their investigation. "How do you know she didn't take a cruise, Miss Mason?"

Brenna placed her bag and laptop computer on the floor. "It's Brenna. Dana was afraid of water. There is absolutely no way she would ever take a cruise."

Jon tilted back in his chair, his elbows on the arms of his chair. "But someone wants us to think she did. Why?"

"Someone wants us to think she's out of town." Eli dropped into a chair in front of Jon's desk. "He or she has gone to a lot of trouble to convince us Dana's on vacation."

"Doesn't take much time to drop postcards in the mail," Jon said.

"But check out the postmarks. They are all from Miami."

"So he or she paid someone to drop these in the mail."

Brenna looked from Jon to Eli and back again. "What does that mean?"

"Like you, I doubt very much that Dana is in the Bahamas or on a cruise ship in the Caribbean." Jon rubbed his chin, bristles scratching his fingers. He'd forgotten to shave again. "She's probably still in the Nashville area. For now."

Brenna paled. "You think they will move her?"

Or worse. Jon hoped whoever had Dana hadn't already killed her. He'd been trying to get in touch with her for days. He knew something was wrong. He should have physically checked on her before now. A ball of ice formed in his stomach. He didn't want to lose her before he had a chance to know her as he'd dreamed.

Eli glanced at their client. "They have to, Brenna. If she's still alive."

Brenna dropped into the other chair. "No. I refuse to believe she's dead. They've gone to a lot of trouble for this ruse. Why do all this to kill her?"

"Cover their tracks." Jon swung back around to his computer. He clicked on the first cruise line and, using some back doors, hacked into the passenger manifests for the three ships sailing in or near the Bahamas. No Dana Cole listed on any of the ships.

He repeated the process for the next two cruise lines listed. Jon's heart sped up on the sixth try. Fun Living Cruise line had a cruise liner the size of the Queen Mary sailing for Trinidad. Their passenger manifest listed Dana Cole in a single occupancy cabin. "Found her or who someone wants us to think is Dana."

Eli and Brenna came around the desk and peered over his shoulder. "Can you tell if she's on the boat or if someone is posing as her?"

Jon raised an eyebrow at his partner. "Give me a few minutes and I'll get you a picture of her as she boarded the boat."

"How?" Brenna asked.

"Security camera." Jon typed in a few more commands and a stream of video flowed on his screen.

Eli moved closer. "What's that? Boarding?"

"Yeah." Jon moved the mouse and clicked, speeding up the video stream. Passengers boarded the cruise liner at a lot faster clip than they did in real time. He checked the list of passengers' boarding time against the video time. "Dana should be coming into view at 9:42 a.m., about two minutes from now."

They all watched passengers stream by until the boarding time read 9:42. A woman stepped into view and handed the attendant her boarding pass which was scanned. Jon froze the screen and blew up the image. He already knew from the woman's body language that it wasn't Dana.

"Who is that?" Brenna's voice revealed her fear.

"The woman who is sailing under Dana Cole's name."

"Is she still on the boat?" Eli asked.

Jon's fingers danced over the keyboard again. He scrolled through information so fast it appeared a large blur. One of the nice benefits of having a photographic memory. He tapped into the real time security cameras and ran through the different images. One view of the passengers on the deck near the pool caught his attention. "Right there. Second lounge chair to the left of the pool."

The buxom blond lay in full sun in a skimpy bikini, her face recognizable in the security camera.

"So she's still on the boat." Eli tilted his head. "We need to find out who this woman is, Jon. Can you email her picture to Fortress?"

"No problem."

Brenna looked up from the image. "Fortress?"

"It's a security firm run by friends of ours," Jon said. "We contract with them for special jobs. They have connections and better equipment than we do." His lips curled. "My boss is a cheapskate. We don't have the best tech stuff."

"Keep it up, partner, and I'll have to cut your salary in half so we can afford all the toys you want." Eli grinned at him.

"Right." Jon turned his head and eyed Eli. "Half of nothing is still nothing and last time I checked the gadgets we need don't come free."

"I'll use my charm and sharp wit. Maybe the Zoo Crew will feel sorry for us and toss a few goodies our way."

"Dream on, Eli. Brent Maddox doesn't think you're as charming as you think yourself."

"You wound me, man."

Jon checked the payment records for Fake Dana. "She paid with a Discover Card."

"Another indication Dana didn't buy this vacation." Brenna tapped the credit card information showing on the screen. "My sister doesn't have any credit cards that I know of."

"She might have gotten one without your knowledge, Brenna," Jon murmured. "She is an adult and almost anybody can get a credit card, including dead people and dogs. People change."

"Maybe. I don't believe my sister has changed so much that she's keeping these kinds of secrets."

A few strokes of the key and a click of the mouse brought up Dana's financial records. A quick scan revealed that she favored Publix grocery store and a local bookstore along with entries from Exxon, McDonald's and Belk. All purchases were made with a Visa debit card.

Brenna gasped. "How did you pull that information up? Isn't that illegal?"

Jon's hands hovered over the keyboard. "Do you want me to stop?" He would stop while she remained in sight, but as soon as Brenna Mason left, all bets were off. He intended to locate Dana by any means necessary, legal or not.

She remained silent a moment, sighed. "No."

He nodded and went back to work tracing Dana's financial trail. The last entry was Thursday, two weeks ago. She paid for dinner at Red Lobster at 9:05 and the trail went cold from there. Jon analyzed her purchase pattern. Dana never went more than three days without some kind of entry.

"What do you know, Jon?" Eli asked.

"Dana's last purchase was at Red Lobster on Thursday two weeks ago. No cash advances. No credit cards." He glanced at Eli. "She dropped off the map with very little cash." Jon gritted his teeth. He had a horrible suspicion Dana was in trouble.

"What do we do now?" Brenna leaned back against the desk and ran her hands through her hair.

Eli checked his watch. Seven o'clock in the evening. "Not much we can do tonight, Brenna. The place to start tomorrow is Sartelli Construction. Right now, everybody's gone home for the night." He glanced at Jon. "You up for a little surveillance?"

"Sartelli?"

"Let's see if he's up to anything interesting tonight."

"What about me?" Brenna asked. "I want to help."

"Okay." Eli grinned. "Have dinner with me."

"That's helping?" Color stained her cheeks. "How can you hit on me at a time like this? My sister is missing, you Neanderthal. I'm not in the market for a date."

"Easy, sugar. You're beautiful and provide camouflage while I ask if Red Lobster employees noticed Dana leave the restaurant."

A small smile curved Brenna's lips. "Well done. Mind if I use that line?"

"Absolutely. I'll expect some thanks on your acknowledgments page."

Brenna laughed. "I'll be sure to mention your contribution. Where can I freshen up?"

"Turn to your right at the door."

"Acknowledgments page?" Jon said. "Brenna's a writer?"

Eli nodded. "Historical romance, stuff my mom and sisters would like." He listened to her footsteps retreat across the suite and waited for the click of the lock. "How much time do we have, Jon?"

A grim expression settled on his partner's face. "We may already be too late." He raked his hands down his face. "This is my fault, Eli. I should have checked on her sooner, but I was too busy tracking down leads on Joe's murder. Dana is a friend." He paused. "A good friend," he corrected. "And I let her down. Hope I didn't focus on solving a murder and contribute to Dana's death."

An arrow of pain shot through Eli's heart. Joe Baker, his and Jon's PI mentor, had been murdered four weeks ago near LP Field, home of the Tennessee Titans. Four years ago, Joe had taken the two frazzled former SEALs who worked occasional jobs for Fortress, a private security company, and trained them in the art of private investigation, selling them his business after two years.

Something or someone drew him out of retirement for one last case. That case lead to the gruff old man's death. He and Jon had just spent the last month in Mississippi helping his widow, Louise, move in with her daughter and settle Joe's estate. He and Jon planned to look into their old mentor's murder. They promised Louise they'd find out who killed her husband and present the evidence to the cops.

"I still say Sartelli is involved in this somehow," Eli said. "Take your laptop on surveillance. See what's cooking in Sartelli's finances. We know Dana couldn't pay for this cruise. Maybe we'll get lucky and there will be a connection with his money."

Jon nodded. "Maybe. Can't see old Marcos footing the bill for a vacation without either going along or expecting some kind of favor in return. Even if that's the case, doubt he'd be stupid enough to pay for it in a way which pointed back to him. I'll check the cost for the cruise package anyway and see if I can connect the dots. Wouldn't hold my breath."

"Wonder if Sartelli had anything to do with Joe's death. Might be interesting to try connecting those dots." Eli straightened at Brenna's approaching footsteps. "Ready?" He grabbed her laptop. "After you, pretty lady." Pausing at the doorway, he glanced back at his partner. "Work fast. Time is gnawing at us with sharp teeth."

CHAPTER FIVE

After a brisk good night from Eli and a promise to pick her up at eight o'clock the next morning, Brenna closed Dana's apartment door, latched the chain and slid home the dead bolt. The refrigerator's hum and the air conditioner's whoosh broke the silence in the apartment. Too quiet. She missed her sister's incessant chatter, her spunky sense of humor. Where was she?

For once, Brenna wished she wrote mystery or suspense novels. She wanted to help, but she didn't write this type of novel or read it much. If she treated this like a suspense novel, could she come up with some ideas that might help Eli and Jon? Eli turned up nothing at Red Lobster. The waitress remembered Dana, but didn't notice anyone following her as she left the restaurant.

She grabbed her suitcase and headed for Dana's guest room, her home away from home. Brenna unpacked her night clothes and mused over the facts they knew. Not much, she admitted to herself. Her sister had been gone for two weeks, hadn't spent any money which didn't bode well for Dana's wellbeing. She'd disappeared off the map, as Jon said. But someone had gone to a lot of trouble to make everyone think Dana was on vacation.

Why? What did she know or what had she learned that would make her a threat? Dana was an administrative assistant. The most dangerous thing in her world was a paper cut. She didn't hang out in bars or nightclubs. Her sister went to work, came home, climbed in bed early, and rose early to start the cycle again the next morning. She didn't indulge in risky behavior.

Neighbor Tim seemed sure of his relationship with Dana. Fat chance of that being the case. In fact, Dana had complained a few times about how strong her neighbor pushed for a more intimate relationship with her. Was it possible Tim had hurt her? Spurned love did weird things to some people.

And what about Sartelli, Dana's boss? As far as she knew, he'd been the last person to see her sister. But Dana was just his administrative assistant. Wasn't she? Brenna considered her encounter with Sartelli. She shuddered. Dana's boss reminded her of a cold-blooded reptile. How did her sweet sister stand being in the same room with him much less being his personal assistant?

Much as she'd love to blame Sartelli, what if he had nothing to do with Dana's disappearance? Did she stumble onto something illegal, something which precipitated violence? If so, where did she run into trouble? Work, the bank, the grocery store or bookstore? Brenna dragged her hands through her hair. Yeah, she had some kind of imagination. Came with the creativity gene. Before long, she'd have her sister secreted in the federal witness protection program. She huffed out a laugh.

All the unanswered questions left her with a growing headache. She dug in the suitcase for her face cream and body lotion. Her spirit needed a vanilla pick-me-up slathered on her skin. After a quick shower to wash away the travel stench and a change into her pajamas, Brenna powered up her laptop and clicked on her email icon.

She deleted dozens of requests to be Facebook friends with people she didn't know and x-rated invitations. How did these people get her personal email address? She had a web mistress who patrolled the email on her author's website. Maybe it was time to expand Gina's duties.

A message from her agent caught Brenna's attention. She was ready to work on something new, anything to distract herself in the quiet moments, waiting for information about Dana. Which proposal had captured an editor's attention? She clicked and read. An invisible band squeezed air from her lungs as she read further into the document.

No sales bites. Nobody wanted the Amish romance or the Medieval one. Not even the prairie romance or the Victorian. But her publishers always bought her books. Sweat beaded on her forehead. Maybe Maggie hadn't contacted all of them yet.

She reread her agent's last paragraph. "The editors we normally work with just aren't interested in any more historical romances right now, Brenna. I hit them all and no nibbles. Two of them mentioned that if you had a romantic suspense or thriller, they would love to look at your proposals for those. The market is hot for these types of books. You are a fabulous writer and I know you can change genres. Take a few days and switch gears. I want a proposal in my inbox by the end of next week."

By the end of next week? Was she serious? She wrote historical romances. Period. How could she switch gears in a matter of days and turn into a romantic suspense author? Every plot running around in her head, every character that talked to her was situated in the past. And to get a proposal in by the end of next week was impossible. She couldn't concentrate on a new proposal while she worried about Dana.

Brenna pressed the reply icon and stared at the blinking cursor. She wanted to shoot off a missive about how she was a historical romance author, an award winning author at that. Some publisher must still publish quality historical romances. She continued to stare at the blank space and blinking cursor.

This was what she had always wanted to do—write. And she was a good writer. Writers write, no matter what, she reminded herself. So she had a choice. Either encourage Maggie to keep looking for a publisher who wanted her work, likely a small independent publisher by the looks of the rejection list, or she could buck up and get on with her job and write.

Brenna's hands shook. Guess she had as many hang-ups as her sister. She hated to change her market. But she was a writer. Did it really matter in which genre she chose to write? In some ways the writing would require less research, at least less historical research. There were so many good romantic suspense authors out there in the market, though. Powerhouses like Elizabeth Lowell, Jayne Ann Krentz, and Nora Roberts ruled the market. Would she be able to compete with such creative geniuses?

She scowled. No, that train of thought led to undermined confidence and writer's block. Brenna had a large, supportive base of readers. Most of her loyal minions would follow her to the new genre. She would have to entice new readers to replace the supporters who refused to read romantic suspense. Build another mailing list. She could do this.

Brenna dashed off a response to Maggie, indicated an agreement to the one week deadline for the new proposal. She closed out the email program and opened her word processing file. The cursor blinked at her from the white, empty page. She tried a couple pitch sentences. Frowned. Spaced down and tried again. She groaned. That sentence was worse than the first two.

This situation with Dana was the only thing on her mind. No other story popped up from her creativity pool.

Well, maybe she should go with it. A young woman disappears. Her sister hires two hot private investigators to look into the situation. Brenna's face flushed. If Eli ever got his hands on her computer and read this, she'd have to crawl in a hole and pull the dirt in over herself. Good thing no one saw the rough draft of anything she wrote. Her loyal fans would be shocked by her pitiful first drafts. If forced to describe her process to fellow writers, she told them she tried to outrun her writing demon, a yammering editor's voice in her head that wouldn't shut up about the lame plot and hokey word choice. As a result, she wrote her first drafts fast and messy. No finesse at all. Not pretty, but the process worked for her.

Brenna typed the premise and shifted over to the character sketches of the male and female protagonists. She grinned as the female turned out to be a romance writer. Well, the experts always said to write what you know. A romance writer with spunk, a sassy mouth, a smart-aleck attitude, the type of woman who took no prisoners.

Eve Dallas better look out. Brenna's smile broadened. Her character, T.J. Sorenson, might beat Lt. Dallas in a popularity contest. T.J.'s love interest would have to be extraordinary to compete with Roarke. Brenna sighed, wished he was real. She could deal with a guy who made enough money to buy planets and spoke with a dreamy Irish accent.

No surprise, the private investigator she created sounded like Eli Wolfe. Looked like him too. She should change that. Wouldn't do for Eli to recognize himself in print. It would be pretty embarrassing for her, too. The private investigator took up too much of her attention considering she'd just met the guy a few hours earlier. He was a great dinner companion, though. Funny, charming with an old world southern manner, and courteous. The waitress at Red Lobster had stopped by their table quite a few times to see if they needed anything further. She seemed disappointed that Eli was interested in information on Dana instead of the waitress's phone number.

By the time Brenna finished the character sketches, the clock showed two a.m. All in all, good progress, considering she was rethinking her characters' personalities and backstories. None of these people worried about social status and social gaffes, or being disinherited by an irate duchess or scalped by renegade savages on the open prairie. The pace in romantic suspense novels was a great deal faster than a world with knights or Native Americans. And she knew squat about modern weapons. Didn't suppose T.J. Sorenson could carry a sword instead of a girly gun.

Brain fuzzy and her thought processes running at half speed, Brenna shut off her computer and stretched the kinks from her back. An hour after turning off the lights, she still rolled from one side of the bed to the other, her mind puzzling out plot points and choice of weapons. No sabers or spears or dueling pistols could show up in the villain's hands. Or could they? Not unless she did time travel, which wasn't likely in romantic suspense. She sighed. A crash course in guns and bombs was in her near future. She hoped her computer searches didn't land her on a Homeland Security watch list.

A floorboard creaked in the living room. Brenna's eyes flew open and she sat up, gaze glued to the dark doorway. Did she imagine that noise, maybe a prodding from her subconscious mind concerning a plot point? Another creak sent her pulse skittering out of control. She knew that creak, a loose floorboard at the entrance to the hall. Was Dana home?

The air conditioner kicked off and left the apartment silent, devoid of mechanical hums. Barely daring to breathe, Brenna slid her feet into a pair of Isotoner slippers and eased her cell phone off the nightstand. Moonbeams filtered through the blinds onto her rumpled covers. She glanced at the window, her eyes widening. She stood there like a goof, silhouetted against the outside light.

Almost silent footsteps and the brush of clothes against the wall told her the intruder moved down the hall. The door to Dana's room squeaked. Could it be her sister? Brenna shifted her position to hug the wall and eased the door open a little further, enough to tell if her sister had returned and was trying not to wake her.

A nightlight in Dana's room gave off just enough glow for Brenna to know the intruder wasn't Dana. Not unless her sister had grown a foot and gained over one hundred pounds in the last ten days. A big man.

Brenna's grip on the cell phone tightened and she clamped her lips on the gasp that wanted to escape. No way to call the police without the intruder hearing. Dana always complained how sound carried through her paper-thin walls. In fact, Brenna heard him rifling through Dana's dresser drawers. What was he looking for? Maybe this was just a common thief and she had the bad luck to be home when he broke in.

He must have found nothing of interest in her dresser because the intruder moved on to Dana's closet. Brenna had to move now or be caught by the stranger when he came to search her room. Should she try to escape by the balcony outside her room or the front door? If she ran to the front door, she had to pass Dana's room and pinpoint her escape route with the same squeaking floorboard that alerted her to the intruder's presence in the apartment in the first place.

She grasped the door, shut it, and eased the knob's lock into place. Pretty flimsy door lock, but at least the intruder would be forced to slow down and kick in the door. Brenna hurried across the room to the French doors leading out to the balcony. She paused, hand on the knob. Her purse. It contained her life—a little money, her ID, and the all-important flash drives with her book manuscripts on them.

She scooped the bag off the floor, dropped her cell phone inside, pulled the long strap across her neck and let it hang down her side. The bag was a little large to carry this way, but she preferred that to leaving it for a burglar to rifle through. The computer was too heavy to haul around in stealth so she shoved the case under the bed and slipped out the door, locking it behind her.

The flashlight in Dana's room continued its pattern unchanged. Good. The intruder hadn't heard her slip out. Brenna rushed to the balcony and swallowed hard. Dana lived on the third floor. If she jumped she could break an arm or leg or, worse, her neck.

She leaned over the edge of the railing as far as she could, bent at the waist. Under the balcony she stood on, the second floor railing glistened in the moonlight. How far below was the railing? Brenna glanced back at the French door to Dana's room. The light had disappeared. In the next instant, she heard heavy thumps against the door to her room.

Brenna grabbed the railing, crawled over the top and let her hands slide down the wrought-iron rails, her feet dangling in the air. For once, she blessed her 5 foot 10 inches of height. If she stretched, her toes touched the railing on the balcony below. She scrabbled for a foothold, kept her hands on the bottom of her railing and reached for the next floor's balcony rail. Just as she heard balcony doors open above her, Brenna slid off the railing onto the second floor balcony and moved close to the neighbor's French doors, prayed they wouldn't wake up to see a stranger looming in the darkness outside their window and grab a gun.

Footsteps clomped across Dana's balcony, the brush of clothing telling Brenna the intruder was looking for her.

She pressed against the glass, hoped he wouldn't lean over the railing and catch her.

After what seemed like an eternity, a soft curse drifted down and the footsteps headed back into the apartment. Brenna waited until she couldn't stand the pressure any more, and repeated the balcony-hopping process down one more floor and jumped to the ground. A final glance at Dana's apartment with the resumed light dancing in her bedroom window and she bolted across the lawn, keeping to as many shadows as she could find.

She glanced down at herself as she fled and winced. White pajamas. Almost as bad as if she wore glow-in-the-dark nightwear. She needed a place to hide to call the cops, but where could she go this time of night? So close to the apartment, if she pounded on doors to wake the neighbors, the intruder would be able to locate her. Besides who would open a door in the middle of the night to a strange woman in pajamas and slippers?

Laundry room. Brenna scanned the area and changed direction. The laundry facilities were located in the next building. She crossed the grassy area between Dana's building and her goal, paused at the corner. Between her and the door was a well-lit walkway. Great, just what she didn't need with her lighthouse-beacon pajamas.

Brenna searched the area again. No sign of anyone else in the vicinity. Maybe if she ran fast she'd avoid detection. She wished she had donned her sneakers instead of slippers. No traction in slippers and her feet hurt from running and scaling the rails like a gymnast on the balance beam. She adjusted her bag and dashed from the safety of darkness into the vulnerability of light.

Brenna yanked on the door and almost wrenched her arm out of socket. She stared in disbelief. Who locked the laundry room at night? Wasn't anyone else a night owl besides her and ghost man prowling through Dana's apartment?

She growled, frustration brewing inside, and raced to the back of the laundry building and ran into a wall of black-clad muscle.

Before Brenna could draw in breath to scream, muscle man clamped a hand over her mouth and shoved her against the brick, further into the shadows. Her head thumped against the wall.

Her muffled scream led to an arm pressed against her throat. Brenna gagged from the pressure. Okay, so screaming wasn't a good idea. And he had her pinned so tight against the wall with his body, she couldn't get a leg free to knee him. If she could jerk her knee that high. Good grief, how tall was this guy? Her nose reached the middle of his chest.

"Where is it?"

Brenna froze at the raspy whisper, her gaze scouring the gloom for her captor's face. Nothing but a shadow, a face surrounded by black hoodie. Who was he? What was he talking about?

"I'm going to lift my hand from your mouth." He moved his arm from her throat. Enough light from a street light revealed the knife he flipped open and pressed against her jugular. "If you scream again, I will slice open your throat. Do you understand?"

Brenna nodded. Terror poured through her veins. Who was this man and what did he want?

Her captor lifted the pressure from her mouth. When she remained silent except for the small whimper she couldn't hold back, he nodded. "Very good. You learn fast. A plus in my business. Now, where is it, Miss Mason?"

Heart slamming in her chest, Brenna's muddled brain processed the fact that this cretin knew her by name. But his voice didn't sound familiar. Not that she could tell much from a guttural whisper. Guttural? The writer in her came out even in the most horrific circumstances. "What are you talking about?"

The knife pressed against her throat. "Don't lie to me."

"I'm not. I don't know what you're talking about. I've only been in town a few hours."

Hoodie pressed his body against hers. Brenna's stomach twisted. What kind of man was aroused by violence? She shuddered. The kind she wanted nothing to do with.

The knife nicked her throat. Brenna flinched as a trail of warmth trickled down her neck. Oh, man. She so did not want to die at the hands of this bozo. Well, she didn't want to die at anyone's hands right now, but especially not at this creep's hands. "Tell me what you want. Maybe I know more than I think." Maybe she could make it up. She was a fiction writer, after all.

"The recording, Miss Mason."

"Recording?"

Another knife prick and another stream. "Lay off with the pin cushion routine."

"Spunk, too." Hoodie chuckled. "I like that."

Nausea blossomed in her stomach. The last thing she wanted was to please Hoodie. "Dana has a recording you want? What kind of recording?"

The sound of a high-pitched whine breached the stillness. A gulf cart swung around the corner on the sidewalk. A man in a private security uniform scowled at them. "Hey! Get a room already!"

Hoodie eased away from Brenna but remained in the shadows, knife pressed against the back of her neck. "Sorry, man, got carried away. Can't keep my hands off my woman."

His woman? Oh, barf.

"Yeah, well, take it inside, dude. We got kids that live here."

"Sure. Sorry, buddy." Hoodie applied pressure to Brenna's neck with his knife hand, silently ordering her to walk in front of him.

The rent-a-cop remained in the cart, waited for them to leave. Brenna blessed his good sense to hang around and make sure they went inside before resuming any activity. She pressed her lips. Like she would willingly let Hoodie touch her in that manner.

A few feet in front of her loomed that corner she'd careened around earlier. What if she sped up a little? Maybe she could put enough distance between her and Hoodie to escape. He couldn't do much with Rent-a-cop as an eyewitness.

Brenna's legs resembled warm rubber with a measure of weakness thrown in the mix. She stumbled and let the momentum put more space between herself and Hoodie. Clearing the corner, she dashed across the walkway and the parking lot. A pair of headlights appeared in the distance.

Brenna changed direction and headed for the approaching lights. Whoever drove the vehicle with those headlights was about to get a real shock because she meant to get some help, even if she had to carjack some innocent person to do it. She gritted her teeth and poured on as much speed as her Isotoners would let her. Behind her, heavier steps pounded on the pavement in pursuit.

A quick glance over her shoulder. Hoodie's face remained hidden in the shadows of his garment, but anger almost shimmered from his every stride.

She sped across the grassy median and dashed toward the tree line beside the road. The car slowed to a crawl. No! She didn't want it to slow down. Brenna zigzagged closer to the approaching vehicle, leaped over flower beds and activated sprinklers. Cold water splattered her clothes and made them feel clammy on her skin. Oh, man. White pajamas and water? Yeah, she was going to die of embarrassment unless Hoodie killed her first.

Vile curses rang in her ears. Gasping for breath and vowing to join a gym if she survived this night, Brenna plunged through the stand of trees. Leaf-laden limbs smacked face and body in her mad dash for safety. Not daring to peek over her shoulder again for fear of running headlong into a tree, Brenna focused on the headlights so close yet still out of reach.

Relentless footsteps and the hair standing up on her neck clued her in to the fact that Hoodie was closing in on her. A hand grasped her shoulder. Brenna twisted away and lunged through the edge of the trees and into the street.

Headlights blinded her. Tires squealed. Brenna careened into something hard, slid to the pavement. Blackness engulfed her.

CHAPTER SIX

"I didn't see her until it was too late." The patrolman ran a shaking hand through his close-cut blond hair. "She flew out of those trees like the hounds of hell were after her. I didn't hit her, sir. I swear. She hit me, or rather my car, and fell to the ground."

Detective Cal Taylor swiveled and scanned the trees coming into view with the predawn light. "Has anyone figured out what or who was chasing her?"

"No, sir. I called for the EMTs and rendered aid until they arrived. The ambulance left a couple of minutes ago."

Cal faced the patrolman again and glanced at his name tag. "Officer Knight, were you able to identify our vic?"

He produced a small notebook. "She's not from around here. Her name is Brenna Mason."

Cal stilled. "Brenna Mason. Where is she from?"

Another consultation of the notebook. "Pound, Virginia."

The detective pulled out his cell phone. "Which hospital?"

"Vanderbilt." Knight closed his notebook. "Do you know this woman, sir?"

"I talked to her yesterday afternoon. She's a client of a local private investigator." One PI who would be very upset when he called about this incident. Cal walked a few feet away from the patrolman and put through his call.

"Did you retrieve the recording?"

He shoved back the hoodie and squeezed his eyes shut, gripping the phone tighter. "Not yet."

"The sister doesn't have it?" Disbelief rang in the tones.

"She didn't know what I was talking about. I attempted to interrogate her, but was interrupted by a security guard at the complex."

"And you let that stop you?"

The icy words sent a spear of uneasiness into his gut. "A body or a missing man would lead to more investigation. I didn't think you wanted more attention brought to anyone connected to the woman."

"I don't pay you to think. I pay you for results which I did not receive. I want that recording, Liam. No more failures or your family will pay the price."

Liam closed the phone, muttered curses under his breath at the cause of all his problems. Dana Cole and her stepsister, Brenna Mason. He had a good job, one that supported his mama and papa in their old age, made them comfortable for the first time in their lives. They didn't have to worry now about where the next bite of food came from.

He pressed harder on the gas pedal and the dark SUV leapt forward on Interstate 24. Nothing could interfere with his responsibilities. He was an only child and it was his obligation and privilege to care for his parents.

Liam's jaw clenched. He would find that recording no matter what it took or who he had to hurt.

Eli's hand fumbled around on the nightstand for the ringing phone. He grabbed it on the fourth ring and, without opening his eyes, answered the bell-toned summons. "Wolfe."

"Wakey, wakey, sleeping beauty."

He groaned and rolled over. "Taylor, this better be good. You woke me from a dream featuring a gorgeous woman, one who actually agreed to go out on a date with me. I want to go back to sleep and see how it turns out." For once, his dreams were pleasant, a rarity these days.

"Forget it. Get down to Vanderbilt Medical Center's emergency room."

Eli sat up, the heavy fog of sleep dissipating in a flash. "Why? What's wrong?" Was it his mom or dad? His sisters? Jon?

"Brenna Mason."

Eli tucked the phone between his shoulder and ear and rolled out of bed. "What happened? Is she all right?" He yanked on a pair of jeans lying close by.

"Don't know much at this point except that she ran into one of our prowl cars a few minutes ago."

He paused while pulling on a sock. "She doesn't have a car. You telling me she stole one and plowed into a marked cop car?" That didn't make any sense. From what he could tell, Brenna didn't have much money, but he supposed she could have gotten Enterprise to bring her a car for a few days without too much money if she rented a compact.

"She literally ran into the car. Someone or something pursued her through the parking lot into the woods. According to the patrolman, she ran out of the woods right beside his car. She plowed into the driver's side and hit the ground."

Eli punched the speakerphone and set down his cell. "Injuries?" He jerked open his closet and tugged on a shirt.

Cal's voice sounded tinny over the speaker. "No word yet. Thought you might like to know." He paused. "You have information I need to know about, Eli?"

"Nope, but give me a few hours."

"I'll hold you to that. See you at Vanderbilt."

Eli ended the call, jammed his feet in a pair of running shoes and grabbed his gun and jacket. Racing down the hall, he hit the speed dial on his cell phone.

"What?"

Eli's mouth twitched. His partner wasn't known for his friendly disposition. "Did Sartelli leave his house any time during the night?"

"No. Why?"

"Cal called. Brenna's at Vanderbilt."

"What happened?"

"Sounds like someone was after her, but I don't know yet. Cal didn't have much information to give me."

"What do you want me to do? Stay on Sartelli or join you at Vandy?"

"Vandy." Eli slammed the car door and cranked the engine. The Camaro's tires squealed as he peeled out into the street. "I want someone I trust on Brenna's door if they keep her in the hospital or a pair of friendly eyes on my back on the drive home. This has to have something to do with Dana's disappearance."

"Thirty minutes." Jon hung up.

Twenty minutes later, Eli strode into the Medical Center's emergency room waiting area and zeroed in on the nurse behind the desk. "Brenna Mason. Where is she?"

"Are you a family member?"

He opened his mouth, determined to get in that room with Brenna, when a detective's badge slid onto the counter beside Eli. "Metro police. We need to see Miss Mason."

The nurse examined the badge and stood. "I'll check with her attending physician. If he says it's all right, I'll take you back."

Eli barely restrained himself from following her through the door. He eyed Cal. "You look wasted, man. Did you sleep last night?"

A wry smile curved the detective's lips. "Between the nightmares and this roll out, not much."

A wave of sympathy surged through Eli. He'd lost count of how many hours he spent watching infomercials or some old John Wayne flicks. His sisters added to his collection of westerns every few months. He hit the mother lode of westerns on his birthday and Christmas each year. You had to love movies where the good and bad guys were obvious. Unlike real life.

The nurse returned. "This way, officers. The doctor is waiting for you outside room 4."

Without bothering to correct her mistaken assumption he was a cop, Eli hurried past hustling medical personnel, hunting for room 4. He spotted the door sign and the doctor at the end of the hall.

The physician held out his hand. "Officers, I'm Wayne Thomas, Miss Mason's physician."

Eli gripped his hand. "How is she?"

"Doing very well, actually. A few bruises and scrapes. Nothing serious, considering she collided with a car." He smiled. "A very lucky young woman, I'd say."

"We need to talk to her, Dr. Thomas," Cal said.

"I don't see a problem with that. We'll be releasing her in a few minutes. Why don't you go in and talk to her while the nurses finish processing the paperwork." He paused. "Is someone waiting for her? She's pretty shaken up."

Heat flooded Eli's cheeks. "I'll take care of her," he said. He'd look after her better than he had last night. He should have camped out in the apartment or at least stayed outside her building to keep watch over her.

He pushed through the doorway. Inside the room, Brenna rested on an upraised bed. He noted the white bandages on her neck and scrapes down her left arm.

Her eyes widened at the sight of him in the doorway. "Eli. How did you know I was here? I didn't have a number to give the nurse so she could contact you."

"I'll take care of that oversight as soon as the doctor releases you." Eli nodded at Cal. "This is Cal Taylor, the detective you talked to yesterday afternoon. He answered the call on your accident and recognized your name. He called me." Eli crossed the room and sat in the chair beside her bed. "How are you?"

Her lower lip trembled for a second. "I won't be running races anytime soon. And by the way, in case you ever want to know, Isotoner slippers are not good running gear."

Cal stepped up beside Eli. "What happened tonight, Miss Mason? Start at the beginning." He pulled out a notebook and pen.

"I had dinner with Eli and he dropped me off at Dana's apartment around 11:00 o'clock. I did some preliminary work on my next book and turned out the light about 2:00 o'clock, but couldn't sleep. An hour later, I heard the floor creak in the hallway and realized someone was in the apartment with me."

Eli's hands fisted. He should have stayed with her or made her stay at his place, but he hadn't thought anyone was interested in Brenna. Another oversight which he would remedy as soon as the hospital released her.

"What did you do?" Cal asked.

"When he went into Dana's room to search, I closed and locked my bedroom door and escaped by way of the balcony."

"It was a man?" Eli asked.

Brenna paused. "I'm not sure, but I think so."

"Okay. We'll come back to that. What happened next?"

"I ran to the laundry room." She shrugged. "I figured somebody would be doing laundry at all hours of the night, but the door was locked. My white pajamas stand out so I couldn't stay under the light. I ran around the back of the building, hoping to find a safe place to call the police. I ran right into a guy with a knife. I'm not positive, but I think it was the same man slinking around Dana's place."

Eli's lips twitched despite the dismay swelling in his gut at her close encounter with a knife. Slinking?

"Can you identify him, Miss Mason?"

Brenna shook her head. "He wore all black, including a hoodie. I never saw his face. I'll tell you this, though. This guy is a skyscraper. I'm 5 foot 10 inches, and my nose hit the middle of his chest."

Cal's brows arched. "Interesting. What did he want from you?"

"A recording. He believed I knew about some digital recording that Dana must have." Her hand moved to the bandages on her throat. "And he wasn't happy with my answers, Detective Taylor."

Eli forced his hand to remain by his side. "He cut you?"

"Nicks." A wry smile curved her lips. "To make his point. Trust me, he was quite successful. That knife was very sharp."

"Do you know what recording he's talking about?" Cal asked. "Did Dana mention anything to you when you talked to her the last time?"

"Something about doing a favor for a friend and it involved her boss."

Eli's gut twisted. A favor for a friend. Did Dana mean what he'd asked her to do? But it didn't involve recording Sartelli. Could Dana have taken this farther than he had asked her to? If she did and Sartelli caught her, what did she capture on digital recording that lead to her disappearance? Maybe something he could use to nail Sartellli's miserable hide to the wall. He didn't want it bad enough to endanger a friend.

"A favor for a friend?" Cal's eyes narrowed. "Did she say who the favor was for?"

Brenna shook her head.

"It was for me."

Brenna's head jerked around. She stared at Eli, her eyes wide. "You? What was she doing for you? Why didn't you tell me this before?"

"It involved another case."

"Joe's?" Cal asked.

Eli nodded. "I asked Dana to keep an eye on Sartelli, let us know who he was talking to, that sort of thing, not record him. I never asked her to do anything dangerous, Brenna. I would never do that. She's a friend."

"Well, obviously, she found out something that upset Sartelli." Brenna turned her scowl on Cal. "Why don't you arrest him or put the squeeze on him? Make him tell you where Dana is."

"We don't know Sartelli is behind her disappearance. It's possible this has nothing to do with her boss. She could have stumbled onto something shady while doing this favor for someone other than Eli. I can't arrest somebody because you want him to be guilty."

"Have you even talked to Sartelli?" Brenna's voice rose.

Color creeped up Cal's neck. "Yes, ma'am. I have. He knows nothing except that Dana's on vacation and he wasn't happy about it. He hadn't expected her to be gone. You disappointed the guy holding you at knife point. How did you get away from him?"

For an instant, uncertainty flickered in her eyes. Uncertainty and something else Eli couldn't identify. She was holding something back. He wished he knew her better so he'd recognize the emotion on her face. Now he had no choice but to weasel the info out of her whether she liked it or not. Anything she withheld made all their jobs harder.

"The complex security guard interrupted him."

Eli leaned closer to the bedside. "Did he help you get away?"

Brenna's gaze remained glued to her hands. "In a way."

"Brenna." Cal remained silent until she looked at him. "What happened? What did the security guard say? Don't leave anything out. It could be important."

She folded her arms across her chest. "He told us to get a room, that there were kids living in the complex."

Eli leaped to his feet. "What? Did this scum bag assault you?"

Brenna scooted further across the bed in an effort to get away from him. "Not really."

"Not really? What does that mean? Did he try to rape you or not?" Anger made his words sound harsh. No wonder she'd held back. He couldn't imagine any woman being comfortable talking about a sexual assault with another man. Maybe Cal could bring in a female police officer to question her closer. He gentled his tone. "Brenna, please. We need to know everything. It might help us find this guy and maybe your sister."

She glared at him. "He pressed me against the wall with his body, okay? The security guy thought we were making out. We were in the shadows and the guard didn't see the knife. Hoodie kept the knife hidden, but he apologized and told the guard he couldn't keep his hands off me. The guard waited for us to move along. I got far enough ahead of Hoodie that when I rounded the corner, I ran away from him. He chased me. I ran into the woods and out into the road straight into a cop car." She shrugged. "That's all I remember until I woke up in the ambulance."

Cal paused in his note taking. "And you didn't see your assailant's face. Did he say anything else, something that stood out?"

She snapped her fingers. "Yes, now I remember. He called me by name like he knew me. And, before you ask, I didn't recognize his voice." She frowned. "One other thing I noticed. Hoodie is very well spoken. You know, mannerly. He called me Miss Mason. This wasn't a random break-in. He broke into Dana's place to look for this digital recording and, when he discovered I was staying there, came after me to see if I had hidden it."

A nurse entered the room with a clipboard in her hands. "Forms for you to sign, Miss Mason, and you'll be ready to leave." After obtaining her signature and giving instructions from the doctor, she left the room with a curious glance at Eli and Cal.

"I need to search Dana's apartment," Cal said in the silence following the nurse's departure. "If you don't have your keys, I can get one from the complex management."

Brenna pointed to the bag sitting on the counter. "I grabbed my purse before climbing off the balcony."

"You climbed off the balcony." Eli dragged his hand down his face. Guilt ate a hole in his gut as he considered how scared she must have been to scale the iron railing of a third-floor apartment and make like a monkey to the ground. He should have stayed somewhere close by. He could have helped her. He'd done enough rappelling in his SEAL days. Didn't like heights, but he'd sucked up the fear and completed his tasks anyway. Eli dropped into the chair by her bedside.

After Cal handed her the bag, she dug through the contents and held aloft a set of keys. She slid one off the ring. "Would you see if my laptop is still under the bed, please? If it's not, I'll need to make arrangements to get another one, even if it means adding to the tab on the credit card, much as I dread the expense. I don't have a choice. My laptop is my livelihood. Deadlines don't take into account middle of the night intruders."

"Sure. You do realize Dana's place is now a crime scene and you can't stay there for a while, right?"

Brenna sighed. "I need clothes, too." She frowned down at her dirty pajamas. "I can't wear these anymore."

"I'll see what I can do about that. Where will you be staying? I need a number where I can reach you."

Brenna recited her cell phone number. "I guess Eli will have to take me to a hotel for a day or two." She smiled at him. "A hotel that won't bankrupt my bank account."

"She's staying with me." Eli helped her from the bed. "She will be with me or Jon from now on."

"I can't impose like that." Brenna swayed on her feet.

Eli grasped her arm. "Save the argument for a later time, beautiful. If you stay in a hotel, Jon or I will have to stay there as well and that will pad your bill. You're saving yourself money this way."

Brenna yanked her arm away. "How about I save myself even more money? You're fired."

CHAPTER SEVEN

Brenna scowled at Eli, fighting to stay on her feet and away from the nearest wall. She felt sorry for the poor baby. Well, not much, but he did look miserable. Her frown deepened. He should look miserable. The sorry excuse for a friend used Dana to do his dirty work which might have led to her disappearance.

"Nice going, lover boy," Jon Smith said. He lounged against the doorway, observing the occupants of the room. "Let me grab some paper and take notes. Wouldn't want to miss the fine points of handling women."

Eli glared over his shoulder. "Shut up. You're making things worse."

"From where I'm standing, that's not possible."

"Do yourself a favor, Jon," Brenna said. "Leave the pages in Eli's playbook alone. Otherwise, your next date will be years in the future." She slanted a slit-eyed look at the flushed PI standing by her side. Good. She hoped he squirmed a long time. Not that it mattered. As soon as she found a hotel, she planned to send Eli Wolfe on his way.

A twinge of uneasiness pierced her anger. How would she find Dana? Where did she start looking? Her first jaunt into the PI world had ended on a downtown street in

Nashville with a yard ape bodyguard drawing down on her. So much for her bravado. She was lucky not to come away from that encounter with more holes than a slice of Swiss cheese.

"Miss Mason, you might want to rethink that decision," Cal said. "Someone wants information from you and he's willing to hurt you to get it. You escaped a few hours ago relatively unhurt. Next time, you might not be so lucky."

Next time? Brenna did not like the sound of that comment. She swallowed hard. "You think he'll come after me again?"

Jon straightened. "Did he get what he wanted?"

"No," Eli said, his voice tight. "He wants some digital recording that Dana had. Did she mention anything about that to you?"

Jon shook his head. "Fire Eli later, Brenna. He might be a jerk, but between us, we'll keep you alive and bring Dana home."

Eli scowled at his partner before turning again to face her. "Besides, Wolfe Investigations doesn't give refunds. You hired us, you're stuck with us, sugar. We deliver your money's worth."

"You need a better slogan." Brenna fought the smile threatening to curve her lips upward in spite of her anger. "Especially in light of the fee you charged me."

"We still owe service for ninety-nine percent of your retainer."

Cal flipped his notebook closed and stuffed it into his shirt pocket. "Despite how this all came down tonight, you can trust these men, Miss Mason."

"Do you?"

He paused at the door and glanced over his shoulder. "Trust Eli and Jon? You bet. Who wouldn't want two former Navy SEALs guarding their six? I owe both of them more than I can ever repay. So, yeah, I'd trust them with my life and have many times over the years. I'll be in touch."

Brenna watched the police detective until he walked out of her line of sight. Her gaze shifted from Jon to Eli. Wow, Navy SEALs. Dana sure knew how to pick friends. Handsome and deadly.

"So, what's it going to be, Brenna?" Eli retrieved her purse from the bed and handed it to her. "Do we search for Dana with or without you?"

Brenna's eyes widened. Determination glittered in Eli's spectacular green eyes. Either she agreed to work with them or he and Jon would run this investigation on their own. She raised her chin, eyed him. Wolfe Investigations owed her, even it if was only ninety-nine cents. And they owed it to Dana to rescue her since it might be their fault her sister was missing. "Fine, you're hired again. Now get me out of this place."

Eli pulled into the driveway of his ranch-style home, shut off the Camaro's engine, and glanced at his silent passenger. Brenna's head remained propped against the seat rest, her breathing slow and even. He hated to wake her, but given the circumstances of the night, if he tried to lift her from the car he'd likely end up with a bloody nose. He'd had plenty of those in training and on ops. Didn't like them. Safer for his face and her hand if he woke her from a safe distance.

"Brenna, we're here. Can you walk to the house on your own?"

The sleeping beauty in his passenger seat stirred, stretched, winced before opening her eyes. "Where are we?"

"South side of Nashville in a suburb near the Davidson county line. We're sitting in my driveway."

Brenna eyed his well-lit home. "What if I refuse to stay?"

Tension tightened every muscle in his body. Did she hate him that much? And why did he care? He'd only met her the previous afternoon. It shouldn't matter what she thought of him. Yet it did. A lot. "We laid out the rules for your safety at the hospital. What's it going to be, Brenna? Stay here with me or get connecting rooms at a hotel?" He paused. "On your dime, of course." Dirty pool, he knew. She didn't appear flush with cash at the moment. Besides, he could keep her safer in familiar surroundings. He knew who came and went at different times during the day and night in this neighborhood. He'd made it a point over two years to stay home at various times, different days of the week, to learn the life rhythm of his subdivision.

More than that, he wanted Brenna Mason to trust him. He'd screwed up. He wanted a chance to redeem himself in Brenna's eyes and bring Dana home. The time clock in his head kept ticking. His gut said time was running out to mount a rescue op, if one were still needed by this point.

Another hard glare his direction and Brenna opened her car door.

Eli blew out a breath and hustled around the hood to assist the still-weaving author up the walkway to his front door. Once inside with the door secured and the alarm reset, he nudged her down the hall to his guest room. "There's a full bath through the door on your left. Towels and washcloths are under the vanity. My sisters stay here once in a while, so they leave their favorite body washes and shampoos in there. Help yourself. I'll grab a couple things for you to sleep in and lay them inside the bedroom door."

"Thanks."

He studied her drawn, sad expression a moment. "Brenna, I am sorry about Dana. We'll find her. We're very good at what we do. Jon and I work with some of the top black ops people on the planet. In the meantime, clean up and rest. Hoodie doesn't know where you are. You're safe."

"That's why I feel so guilty. I'm safe. Dana isn't. Again."

Eli raised his hand, brushed the back of his knuckles over her velvet cheek. So soft. "We'll find her." He turned her around and urged her toward the bathroom.

Two hours later, Eli sat at his kitchen table, cell phone pressed to his ear, sipping on a cold Coke, and waiting for his former SEAL teammate to answer his phone. He also listened for any noises indicating Brenna was awake in the guest room. He didn't really want her to hear what he feared could be happening with Dana.

"Yeah, Maddox."

Eli leaned back in his chair. "Anything yet?"

Maddox growled. "You just called me thirty minutes ago, Wolfe."

"You have people everywhere. Figured you might have something by now."

"Yeah and I'm your fairy godmother waving a magic wand. All my people are busy running ops. I'm short staffed. We're spread thin, too thin. You should be in the field yourself right now. Jon, too. Not like I don't have plenty of work for you. I had to turn down a couple contracts this week because I don't have enough people free."

Regret raced through his system. He would give almost anything to be back in the fray, anything except the sanity of his best friend and teammate. "I hear you, Maddox. Tempting though it is, I'll have to pass for a little longer."

A pause, then, "Jon's not ready?"

Eli bit back a bitter laugh. Not hardly. The op he and his partner had deployed on three months ago with the Zoo Crew almost cost Jon his life. If Eli had been five minutes later, Jon would be buried at Arlington National Cemetery right now. "He's getting there. What about the leak?"

"Plugged."

Eli's lip curled. He didn't ask details, didn't want to know. From the tone of Maddox's voice, the leak had been plugged permanently. No less than the traitor deserved. He'd sold the Zoo Crew to the highest bidder along with the stolen plans for the new missile system Fortress had been contracted to retrieve for an unnamed American defense contractor.

"It's been too long," Maddox said, his voice soft. "You know that, right? This whole situation doesn't look promising for a search-and-rescue op. This is probably going to be a recovery mission."

"Yeah, I know." Eli dragged a hand through his shower-damp hair. "It's been ten days too long. No ransom demand, but no body either." Stupid to be optimistic. He'd been through enough missions as a SEAL to know you hope for the best but plan for the worst. Another glance in the direction of the guest room. He didn't want to be the one to break Brenna's heart, prayed he'd never have to tell her the unthinkable.

"Doesn't mean Dana's still alive. You know the stats, Eli."

Yeah, he did. Didn't mean he liked them. Chances were good Dana had been killed within a few hours of her disappearance. "I'm hoping the kidnappers want information from Dana bad enough to keep her alive until they get it."

"Then you better find the recording before they do."

Maddox didn't have to say the rest. If Hoodie found the recording before they did, Dana would be an unnecessary and expendable liability. The likelihood of someone killing his friend made him want to hurl his donut breakfast. "Keep tabs on her passport."

Maddox snorted. "Doubt the kidnappers will go through legit channels to get her out of the country. I'll flag it anyway."

"I know, but just in case we're reading this wrong and she leaves the country under her own steam." Couldn't imagine Dana doing that in light of her past with her stepfather. She wouldn't want to worry Brenna.

"Done. Now, stop calling me every half hour unless you have new info to share. I've got three other situations around the globe blowing up right now. I'll be in touch."

He dropped the phone and rubbed his eyes. Man, he needed a huge hit of caffeine. Eli rose and filled the coffee pot with water. He scooped ground coffee from the can and dumped it into the filter. While the aromatic brew dripped into the pot, he eased the curtain back and scanned the neighborhood. The Cordells drove past in their new Escalade. Eli smiled at the sight of the frail senior citizen behind the wheel of such a large SUV. Looked like a kid in the driver's seat except for the gray hair.

He froze. No sign of a struggle in Dana's apartment. She disappeared after dinner at Red Lobster, but where was her Mazda? If they could locate Dana's car, it might give them another avenue to pursue.

Eli snatched his phone from the table and punched in Jon's number. "Did Cal say anything about Dana's car?"

"Hasn't located it yet."

"Think you can find it first?"

Sounds of keys clicking, then, "I'll hack into the traffic cams and track her from Red Lobster." And Jon ended the call. A wry smile crossed Eli's lips. His co-workers didn't waste time on niceties.

"What's going on?"

Eli spun around. He stared at the gorgeous writer who did incredible things to his oversized t-shirt and sleeping shorts. They had never looked that good on him. He needed to say something, but he had a feeling Brenna wouldn't appreciate comments from a near stranger about how stunning she looked first thing in the morning. She looked rumpled and adorable. Her flushed cheeks indicated she'd slept at least a little before wandering to the kitchen. Not enough sack time, he knew. From what he'd gathered at the hospital, she hadn't slept at all before Hoodie broke into Dana's apartment.

He also considered the fact she didn't sound grumpy before a cup of coffee a real plus. "Jon's going to search for Dana's car on the traffic cams."

"You think he can find her car?"

"I'd put my money on Jon any time. In the meantime, would you like coffee or maybe a shower?"

A sheepish smile curved her lips. "Coffee first. Besides, I don't have anything to change into yet."

"Ah, never let it be said that Wolfe Investigations doesn't take care of its clients. I called Cal and asked him to drop off your luggage and laptop. He should arrive in the next few minutes." He poured a mug of coffee and handed it to her. "Cream or sugar?"

Brenna sighed. "No, thanks. I need straight up and strong today."

Eli noted the dark circles under her eyes. They matched the circles under his. "Maybe you can catch a nap later."

"I'll sleep after we find Dana."

"Brenna, you have to take care of yourself. You can't help Dana if you collapse from exhaustion."

"What about you? Did you sleep?"

He sipped his coffee, eyed her over the mug's rim. "I've been on the phone and put out feelers for information in the intelligence community and Fortress's network. I'll sleep later when Jon's here to keep watch. I also slept four hours before Cal called about you. You, on the other hand, worked until Hoodie broke into Dana's place. Jon and I are trained to work on little to no sleep. You aren't."

Brenna yawned, her jaws popping. "Okay, you made your point. I might try to sleep later, but I doubt it will work. I keep thinking about Dana, wondering what's happened to her, trying to figure out why someone took her. It doesn't make sense, Eli. I don't have much money. I would sell everything I own in a heartbeat to get her back, but no one's asked for money, only a recording I know nothing about and can't find."

Eli squeezed her shoulder. "We won't stop looking until we find her."

"Promise?"

"No matter how long it takes or how far they take her." He just hoped they found her before it was too late.

Dana stumbled into the room, shaded her eyes against the bright lights.

"Sit here, Ms. Cole."

A cold hand clamped on her arm and moved her to an examination table. Dana sat as far away as she could from the man wearing a white lab coat and surveyed the room. Scattered medical equipment and supplies lined the walls and countertops. "Who are you?"

"I'm a doctor. My name doesn't matter." He pulled on a pair of rubber gloves. "Hold out your arm, please."

"Why?" Her eyes widened at the sight of tray he dragged closer, one laden with test tubes and hypodermic needles. "No more drugs."

"Don't be ridiculous, Ms. Cole." He frowned at her. "I'm simply taking a blood sample."

Dana's pulse raced. Why did he need a blood sample?

Ape man stepped inside the examining room, his expression hard. "Got a problem here, Doc?"

"She's not very cooperative, Reggie. I need a blood sample."

Faster than Dana believed possible for such a large guy, Ape man crossed the room, grabbed her throat with one hand and shoved her against the wall. "Stick out your arm." He increased the pressure, leaning forward until his mouth brushed against her ear. "If you want your sister to

78

remain free and healthy, you'll give the doc what he needs. Your choice. You or your sister." His tongue caressed her ear. "Does she taste as sweet as you, Dana?"

Dana shuddered, revulsion growing stronger by the second. She couldn't let these thugs hurt Brenna. "Leave her alone." Gritting her teeth, she extended her arm. Ape man released her and stepped back though he remained close enough to ensure her cooperation. The doctor tightened the rubber tourniquet around her arm, swiped the skin with alcohol and drew the sample.

He capped the tube and labeled it. "Remove your clothes, Ms. Cole."

She froze. "Excuse me?"

The doctor scowled. "I need to do an examination, make sure you're healthy. Remove your clothes now. I'm due at the office in a few minutes."

Why did he need to determine her health status? Maybe the kidnappers had contacted Brenna for money or something and she'd demanded proof of life or health. She hoped they hadn't asked for money. Brenna didn't have much. Contrary to popular opinion, most contracted authors didn't make enough money to quit a day job. Brenna had been able to stop reporting, but she didn't live an extravagant lifestyle. And her sister still supported her financially because Dana's salary was so small at Sartelli Construction. She liked her job enough that Brenna had encouraged her to stay and apply for higher positions as they came available if they interested her. Dana's gaze darted to the grinning hulk by the door. "Not with him in the room."

Ape man's eyes glittered. "Want me to help, Doc? It would be my pleasure."

"Step outside for now, Reggie."

The door closed behind Ape man with a quiet snick. Dana's hands moved to the buttons of her shirt. "Why are you doing this for them?"

"I am paid well for my services and forgetful memory."

"But they threatened to hurt my sister. Don't you care?"

"About your family? No, my dear, I don't. Remove the trousers, too, please." He motioned Dana back to the examination table and slipped the ends of the stethoscope into his ears. He listened to her heart and lungs before checking her reflexes. "Excellent." The doctor hurried to the counter at the far end of the room and picked up a camera. He opened a drawer, grabbed a gallon-sized storage bag with red material inside, and tossed it onto the table behind her. "We're almost finished. Now, take off the rest of your clothes and put that on, Ms. Cole."

Red. No. Oh, no. Couldn't be. Dana began shaking. "But why? This isn't necessary."

"Oh, but it is. We must have proof that you are in top physical condition. You'll bring a much higher price."

So this was about money. Where would Brenna get money to buy her freedom? How was she ever going to earn enough to pay back her sister for ransoming her? She opened the bag and dumped the contents. Hands trembling, Dana unfolded the material. A red bikini. Blood drained from her face. Nausea swelled in her stomach until she rushed to the nearby sink and threw up.

Brenna unbuckled the seatbelt and stepped into the sweltering heat. "It's not even noon yet. How can it be this hot already?"

Eli shut the car door and hit the lock button on his remote. "August is worse. This is only a hint at the weather to come in a few weeks."

"Why are we here?" Brenna stared at the Sartelli Construction headquarters, a three-story black glass and steel structure which gleamed in the summer sun. Heat waves radiated from the sidewalk as she stepped into the humid air from the air-conditioned comfort of Eli's car. "Sartelli wasn't a fountain of information in our last encounter."

"While Jon's searching for Dana's car, we're tracing her movements the day she disappeared. We know she started her day here at 8:00 that morning and it ended with Sartelli. Let's fill in the blanks about what happened between those hours. Maybe we'll get lucky."

Seemed like a colossal waste of time to Brenna. She knew deep in her gut that Sartelli was involved in Dana's disappearance somehow. "Do you think this is going to help? We have to find her, Eli. Why are we wasting time on this?"

Eli opened the building door and ushered her inside. Although the handsome PI had warned Brenna he would once again resume the role of her besotted boyfriend, she still jumped when his arm slid around her waist.

"Easy, sugar," he murmured, his arm tightening.

"Sorry," Brenna whispered.

Eli eased her closer to his side with a low intimate chuckle that made her cheeks burn even though she knew he played a role for the Sartelli workers and security cameras. "Pretend I'm that lucky guy waiting for you back home."

Brenna snorted. The guy waiting for her lived in the pages of her next book. "No guy."

He kissed her on the ear. "Too bad for the Virginia boys. Great for me."

She eyed him. "You're into long distance romances?"

"In the short run, sugar. No relationship will thrive under those circumstances, although I might be real tempted to try if I stood a chance to win your heart. You would be worth every bit of expense and trouble."

Brenna's brows rose. The women in Nashville must be nuts to pass up this guy. Handsome and a sweet talker as well. "You expect me to believe some beautiful woman isn't waiting until your back is turned to scratch my eyes out?"

Eli grinned. "Other than you, the women in my life are related to me and they haven't taken out a girlfriend yet."

She hoped they didn't start now. Brenna's cheeks heated, astonished that she forgot this whole boyfriend/girlfriend act was just that—an act. She needed to guard her heart. It would be too easy to let Eli Wolfe slide right through her defenses. And that would net her a heartbreak, an ailment her health insurance couldn't fix.

"May I help you?"

Eli winked at Brenna and turned to answer the blond receptionist watching their approach with curiosity. "I'm looking into the disappearance of Dana Cole. I need to talk to her co-workers. Can you help me with that?" He slid his card across the receptionist's desk.

"I heard about Dana. It's so hard to believe she's missing. You never expect that kind of thing to happen to someone you know. We all thought she was having a great time on some cruise to the Bahamas. I hope you can find her."

"You can count on it. I won't stop looking until I bring her home. That's why it's so important for me to talk to her friends and co-workers. Time's working against us."

"Take the elevator on your left to the third floor. First office on your right. Dana's friend, Grace Peters, is filling in for her. If anyone can give you information that might help, it's Grace."

"Thanks for your help."

An elevator ride later, Brenna and Eli opened the door to Dana's office. The woman sitting behind the desk glanced up. Her eyes widened. "Eli. Brenna. Have you heard from Dana?"

She shook her head. "How are you, Grace?"

Tears filled Grace's eyes. "I've been so worried since Mr. Sartelli told me you believed Dana was missing. I thought she was on an unexpected vacation with a man she'd met and didn't want to tell anyone details. She's really private about stuff like that. In fact, I don't think I've heard her mention any man she was dating. What do you think happened to her?"

"That's what we're going to find out," Eli said. "Would you be willing to help?"

"Yes, anything."

Eli leaned close to Grace. "Where's Sartelli?" he asked, voice soft.

"In Mt. Juliet at a construction site. He's doing an inspection."

"Great. How about going to lunch with me and Brenna? My treat."

"Take me to Qdoba and you've got a deal." Grace yanked open a desk drawer and lifted her Coach bag.

A shaft of pain speared Brenna at going to Dana's favorite restaurant without her sister. She swallowed hard against the sudden lump forming in her throat.

Eli's arm shifted to Brenna's shoulders and squeezed. She glanced up and found him watching her. One eyebrow quirked upward, as though he were asking if she could handle it. Brenna's vision blurred, but she nodded. She could do this.

"We'll meet you at the restaurant," Eli said. "That way you'll have your car so you can return to work on time. Wouldn't want your boss to be angry because you're late." He urged Brenna back to the elevator.

The doors closed as the first tears fell. Brenna covered her face with her hands and sobbed. Eli's strong arms closed around her.

"Hold on, Brenna," he murmured in her ear. "I promise you, we'll find her."

Eli carried the trays to the table, sat and breathed in the pungent aroma of grilled onions and green peppers with a hint of black beans, all scents guaranteed to make his mouth water. His breakfast donuts were a distant memory. He waited for Brenna to fill the drink cups and sit beside him before he began questioning Grace. "Anything unusual happening since Dana's disappearance?"

Grace's brow furrowed. "Mr. Sartelli's been grumpy, yelling at everybody." She scowled. "Especially me."

Eli smiled. "Yeah? What's so unusual about that? Sartelli is about as charming as a snake on good days."

Grace laughed. "You're right. I guess his behavior isn't out of the ordinary."

"What was Dana working on?" Brenna asked. "Any special project for Sartelli?"

She rolled her eyes, sipping her soda. "Dana has her hands on almost every project at the company and a few more on the side. Filling in for her is driving me insane. I don't know how she kept up with it all."

Nothing significant yet. Maybe Brenna was right. This might be a huge waste of time, time Dana didn't have. Eli pushed back the frustration eroding his patience. "What projects? Do you remember them?"

"A new strip mall in Mt. Juliet for one, an office building in Hermitage, another in Madison, and the campus for a private high school up in Gallatin."

"You said Dana was working on outside projects, too. Do you know anything about those?"

"Helping with preparations for Maria Sartelli's wedding and a charity event to be hosted at the Vanderbilt Plaza Hotel next month. Mr. Sartelli volunteered Dana to work with his wife, Elena."

Eli whistled. "Bet that was an aggravating assignment." Never an easy person to be around, Elena Sartelli turned into a tyrant when dealing with charities or her family. Public perception of her as a doting mother or a community benefactress trumped any other priorities. Old Marcos ranked a distant third.

"Not half as irritating as all those phone calls for Dana. Same woman with the same message. She sounds pretty desperate to talk to her."

"Did she say what she wanted?" Brenna asked.

Grace shrugged. "Sorry."

"Do you remember the name?" Eli pulled out a small notebook and pen.

"Helen. Can't remember the last name on the messages I wrote down. She calls at least a couple times a day."

"It might help if we had her number. Could you get that for me?" Eli waited, wondered if Dana's friend considered the information confidential. He'd prefer Grace volunteered the number, but if she didn't cooperate, Eli wasn't averse to a little night reconnaissance mission to retrieve the information. Jon was better at breaking and entering than he was. He suspected his partner would insist on tagging along if it meant a possible clue to Dana's whereabouts.

Grace sipped her drink, a thoughtful expression on her face. "Well, I suppose it's all right since this isn't connected to Sartelli Construction. I don't want to put my job in jeopardy."

"We understand, Grace," Brenna said. "We don't want you to do anything that might cause problems with Mr. Sartelli. Do you remember the number or should we follow you back to the office?"

"I think I might have one of the messages in my purse." Grace pulled the purse onto her lap and dug for a minute. "Here it is." She handed Eli a crumpled pink note. "Helen called again just before I left the office to come here. I stuffed it in my purse instead of filing it with all the others. Didn't figure it mattered whether there was one more of the same message in that pile."

Eli scanned the standard phone message form. Helen's last name was Lynch. Phone number was local, too. He folded the note and slipped it into his pocket. "Thanks, Grace."

"You think this woman will help you find Dana?" Grace sounded skeptical.

"We have to run down every possibility. A lot of my work entails chasing leads, even ones that wind up as dead ends."

"Whatever. It's your time to waste." Grace stood, slinging her purse over her shoulder. "Let me know if I can answer more questions."

"One more thing," Eli said. "Did Dana leave work before quitting time for any reason that last day?"

She tilted her head, frowning. "Now that you mention it, Dana delivered some papers to Mr. Sartelli at lunch. He'd forgotten them on his desk. Maybe some invoices for the school campus he's building." Grace paused. "Oh, yeah, Dana also stopped by the Sartelli place after that."

Eli's brows rose. "And you remember all this two weeks later? That's some memory, Grace."

The woman flushed and shrugged. "Dana picked up lunch for me that day. To be honest, I was kind of angry with her because she returned to the office at three o'clock. I was about to starve to death. Sounds really trivial, now, doesn't it? It seems petty in light of Dana's disappearance." Grace sighed. "I have to go. Let me know if I can help with anything else."

She waved and hurried across the parking lot to her late-model Lexus. Nice car. Eli wouldn't mind driving one like that himself. Had to admit, he still preferred speed over luxury.

Eli's cell phone vibrated and drew his attention away from Dana's friend. He checked the cell phone's two-word message. Excitement bloomed in his gut.

"What?" Brenna asked. "Is it something to do with Dana?"

He stood and gathered their trash. "Jon found Dana's car."

CHAPTER EIGHT

Brenna scrambled out of the Camaro and hurried to Dana's maroon four-door Mazda. There had to be something here to help them find her sister. Eli's warning on the drive to the airport not to get her hopes up echoed in her mind. She reached for the door handle only to have a strong hand grab hold of her arm.

"Don't touch the car, Brenna."

She fought to get free. "Let me go. There might be a clue, some hint as to what happened to her. I have to know. Please."

"Not this way, sugar. We can't leave our prints behind or smudge prints the kidnapper might have left." Eli slid his around her waist and jerked her back against his chest. "Calm down or security will cart us off and call the cops. We'll get the answers, no matter what it takes."

She froze. His arm felt like a steel band across her stomach. Brenna turned her head and noted the telling expression on his face. His implacable resolve penetrated the near desperation more than anything he said. She believed he wouldn't quit until he brought Dana home to her. Panic receded, left her shaky and holding onto her composure by sheer force of will. She couldn't lose it now.

Dana needed her to be calm so she could think. Brenna knew her sister better than anyone else. She must be able to think in order help her sister.

"Do you have a set of keys to her car?"

Her stomach knotted. "No." So close to be stopped by a locked door. "I don't suppose you can break the window in broad daylight without anyone noticing."

"Nope, but I don't have to break in. I've got something better." He pulled out his cell and sent a text message she couldn't read without twisting herself into a pretzel.

A small smile curved Brenna's lips. "Oh, yeah? What's that?"

"Not what, sugar. Who."

"Jon?"

"You got it."

"That man is a walking computer, isn't he? I have a feeling many of his skills aren't legal."

"Let's just say he's well trained by street life and the military. Even I don't know all that Jon can do and I don't ask. Sometimes it's safer not to know what he's capable of." Eli stiffened. "We've got company coming. Security. Turn around and kiss me like you mean it."

Brenna's heart sped into overdrive. "Will I ever get a chance to kiss you without an audience?" She turned, slid her hands up his arms and locked them behind his neck.

Eli grinned. "Any time you want, sugar. I'll look forward to it."

She raised her head the scant few inches that separated them and pressed her mouth to his. She tasted Coke, mint and Eli. Brenna eased closer and tightened her grip on his neck. Eli's arms circled around her back as warmth that had nothing to do with the weather surged through her body. A soft sigh escaped as she changed the angle and deepened the kiss. Kissing Eli Wolfe could become very addicting, she decided. An addiction she wouldn't mind exploring if the circumstances weren't so dire.

Somewhere in the distance she registered the sound of a golf cart passing and growing fainter along with the rising whine of jet engines on one of the nearby runways. Long minutes later, Eli lifted his head. Brenna was gratified to note his rapid breathing mirrored her own.

He leaned his forehead against hers. "It's good we had an audience. You almost knocked me off my feet. By the way, you owe me a piece of gum."

Brenna's face flamed as she realized the mint taste in her mouth came from Eli's gum, now pressed against the inside of her cheek. "You want it back?"

Eli's gaze darkened and dropped to her mouth. "A very tempting offer, but we need to stay focused."

"Right, focused." Brenna made herself unlock her arms and step back. "How much longer will we have to wait for Jon?"

His soft laughter told her the answer. She sighed. Great. She had been so entranced by the distraction staged for the security guard's benefit she hadn't paid attention to the goal. "I missed the main event, didn't I? When did he unlock it?"

"Oh, about the time I lost my gum."

"This is so embarrassing."

Eli captured her hand and raised it to his mouth for a brief kiss. "I think it's cute." He urged her closer to the Mazda.

Cute? What about breathtaking or stupendous? Maybe the distraction had all been on her side. She scowled. "You didn't miss Jon's work."

He drew her to a stop inches from the car and cupped her chin in his hand, raised her gaze to his. "I'm good at multitasking, Brenna. Had to be a multitasker in the SEALs. Make no mistake, though, sugar. I was in the moment every bit as much as you."

Brenna smiled. "Right answer, another one that might appear in my next book."

Eli tugged his polo shirt free from his jeans and opened the car door with his covered hand. "When you hit the New York Times bestseller list, I'll expect appropriate compensation in return."

"I'll keep that in mind."

"Keep your hands in your pockets, but look inside Dana's car. Notice anything that shouldn't be there or maybe something that's missing?"

Brenna leaned closer and peered into the interior of the hot Mazda. Nothing seemed to be missing. Dana's CDs were in the door. She frowned. They didn't rattle when Eli opened the door. Had Dana bought a new one? The air freshener hung from the rearview mirror. No trash or loose bits of paper. Like always, even Dana's car reflected her neatness fetish.

"Want to look in the back?" Eli asked.

She nodded, still thinking about the CDs. Dana bragged about any new music she bought. Another plane took off, the noise making any verbal comments to Eli impossible. Brenna eased closer to the now open back door. A scent caught her attention. She sniffed. What was that scent? It sort of smelled familiar. Not Dana's perfume since she didn't wear any. Her fragrance of choice was vanilla-scented body wash and shampoo, same scent as Brenna preferred.

Cologne, maybe? But whose cologne? Dana wasn't dating anyone, at least no one Brenna knew about. Were Eli and Jon right? Had her sister changed enough not to feel compelled to tell her everything?

She sniffed again. Something about that scent bothered her enough to make her stomach twist.

"What is it, Brenna? Did you find something?"

"Not really. A scent I can't identify." She turned her head to look deeper into the car's interior. The sun's reflection glittered off a bottle in the side pocket of the passenger door. Brenna bent closer, drawing in a deep breath. The smell grew stronger as she neared the door. "There's a bottle of cologne back here and it doesn't belong to Dana."

Eli knelt beside the door. "You sure?"

"Positive."

Once again using his shirt-covered hand, Eli eased the bottle high enough to read the label. Obsession.

Brenna gasped. "No way. Dana would never carry this in her car."

"Why? Talk to me, Brenna."

"I knew that scent was familiar. That's the cologne our stepfather always used. Dana hates that cologne." She stood. "Could we be on the wrong track with Sartelli? Maybe Ross is involved in Dana's disappearance. What if he took Dana?" The possibility horrified her. Dana had seen a therapist for a couple years after Ross's arrest. She'd spent many nights holding Dana when she woke from nightmares screaming for Ross to get away from her.

Eli frowned. "But why send Hoodie after a digital recording?"

"I don't know. It doesn't make sense." Brenna bit her lower lip, considered the implications of a connection with Ross. "You think I'm grasping at straws, don't you?"

He slid the bottle back into position and closed the door. "We need to call Cal and let the crime techs work on Dana's car."

"Go ahead." Brenna moved back to the still open front door. "I want to check these CDs. Dana must have bought something new. It's probably nothing, but the CDs didn't rattle in the door like normal." She followed Eli's example and used her shirt to cover her hand and removed the one cover she didn't recognize. "Eli, look at this."

She showed him the white CD with the clear cover. The CD was hand labeled with the letters SC. Sartelli Construction? "This is for pictures, not music."

"Is your laptop still in the trunk?" Eli asked.

"I never leave home without it." She smiled. "The computer is fully charged. I think we can find a use for it, don't you?"

"I love a woman who's beautiful and smart."

Brenna darted a look at Eli. He thought she was beautiful? Butterflies danced in her stomach. Wouldn't that be nice? Complicated, but good. Yeah, she wasn't big on long distance romances either. If he meant what he said. She reminded herself about the courteous southern gentleman part of Eli's personality.

Eli unlocked his trunk with the remote and raised the lid. "I won't sabotage Cal's case by taking the CD, but I don't mind copying the thing before he gets here. We'll put it back as soon as we have what we need." He unzipped the carrier case. "You do the honors."

Brenna turned on her laptop and copied the CD onto her computer's desktop. "Got it. What's next?"

"Now we call in Metro's finest."

Thirty minutes later, Cal Taylor eyed Eli with suspicion over the roof of Dana's car. "You better not have messed with anything, Wolfe."

"Would I do that?"

Cal snorted. "If I find so much as a hair from your head in this car, you might find yourself wearing a pair of handcuffs."

"You're breaking my heart here, Cal." Eli shook his head in mock disgust, his arm draped around Brenna's shoulders. "I'm smarter than that."

"Yeah, that's what I'm afraid of."

"Do you need us for anything else?"

The police detective scowled. "Your usual pattern is to hang over my shoulder and dog me for information. What gives, Wolfe?"

Eli turned Brenna toward the car. "You'll let me know what you find?"

"Works both ways, Eli."

Cal's soft response brought Eli's gaze back to his friend. Cal Taylor was a smart man. Eli fought back a smile. Taylor suspected the car had already been searched. "Check the pockets of the doors."

"Was the car locked?"

"Yep."

"Does Brenna have keys?"

"Nope."

"Do I want to know how the doors are now unlocked?"

"Nope."

Cal sighed. "Figured you would say that. Tell Jon he owes me for ignoring his skills again."

Eli grinned and opened the car door for Brenna.

Twenty minutes later, he and Brenna walked into Jon's office, computer in hand. The computer wizard glanced up from his screen, coffee mug halfway to his mouth.

"What did you find?" Jon asked. He sipped the steaming brew in his cup.

"A couple of things. A bottle of Obsession cologne for men in the backseat."

Jon's eyes narrowed and the muscles in his jaw flexed. "What else?"

Hmm. Eli eyed his friend and partner, wondered if he had missed something over the last few weeks. Did Jon have more than a soft spot for Dana? Guess the real question was if he did, were Dana's feelings involved? Her heart would have to be seriously tangled up with his teammate to take the risk of being vulnerable with a man again. Someone needed to address this thing with Ross Harrison. He'd like to be the man to do it. Had a feeling his partner would be the one to handle it. "A CD. Might have pictures burned on it. We copied it to Brenna's computer before we called the cops." He unzipped the case, flipped up the screen and awakened the computer from sleep mode. "Cal said you owe him one."

Jon's lip curled at one corner. "Maybe. Send a copy of the CD to our email. We might need our equipment to enhance picture or audio quality."

A few taps of the computer keys and Eli sent the file to the office email. He noticed Brenna chewing on her lower lip again and her hands trembled. Lack of sleep and stress making their presence felt? "Brenna, it will take a couple of minutes to transfer the file. Why don't you go to the kitchen and grab some bottled water for all of us? First door on your left. If you need a chocolate fix, there's a vending machine on the floor below. My sisters say chocolate fixes all manner of ailments."

"Oh, man, the chocolate sounds good. I'll be back."

He waited until he heard Brenna's footsteps on the tiled kitchen floor. "Jon, do you know about Dana's stepfather?"

His partner froze, hands hovering over the keyboard. "No." He lowered his hands to the sides of the keyboard. "Tell me."

In succinct sentences, Eli explained Dana's nightmarish past. When he finished, Jon's hands were clenched, knuckles white. "The stepfather wore Obsession. Brenna says Dana despises that cologne and would never have the bottle in her possession, let alone her car."

"Where is he?" Jon asked, his tone devoid of any emotion.

Eli flinched. He recognized the signs of bone-deep fury coursing through his friend. Ross Harrison didn't know it, but he had a painful appointment soon with Jon's fists. Nothing less than the creep deserved. Eli wouldn't lose one minute of sleep over Harrison's fate. "Haven't had time to chase that down yet. There's no indication that he's involved in Dana's disappearance."

"I'll find him." Jon's eyes narrowed. "He'll talk."

Oh, yeah. Harrison would talk and regret laying a finger on Dana. Jon's methods always worked which was why he'd been tagged repeatedly as interrogator when they captured terrorists on ops. In Harrison's case, Jon would choose the most painful methods at his disposal. Effective and brutal. Yeah, he'd get answers from Dana's slimy stepfather.

Brenna's footsteps echoed in the hall outside Jon's door. She entered the office carrying three bottles of water and three bags of Peanut M & Ms.

Eli's brows rose. "Are you that hungry, Brenna?"

She flushed. "I hate eating junk food alone. Dana shares with me when I buy these. They are her favorite." Brenna's eyes glistened. "I thought since you are her friends, you might join me."

"Thanks." Eli took one bag for himself and tossed the other to Jon. He said nothing when his partner dropped the candy on his desk and returned to the keyboard. Jon needed time to process the information he'd had dumped on him before he felt controlled enough for a verbal response.

A few clicks of the mouse later, a thumbnail series of pictures appeared on the screen. Jon enlarged the first, a picture of a construction site. The name Sartelli Construction appeared on the sign in the foreground. More pictures emerged of the same site, different angles in each shot of the guts of a strip mall. Eli frowned. "That may be the Mt. Juliet site. Are they all of the same place?"

Jon shook his head. Under his hand, the mouse skimmed down to the next row of thumbnail pictures and he enlarged the first photo. "Cinder block building. Several of them."

"Probably the school Sartelli is building."

Brenna leaned closer. "Who's that in the background?"

Jon clicked a couple of buttons and enlarged the picture again. A blond appeared. The picture was so blurred Eli couldn't see her features. "Can you clean it up?"

His partner fiddled with the picture more, but the result was marginally better. "I can send it to Fortress."

"Do it. Let's check the rest of them."

More shots of the various Sartelli construction sites appeared in dizzying succession under Jon's direction. On the last shot, Jon frowned. "Eli, this is a video clip."

"Let's see what Dana shot."

"Wait a minute. Dana didn't have a video camera." Brenna set her bottled water aside. "How could she shoot this?"

"Probably with her phone," Jon said.

"She only had a pre-paid phone, one without a camera."

"I upgraded her phone," Jon said.

"Why?" Eli asked.

"She needed it. Her phone was over a year old and kept dropping calls. Sartelli barely paid her enough to keep solvent."

Not even that much pay according to Brenna. "I didn't know she was struggling that hard, Jon, or we would have found a way to pay her for the help." Eli studied his friend and thought about what Jon didn't say. The only way he would have known about the cell phone problem was if his calls were the ones being dropped. Eli hadn't noticed a problem when she called his cell. "Why didn't you say something?"

Jon swung around, his expression hard. "I tried to pay her through Wolfe Investigations. She said she wouldn't take money from friends, especially when it required almost no effort on her part."

"You asked her to keep tabs on Sartelli's schedule," Brenna said. "Why did she take these pictures?"

Eli scanned the prints Jon handed him. "These are shots taken with a digital camera. Sartelli probably asked her to take them. It's common to take pictures of construction projects in progress."

"Ready for the video?" Jon asked.

"Play it."

Eli sat on the edge of the desk and eased Brenna closer to the computer. Grainy images of a couple of men carrying something moved across the screen. The video had been shot at dusk, so the lighting was poor on top of the distance. Something about the movement of one of the men caught Eli's attention. "That could be Mendoza. He's the right size. Beefy."

"Sartelli's thug?" Brenna asked.

"That's right, sugar. Wonder where Dana recorded this? Do you recognize the building, Jon?"

"It's not at the Sartelli place. Wrong shape."

"Huh. That leaves the rest of Nashville and the surrounding counties. Guess we're narrowing down the possible places to check out."

Jon ignored him.

The video clip showed the two men disappearing into a building and then stopped.

"Can you do anything with the video?" Eli asked.

"Maybe." Jon enlarged the image and clicked through a series of dialog boxes faster than Eli could read them. The clip started again, this time the background image was lighter and the figures larger.

Brenna gasped. "Eli, they're carrying a woman."

CHAPTER NINE

Brenna leaned closer to Jon's computer, studying the woman the two men carried. "She's blond, like the woman on the picture that Dana took." She turned to Eli. "Do you think this is what Hoodie was talking about? Could this be the recording he wanted?"

"Maybe. Wonder what Mendoza's involved in? If Sartelli knows, then his yard ape isn't straying into side work. He's carrying out the orders of his boss."

"I don't recognize the other guy," Jon said. "He's not one of Sartelli's foot soldiers."

"How do you know?" Brenna asked. "Have you been watching him?"

"For three weeks."

"Why?"

Jon glanced at Eli who shrugged. Brenna stiffened. "Okay, what gives? That's the second time in as many days you shared a meaningful look. I want to know what the big secret is."

"We think Sartelli's responsible for the death of a friend," Eli said. "His name was Joe Baker. Joe mentored Jon and me in private investigation work."

Brenna moved around to the front of Jon's desk and sat in a director's chair. "What happened to him?"

"Joe called me about a month ago. He said he was meeting an informant and if the info was good, Joe wanted us to work a case for him."

She frowned. "Why didn't he investigate the case on his own? He was a private investigator, right?"

"He'd retired and sold the business to us. Joe was traveling the US with his wife in their motor home and fishing in the lakes and streams wherever they camped. Said the world's biggest large-mouthed bass was waiting for him to sink his hook in the water." Eli's voice grew huskier the longer he talked.

"What brought him out of retirement?"

Jon stood and paced to the window. "We think it had something to do with a missing person case Joe couldn't solve. A 16-year-old girl from Boston named Kaylee Young. The Boston PD traced her to Nashville, but the trail went cold. The detective was a friend of Joe's and thought he could pick up the trail. Joe tracked her to The Watering Hole, but that was all. Nothing else ever surfaced, almost as if the trail stopped at the door."

"The Watering Hole?" Brenna blinked. "Sounds like a bar or something. What would an underage teenager be doing in a place like that?"

"It is a bar. Fake IDs are easy to get on the street," Eli said. "And based on her picture, Kaylee looked older than her age. Dana's neighbor, Tim, is the manager of The Watering Hole."

Brenna sighed. A connection to Dana's neighbor. Did her sister suspect Tim was involved in something shady? "Do you think Tim is connected to Kaylee's disappearance?"

"We don't know," Jon answered, turned toward her. "It might be a coincidence Tim appeared on the scene around the time Kaylee vanished from Nashville. He doesn't have a criminal record, if that's what you're asking. No arrests as a juvenile, either."

And, of course, Jon had checked with no obvious repercussions, like jail time for hacking into law enforcement databases. The former SEAL was scary good.

Coincidence didn't exist in her story worlds. Any event happened because she planned it or her muse knew when something should occur and a significant plot point snuck onto the computer screen, always leaving her wondering where the idea or inspiration came from. She suspected real life was the same. Ice poured through Brenna's veins. "But you think it's connected, don't you?" First Kaylee, now Dana missing. Could Tim be involved in either disappearance or both?

"Maybe." Eli tossed his empty water bottle in the trash. "None of us could find any proof."

Another idea surfaced. Her eyes narrowed. "Did you ask Dana to keep an eye on Tim, too?"

Eli shook his head.

"She did know about Kaylee," Jon said. "She saw her photograph on my desk a few weeks ago."

Eli's cell beeped. He pulled it out and read the text message. "Jon, Maddox sent us a link. He thinks it might be related to Dana."

Three long strides and Jon had seated himself at the computer keyboard again. He refreshed the emails and clicked on the link.

Brenna hurried around the desk, her throat tight. She prayed Fortress had found something, anything to help them locate her sister. Right now, she, Eli, and Jon were all grasping at whisper-thin threads. She felt Eli's solid chest behind her back, his hands on her shoulders. The silent support came at the perfect time.

Seconds later, a picture appeared on the screen, Dana wearing a red bikini, her face tear-stained. The caption underneath, "The newest Scarlett Beauty. Bidding ends in

48 hours." A clock counted down the time in the upper left hand corner of the screen.

"No." Brenna's hoarse voice pierced the utter stillness of the office. In her purse, her cell phone beeped. With a shaking hand, Brenna yanked open her bag and dug inside until she located her phone. A text message from an unknown number. "Eli."

"Open it," he said.

She punched the button to read the message and shuddered. "Like the picture? You can stop the clock. The recording in exchange for Dana. Fail to deliver and she will be sold to the highest bidder."

Jon grabbed his coffee mug and hurled it against the far wall.

Eli gathered a trembling Brenna into his arms. "Jon, take a few minutes. Go clear your head. I'll talk to Maddox."

His partner said nothing, just stalked out of the office. A minute later, the outer door slammed hard enough to rattle the windows.

"Who would do this to Dana? To any woman, for that matter. Eli, they're auctioning her off like a side of beef or something."

Eli's gaze flicked back to the gut-wrenching picture. Did the kidnappers mean to do what they threatened? That required connections to human trafficking. Having to rip open a still healing wound made him want to heave. Memories of his failed final SEAL op surged to the surface, refused to stay behind the cement wall he'd built in his mind, the wall which helped him maintain his sanity.

He didn't blame Jon for smashing his coffee mug. Unfortunately, shattered pottery wouldn't erase the faces of the women and children who had died in that foreign compound. SEAL Team 5 had been an hour too late to save the ambassador's daughter and the other victims. Their bloody ghosts populated his nightmares.

Eli dragged his attention back to the present and Brenna. Maybe the kidnappers were adding pressure, hoping to force Brenna to turn over the recording. They must know she wouldn't hold it back if it meant her sister's safe return. He feared the countdown clock was all too real. The question he needed answered—how long ago was the photo taken? It could have been taken ten days ago and only loaded onto the Internet recently.

It made a difference in how he and Jon responded when they found Dana. And they would find her, whether she still lived or not. If Dana remained alive, they would go after her in stealth mode and extract her. Once she had been taken to safety, they would dismantle the organization and deal with the scum bags who ran the business. If they got lucky, they might find out who bought the Young kid.

A wave of cold fury swept through him. If the traffickers killed Dana, all bets were off.

He pressed a kiss to Brenna's forehead and eased her into Jon's vacated chair. "Let me talk to Maddox, see what else he's learned."

Eli placed the call to Maddox's direct line.

"That her?" Maddox asked, once again forgoing manners for expediency. In his business, a minute one way or another meant life or death.

"Yeah. When was it posted?"

"About two hours ago. The computer analyst tripped the clock when he forwarded it to your email account."

"The sister was sent a text message. We found a video clip on a CD in Dana's car. Might be what the kidnappers are after." He leaned over Brenna and grabbed the mouse. "I'm sending you a copy of it right now. Have the analyst clean it up." A few clicks later, he sent an attached copy to Maddox. "Anything you can give us would help at this point because we've got zip."

"I'll get back to you." A dial tone sounded in his ear.

Brenna scooted her laptop across the desk and brought up her Internet connection. "Do you know anything about the Scarlett Beauty reference?"

Eli stilled. "You don't want to go down that rabbit hole, Brenna."

"Why? It sounds like a reference to a business or something."

Yeah, or something, all right. "Sugar, trust me. You don't want to dig too deep. Let me or Jon do the research." Whatever she found would give her nightmares. She didn't need to sully her dreams with the garbage Eli knew they'd find connected to Scarlett.

Brenna eyed him, her lips pressed tight. "You might know about special forces stuff and PI tactics, but I know research. I write historical romances, remember?"

"This isn't research for a book. Life can be ugly. Human trafficking is one of the ugliest things one human being can do to another. You won't like what you find."

"What do you know about it?"

"A lot more than I ever wanted to know. Enough that I don't sleep most nights." And when he did sleep, those same accusing faces haunted his dreams. One hour too late.

Brenna tilted her chin, defiance in her face. "It looks like Dana's living it. If I can help you find her by researching that organization, I'll do it."

Jon walked back into his office, his face totally devoid of emotion. "Out. Both of you."

"Maddox says the picture was posted two hours ago. He's still digging. I also sent him a copy of the video clip." Eli pulled Brenna to her feet. "Bring your computer to my office, sugar. We'll track down Helen Lynch. Maybe she can give us another link in the chain to find your sister."

"Why did you drag me out here with you?" Brenna studied the Lynch home through the Camaro's windshield.

The ranch-style red brick home had multiple fire bushes and boxwoods along the drive. Flowering rosebushes lined the outside walls of the home. Her mother would have enjoyed the landscaping. She would have chosen pink roses instead of the red favored by the Lynches. "I could have been more help doing research than being your arm candy."

Eli turned off the ignition with a soft chuckle. "Believe it or not, that is why I brought you. Ms. Lynch didn't sound comfortable with a stranger coming to her home. I can't blame her for that. Figured she might be more helpful if a gorgeous woman was with me."

Brenna turned her narrowed gaze on her companion. "Gorgeous, huh?"

"Oh, yeah. Total knockout."

"Piling it on a little thick, aren't you, Wolfe?"

"Is it working?"

"Am I supposed to be oblivious to everything in the room but you?"

"Well . . ."

"Because let me tell you right now, Wolfe, I don't simper and fawn over anybody unless it's a baby. You don't qualify, buddy."

Eli laughed and opened the door.

They followed the concrete path to the porch. A middle-aged woman opened the door within seconds of the bell chiming.

"Ms. Lynch?" Eli said. He handed her his card. "I'm Eli Wolfe. This is Brenna Mason."

The woman examined his card and appeared satisfied with what she read. Brenna wondered if the woman realized that anyone could have cards printed at a quick-print shop or order them on the Internet. She should have asked for Eli's investigator's license. Then again, if Brenna had been confronted by Eli Wolfe before Dana's disappearance and the apartment break-in, she might not have asked for the ID either. Would she ever feel safe again?

"May we come in?" Eli asked. "Like I mentioned earlier on the phone, we need to ask you some questions about Dana Cole."

"I don't know that I can help you, Mr. Wolfe. I met Dana once. She was supposed to get in touch with me, but she never called."

"Please, Ms. Lynch." Brenna stepped closer. "Dana is my sister. She's missing. We need your help."

Helen Lynch's face blanched. "Missing?"

"Yes, ma'am," Eli said. "Would you be more comfortable if we talked out here?"

She stepped back. "Come into the kitchen. It's too hot to talk outside."

Brenna walked through the door and traipsed into the kitchen a few feet behind Eli and Ms. Lynch. He'd warned her ahead of time to let him walk ahead of her for safety. He didn't know what they were walking into, doubted it was dangerous, but insisted on the precaution anyway. She took a few seconds to scan the photos lining the walls. A blond girl in various stages of life. Ms. Lynch's daughter, from the close resemblance. Very pretty girl.

"Would either of you like some lemonade? It's fresh, from scratch."

"Appreciate it. Nashville summer heat and humidity are pretty fierce," Eli said.

"Thank you, Ms. Lynch." Brenna smiled at the woman.

"It's Helen. Lemonade is Julie's favorite drink." Her eyes glistened with sudden tears. "I keep a pitcher in the refrigerator, hoping."

"Julie? Is she your daughter?" Brenna asked. "I saw the pictures in the hallway."

Helen wiped tears from her cheeks. "Julie's missing. The police think she ran away three weeks ago." She opened the cabinet and removed three glasses which she filled with a light yellow liquid from a glass pitcher.

"But you don't." Brenna accepted the glass with a smile and sipped the icy drink. "Oh, this is great, Helen. Perfect."

The woman smiled. "Fresh-squeezed lemons make all the difference." Then the smile was gone. "Julie didn't run away. It's just us now." Helen sat at the kitchen table, waving them to chairs across from her. "Ben, my husband, died on patrol last year in the Middle East."

"What branch of the military, Helen?" Eli asked, his voice quiet.

"Army. He was with the 101st Airborne. Anyway, Julie and I are close. She's seventeen, a senior, and we've been making plans for her to go to college next fall. She wants to be a doctor. We haven't had any fights. Her boyfriend, Chad, is beside himself with worry. They weren't having any problems, either. She's just gone."

Eli pulled out his notepad. "What's Chad's last name?"

"Elliott."

"Know how I can contact him?"

"He's a good boy, Mr. Wolfe." Helen's hands clenched around her glass. "He wouldn't hurt Julie. They've been dating since the seventh grade. He treats my daughter like she's made of blown glass. My husband thought well of him, too."

"I'm not saying he hurt your daughter, but Chad might know something that Julie didn't share with you. You know how kids are these days."

Helen sighed. "They confide in each other. I know that, but the police already questioned him. He didn't know anything."

"It's been a while. He may have remembered something else or the news of Dana's disappearance might help him connect some things that didn't seem important a few weeks ago."

After a sip of her drink, Helen gave him the phone number.

"How is Dana involved with your family?" Brenna asked. "She never mentioned you or Julie."

"Julie has been working for Sartelli Construction in the afternoons. She helps with whatever odd jobs Dana finds her to do. After Julie went missing, Dana called every day, checking to see if I had heard from her."

"When was the last time you heard from Dana?" Eli asked.

"Almost two weeks ago. A Thursday night. Dana said she might have an idea what happened to Julie, but she needed to check something before she said anything more." Helen shrugged. "I didn't hear from her after that. I figured she grew tired of me calling all the time, but I was desperate."

Brenna's throat tightened. That was the night Dana had been to Red Lobster with Sartelli. Could Dana's disappearance be linked to Julie Lynch's? Of course it was. The disappearances were around the same time and were similar enough to be nothing less than a real connection. And the police had no leads to Julie's whereabouts. How were Eli and Jon and their private security employer going to find what law enforcement missed?

"Tell us about the day Julie disappeared," Eli said. "Did she work with Dana that day?"

Helen nodded. "She called me from the office and said she was driving to the Sartelli home. She was to address invitations to some charity event Elena is hosting. The police questioned Mrs. Sartelli. She didn't know anything, just said Julie never showed up."

"What about her car?"

"The police still haven't found it."

After making sure Helen had both her and Eli's cell numbers, Brenna and Eli drove away from the home.

Thoughts wound through Brenna's mind in an endless circle. What could Dana have learned about Julie Lynch's disappearance? Brenna wished she had pushed Dana harder, insisted that she spill what troubled her weeks ago. If Julie disappeared because of her job, Dana would have done anything necessary to find her since she'd helped the young teen land the work. The same thing Brenna should have done for Dana that fateful summer. She should have pushed harder for information then, too. Would she never learn?

Eli broke the silence a few blocks from the Lynch place. "You up for another stop?"

Jon ended the call, fury burning a hole in his gut. Maddox's tech geek had learned nothing new in the last few hours. His old SEAL buddy either needed new computer talent or more quantity. How hard could it be to track down the Internet service provider hosting the Scarlett's Beauties website?

The police had stonewalled him, claimed their crime scene techs needed more time to process Dana's car. Cal hadn't responded to the message Jon left thirty minutes earlier. All of which left him with a desire to knock a new hole in the wall.

He studied the sharpened image of the girl sent to his email inbox from Fortress a short while earlier. Jon tweaked and rotated the image, and clicked the print button.

He frowned. What was a young girl doing at a construction site? From the equipment showing in the foreground, it was an active site, too dangerous to be wandering around even in daylight. And why didn't the construction crew chase her off?

Jon highlighted a worker on the left side of the image and enlarged the face. His lip curled. Well, look at that. Same tango that helped Mendoza carry the woman in the video clip.

After a few clicks of the mouse, he grabbed the phone. "It's Jon. I sent you a photo. Need an ID." He listened to the irate voice on the other end of the line, fist slowly clenching. "How soon? Yesterday. Clock's ticking. We're at less than forty-five hours."

"When did you last see Julie?"

Eli studied the teenager in the waning afternoon light at Centennial Park. Very clean cut for a kid his age, he decided. Most teen boys he knew sported longish hair, tattoos, and a few piercings. Of course, that assumption was based on his four nephews, ages 13 to 19. Come to think of it, that description fit his nieces, too.

Chad Elliott's hair was cut over his ears and off the collar. No piercings or tattoos visible. A polo shirt and non-holey jeans with pristine white running shoes completed the image of a young man with a goal in life and a plan to meet said goal.

Chad leaned back against the picnic table, his gaze focused on the ducks swimming in the nearby pond. "The Friday she disappeared. We had lunch together before she went to work."

"Did she seem okay?"

The teen dragged his gaze back to Eli. "What do you mean?"

"Was she upset or worried?" He waited, noting the tightening of the boy's jaws. Chad's gaze returned to the ducks. Hmm. Eli sat next to him. "Look, Chad, you can tell me anything. I'm not a cop or a relative. I'm looking for a friend and I think her disappearance may be tied to Julie's."

"Who's the friend?" he asked, his voice laced with suspicion.

"Dana Cole."

Chad's head jerked around. "Dana's missing, too?"

"She disappeared almost two weeks ago. Do you know her?"

"Spoke to her a few times when I picked up Julie after she finished work. Dana's a nice lady. Helped Julie get her job at Sartelli Construction when no one else would give her a chance. She didn't want to work at a fast food place. Julie worried about burning her hands."

"I thought she had a car of her own."

"Mrs. Lynch's car is unreliable, so sometimes she would drive Julie's Beetle to work. I've been on Mrs. Lynch's case to get something newer, but she's afraid to go car shopping. Julie's dad took care of the car stuff from the time he and her mom started dating."

"I see. Back to my question, Chad. Was Julie upset or worried at lunch that day?"

The teen's gaze dropped to his feet. "Yeah. I upset her. It was my fault."

"Yeah? What happened?" Eli glanced at the nearby picnic table where Brenna sat, working on her computer. He scanned the area. The back of his neck itched, the kind of itch he paid attention to on missions. Nothing caught his interest, but the feeling didn't fade. He needed to end this interview pronto and take Brenna to a safer location.

"I wanted to move our relationship to a new level." The flush in Chad's face deepened.

A flash of sympathy rolled through Eli at the boy's embarrassment. Had to appreciate the careful way he phrased his statement as well. He'd bet no locker room trash talk came from this kid. "Julie didn't?"

"She wanted to wait. Said we weren't old enough, that she wanted a wedding ring on her finger first."

Eli nodded. "Smart girl. You tell the police?"

Silence greeted his question at first, then the boy turned to face him. "I couldn't."

"Why?"

Another silence.

Eli watched the ducks paddle around the pond and dive for bread dropped on the water by a few kids. "Were you afraid the police might be right, that Julie ran away because of you?"

"Yeah."

He decided a change of topic was in order. He'd tortured the poor kid enough about that subject for now. Didn't suppose he'd want to discuss that sensitive topic with the cops either. "How do you feel about Julie's plans for college?"

Chad relaxed, shrugged. "Fine. We both want to attend Vanderbilt University next year."

"Is that right? You okay with her planning to be a doctor?"

The boy shot him a wary glance. "Sure. Why shouldn't I be?"

"That's quite a lofty career goal. Won't leave much time for a boyfriend over the next few years." Eli twisted to face him. "Most guys your age would have a problem with that. Do you?"

The first real smile curved Chad's upward. "No more of a problem than Julie will have with it. I'll be studying medicine, too."

"Good for you. You guys choose a specialty yet?"

"Julie plans to be a surgeon. I want to specialize in pediatrics. Kids have their own brand of magic. Nothing gets them down for long. They just sort of bounce back, even when they're sick. I want to be part of keeping them healthy."

Yeah, he got it. His nieces and nephews dispensed that magic on him whenever they were in the same room. Somehow they silenced all the ghosts. Eli stood and held out his card. "Thanks for your time, Chad. If you think of anything that might help, call me." He shook the teen's hand. "And for what it's worth, I don't think Julie would run away from you and the relationship issues. Got a feeling she's too smart to do something like that. From what I've learned about her from you and her mom, Julie's got enough self-confidence and career focus to kick you to the curb if you pushed too hard."

Chad smiled. "Yeah, you're probably right. Thanks, Mr. Wolfe."

After the teenager left the park, Eli scanned the area again. Needles still pricked the back of his neck. Not good. Time to get Brenna out of the park. "Let's go, sugar."

"Can you give me a minute or two? I need to finish this paragraph."

"Hurry. Something isn't right out here, but I can't pinpoint it." He quartered their surroundings, positive someone watched, maybe with a scope. It never paid to ignore the sensation burning his skin, almost as if a laser sight focused on him.

"Got it." Brenna took out her flash drive and bent over to slip it in her purse.

A flash of light caught Eli's attention. Reacting without thinking, he dove for Brenna and slammed her to the ground, his body covering hers.

The echo of a gunshot splintered the afternoon quiet.

CHAPTER TEN

Brenna tried to raise her head, but found it impossible to shift her more than 200-pound special forces protector enough to see what was happening. Her brain kicked out of slow mode and replayed the sound in her mind.

Holy cow! A gunshot?

Eli's deep voice rumbled in her ear. "Are you okay?"

Brenna managed to turn her head and froze. Eli's voice was rock steady as was the hand holding the gun inches from her face. Did nothing ever rattle this SEAL? "I'm fine. You?" Her own voice sounded a little breathless. No doubt the result of her heavy SEAL cover rather than flying bullets. If he could be unaffected by a bullet, she could at least do a credible job of acting like she had it together instead of admitting she wanted to run away screaming.

"Don't move."

She scowled. She couldn't do more than breathe at the moment. Good grief. Eli Wolfe's muscles must be made from pure steel. The guy put out some serious heat, not a plus on this scorching July day. "Is the shooter gone?"

"I think so."

A couple of college aged men raced toward them. "Hey, you guys okay?"

"Yeah," Eli said. "Did one of you call the cops?"

"I did," the red haired man said. "They should be here in a few minutes. You don't look so good, man. You sure you're okay?"

Brenna twisted hard.

He grunted. "Hold still, sugar."

"Let me up. Right now, Wolfe."

As soon as Eli eased his weight from her back, Brenna scrambled to her knees. Blood dripped down the side of his face and galvanized her into action. "You," she said, pointing to the shaved head man. "Go to McDonald's and get some napkins." As he sprinted across the park, she turned to Red Hair. "Keep watch for the police. Send them over to us as soon as they arrive."

Eli eyed her from the ground, amusement dancing in his eyes. "Any instructions for me?"

Brenna shoved aside the smoking remnants of her laptop. "You are in hot water, Wolfe. You getting shot was not part of my service package. Sit on the bench and shut up."

"Don't you think you're overreacting a little, sugar?"

"Overreacting, huh? Someone shot at us and got lucky enough to hit you. Blood is streaming down your face and the shooter got away. Does that pretty well sum up the situation?"

Eli's mouth twitched as he seated himself with his back to the picnic table. "It's just a scratch."

"Here you go, lady." Baldy handed Brenna a stack of napkins and a bottle of cold water. "You might need this."

"Thanks." After pouring liquid onto a napkin and handing the bottle to Eli, she wiped the blood from his face with one hand while using the other to apply light pressure to the wound on his head.

"It's not as bad as it looks, Brenna," Eli said.

"How do you know that? You don't see your head. You might need stitches or something." Her voice shook.

Brenna firmed her lips. She hated to sound scared, but she was terrified for Dana, Eli, Jon, and herself. Someone could have been killed. Later, when she could process everything in private in the shower, she'd deal with the fact someone tried to kill her.

"Head wounds always bleed a lot. Trust me, sugar. This is a scratch."

She swallowed hard and finished cleaning his face before meeting his gaze. He sounded sure. How could he be? He didn't see the ghoulish mask, the perfection of his features marred by a curtain of blood. Then again, she reasoned, if the wound were deeper or more serious, they wouldn't be having this bizarre conversation. "Voice of experience, I take it."

Eli shrugged.

What had she expected from a SEAL? Anything short of a life-threatening wound might not merit more than his cursory shrug. At that moment a couple of patrol cars skidded to a halt near Red Hair. Behind them, an ambulance pulled in.

When the EMTs drew close, she tried to move away, but Eli grabbed Brenna's hand and tugged hard. "Sit right here beside me. You don't go anywhere without me, remember?"

"I'll get in their way."

"Tough. They'll have to work around you."

The determined expression on his face forestalled more protests. For the next few minutes, she, Eli, Red and Baldy answered questions for the police while one of the EMTs worked on Eli's head wound.

As the EMT put away his medical supplies, Brenna asked, "Anything in particular we should do about this injury?"

"He needs to contact his doctor as soon as possible. Your friend probably needs antibiotics to prevent an infection."

"I'll take care of it," Eli said. He grinned at Brenna. "Told you, sugar. The bullet just kissed me."

Right. Her stomach knotted at what might have happened if the gunman's aim had been more accurate. Based on the police questions, she figured they planned to write this up as a drive-by shooting. She knew better and wondered why Eli hadn't bothered enlightening them. Didn't he trust the Nashville police?

She decided to keep silent for the moment and waited for the questions to end, the patrolmen to leave. In the meantime, she studied the remains of her laptop. She foresaw a trip to Best Buy in her immediate future. With the balance of her bank account nearing a critical stage, she would have to settle for an inexpensive computer. All she really needed was Internet capability and a word processing program. Everything else could wait.

After questioning her one last time and admonishing both of them to call if they remembered anything new, the police left. Brenna held out her hand to Eli, wiggled her fingers. "Keys."

Eli's eyes narrowed. "You want to drive my car?"

"Humor me, tough guy. Give me the keys or I'll call Jon or your detective friend. Think of me as your own personal chauffeur for a few hours. You can tell me which way to go in between the phone calls."

"Chauffeur, huh?"

"I promise not to get a scratch on that beauty."

"Do I get a reward for letting you drive my pride and joy?"

Brenna snorted. "Get real. It's transportation." She squelched a grin at his immediate scowl. "But since you spilled buckets of blood protecting me, we might negotiate. What's the price for babying your car?"

"Three signed copies of your latest book and a date with me."

"We already had a date, remember?"

Rebecca Deel

"Dinner at Red Lobster doesn't count. That was camouflage. I mean a real date where I don't have to watch our backs for tangos or kidnappers."

"Deal. Now hand over the keys."

Eli tossed her the keys with a chuckle. "Wow, if I had known it would only cost a little blood to get a date with you, I would have offered up half a pint sooner."

Tears blurred her vision. "Don't, Eli."

"Hey." He stepped in front of her and folded her into his arms. "Everything is going to be fine. I'd say we're on the right track, sugar. Someone doesn't want us nosing around asking questions about Julie's disappearance and we're almost positive Dana's disappearance is connected to hers. Just hang in there with me."

"They could have killed you. I didn't mean for you to get hurt. I'm so sorry."

"I'm hard to kill, baby. Trust me. Men a lot more dangerous than these guys have tried to take me out and failed." He shepherded her to his car. "Let's get out of here. The clock's ticking."

Eli pulled on a fresh polo shirt, damp hair clinging to his head. He leaned closer to the bedroom mirror and inspected the two-inch long gash marking the side of his head. He grabbed his cell phone and called Jake Davenport, one of the Zoo Crew's medics. Eli had a stash of antibiotics in his Go bag. All Fortress operatives carried medical supplies in their bags along with the requisite tools of their trade. Maybe he'd get lucky and the meds needed would be in his bag. If not, he figured Davenport would have the meds he needed handy.

One ring and a deep voice mumbled, "Davenport."

Eli explained the injury to the medic and answered a barrage of medical questions before his teammate named an antibiotic and dosage standard in all their kits. "Thanks, D."

"Lucky you have a hard head, Wolfe. How's Jon?"

"Getting there."

"Hey, man, you're not talking to Maddox. I hear Jon's threatening bodily harm to any operative who doesn't deliver information at the speed of light. What gives?"

Eli leaned one shoulder against the wall and eased the curtain aside to check the perimeter for changes. "Friend of ours was kidnapped ten days ago. Got a deadline approaching fast and almost zero leads." Lengthening shadows added the need for a slower scan. Still nothing.

"A woman?"

"Yeah."

"His?"

Eli started to say no until he remembered the interesting revelations from his partner. A new phone for Dana, notes, phone calls. All under Eli's radar. Jon might consider Dana his. Not sure their beautiful friend felt the same way. "Maybe. The worst part is she's probably in the hands of human traffickers."

Davenport whistled. "So it doesn't matter whether he's ready for another op."

"No." Muscles twitched in Eli's jaw. "We'll do whatever is necessary to free her." No matter the cost. They weren't going to lose anyone else to human traffickers.

Jon parked his black SUV under heavy shade and shut off the engine. Not many lights worked on this street so his vehicle faded into the gloom, making it close to invisible to the casual observer. Suited his purposes. Jon didn't care who knew he was searching for Dana. He didn't want Eli caught in the backwash if he needed to use extreme measures in uncovering information to rescue Dana.

He wouldn't leave her in enemy hands, not like his former Zoo Crew teammate had left him months ago. His jaw tightened and anger boiled at the memories punching through the mental barrier he'd built to contain those unforgettable days he'd spent as a guest of terrorists. He still had the scars as a reminder.

Jon reached up, shut off the overhead light, and opened his door. According to Maddox's source, Eric Thomas lived two blocks over in a house inherited from his mother. Rumors in the underground said he helped his mother on to her eternal reward. Told him what kind of person he was dealing with. Scum of the earth. No surprise since he had some connection to human traffickers. Jon scowled. Lot of people he'd become acquainted with over the years in relation to his jobs on and off the books were more interested in money than people.

He scanned the deserted street. Jon slipped into the shadows and walked through a stinking, garbage-strewn alley. On some level, he registered a sour taste in his mouth from the stench. At the mouth of the alley, he paused in the deepest shade, listening, observing. Satisfied he'd attracted no attention, he moved forward, crossed barren yards and plunged into yet another alley.

Minutes later, Jon eased over a wooden fence into Thomas's back yard and remained motionless, listened in vain for sounds of a pet. Good. No dog. He'd brought hamburger meat laced with a sleeping drug safe for canines, but he would have been guessing at how much to give a dog weighing less than a hundred pounds.

He shifted his attention and observed the dark house. No movement, no lights. The intel indicated Thomas was at home most Monday nights for a weekly poker game with his buddies. Game didn't start until nine o'clock. It was only seven o'clock now. Left him two hours to learn what he needed. His mouth quirked. Plenty of time.

When full dark cloaked the surroundings in an impenetrable gloom, Jon crossed the yard and unscrewed the single light bulb burning by the door. He hoped Thomas or a neighbor would think the light had burned out.

He removed a set of lock picks from his jacket pocket and, within seconds, heard the satisfying snick of the lock giving to his tools. No alarm, either. His lip curled. Guess the man figured his bad-boy image would protect him from being the target of a crime.

Not today.

After a cursory search through the residence showed nothing except an appalling lack of cleaning skills, Jon settled down to wait in the darkened living room, lights disabled. He spent the time fitting the pieces of Dana's disappearance together as if working a jigsaw puzzle. Each time memories of his time as a prisoner of terrorists interrupted the puzzle assembly, he shoved them back behind the mental wall and resumed manipulating pieces of data. He would find Dana no matter how long it took. And when he did, he'd begin the long, slow process of winning her heart. Knowing now what she'd been through, he figured that was the only type of campaign that gave him a shot with her. And he wanted that shot with a passion. Dana was special, well worth any amount of time it took.

Twenty minutes later, a key jangled in the front door lock. Plastic bags rattled as Thomas shifted them from two hands into one. A flip of a light switch. The room remained dark. An explosive curse followed by a deep grumble as he kicked the door shut with his foot.

Jon, on his feet, waited until Thomas passed within a foot of his position before he moved. Within seconds, Thomas cried out, landing face first on the floor, bags scattered, arms immobilized from behind. More struggles which suddenly ceased as Jon made liberal use of his knowledge of painful pressure points and holds. "Who are you? What do you want?" Thomas demanded.

"Information."

"I don't know nothing."

Jon chuckled while adding more pressure, enough to cause Thomas sharp pain. God bless the Navy SEAL training. Came in handy. "You better hope you do know something, Thomas, or I won't have any reason to leave you breathing." Despite not having plans to kill Thomas, the enemy sensed if you weren't committed to a course of action. To save Dana, Jon knew he would do whatever was necessary. The acrid scent of Thomas's fear tainted the air in the room. "Will anyone miss you, Thomas? Maybe your mother? Oh, wait, she can't miss you. You killed her already, didn't you? Bet it didn't take too long. She was within two months of dying from pancreatic cancer. Did you convince yourself you were committing a humanitarian act by helping her to the Pearly Gates a little faster?"

Thomas froze.

"Since you're not exactly Ghandi, guess that means no one will care if you're dead." Jon waited, ready with more painful tactics if Thomas still proved uncooperative. Thanks to his black ops training, he knew many ways to elicit information from reluctant witnesses. Some left the recipients undamaged. Others didn't. To recover Dana, he wouldn't lose one minute's sleep over using every interrogation skill in his arsenal. In fact, he welcomed the chance to vent the fury raging in his gut, the guilt that ate at his insides like acid. Ten days she'd been missing and Jon had been too busy looking into Joe's murder to more than wonder at her silence before returning to the search. He knew better. The living always trumped the dead. Joe would have been appalled. Never again, Jon vowed. Dana would never again take second place in his priorities.

Jon felt his quarry's capitulation before Thomas's words confirmed it. The body language was a dead giveaway.

"What do you want to know?"

"I'm looking for a woman. Name's Dana Cole."

Thomas tried to turn his head and get a look at the man who pinned him to the floor. He doubted the man could identify him in the pitch black room, but he couldn't take the chance on leading anyone to his partner. Jon increased the pressure on a nerve which he knew caused excruciating pain to radiate down the legs.

Thomas let out a high-pitched howl which seemed to bounce off the living room walls. Jon released enough pressure so the pain was tolerable. Barely. "Next time I won't be so nice."

"I'm sorry, man. Sorry." He sobbed.

"Let's try this again, Thomas. Dana Cole."

"I don't know nobody named Dana."

"Wrong answer." Jon ramped up the pressure on the nerve long enough to leave Thomas squealing and begging for mercy.

"I swear, man. Her name don't sound familiar. I know lots of broads. Can't remember all their names, you know? Tell me what she looks like. Maybe I've seen her."

"Long black hair, green eyes, small height, slender build."

"She got a tattoo or something I'd notice? I mean, that sounds like a lot of women I know."

Jon rested his full body weight on the one knee pressed into Thomas's kidney. The stench of warm urine filled the room. "She works at Sartelli Construction." Not for much longer, if Jon had anything to say about it. If necessary, he'd take on extra jobs for Fortress so he could pay her salary at Wolfe Investigations before he'd let Dana step foot on Sartelli's turf again. She was too important to him to lose her to the likes of Sartelli. Even if she rejected him, which she'd be smart to do, he'd still make sure she worked a safer job. Maybe Maddox could find a job for her at Fortress.

"Name don't mean nothing to me." The fear leaching through in his voice spoiled the bravado of his words. Some people were ultimate liars. Thomas wasn't one of them.

"What a shame, Thomas. I really didn't want to kill you, but you're not helping me out here."

"You don't understand, man. They'll kill me if I talk."

Jon leaned forward, eliciting another groan from the man underneath him, and whispered, "I'll kill you if you don't tell me what I want to know, and I promise, you'll be in such agony you'll beg me to end your life long before I slit your throat."

"Okay, okay. Please."

Again, Jon eased the pressure just enough for Thomas to talk with a sharp reminder of pain. "Sartelli Construction," he prompted.

"I do some work for them on the side."

"For Marcos Sartelli?"

"Maybe. I don't know for sure. I've never seen Sartelli."

Not surprising. Would be pretty careless of Marcos to let himself be tied to anything illegal. He'd learned how to cover his tracks from old school thugs in Italy. "What side work, Thomas?"

"I help a guy with moving stuff."

Jon's internal clock told him Thomas was stalling, hoping the arrival of his poker buddies would save his worthless hide. While he could take down all four men soon to arrive, Jon preferred not to risk a neighbor calling the cops. He pulled a small Smith and Wesson knife from the sheath on his arm and angled the blade across Thomas's throat. "My supply of patience is running low, Thomas. Either you start talking in paragraphs instead of three-word sentences, or I'll skip play time and slice your jugular now. You'll be dead in two minutes."

"I swear, man. I help this guy move stuff. Sometimes we truck equipment from one construction site to another."

"Someone photographed you carrying an unconscious woman with one of Sartelli's goons, scum bag. Who was the girl?"

Thomas stilled beneath Jon. "Someone took a picture?"

"Your ugly mug is very recognizable. That's how I tracked you down so fast. Who was the girl?"

"I don't know."

Jon's knife left a one-inch bleeding scratch on Thomas's neck. "Who was the girl?"

"Ow! Please, no more. I don't know her name. Honest. Just some drunk college girl. Gage thought it would be funny for the party girl to sleep it off and wake up on a construction site. You know, teach her a lesson. Shouldn't drink if you can't hold the booze."

Jon almost snorted at the drivel spilling from Thomas's lips. "What's your excuse for the twenty-four pack of beer on the floor? Just so you know, that girl wasn't in college, Thomas. She's still in high school and disappeared the night you left her at that site. Guess what that makes you? An accomplice. I bet a cop would love to slap cuffs on you and haul you to jail for kidnapping." An anonymous tip to Cal's office was on Jon's agenda soon.

"Hey, no way, man. I don't know nothing about no kidnapping. I'm innocent."

"Not buying it, Thomas. Where did you pick up the girl?"

"Some dude's apartment."

Jon changed his hold on Thomas's arm, twisting it higher. The man screeched with pain. "Name or address."

"Some place off Bell Road and Zelida. Don't know the guy's name or the complex."

Jon's blood ran cold. Dana's complex. "I want an apartment or building number. Think hard before you answer, Thomas. Lie to me and I'll know. I won't be happy. Might even have to break a few bones to make my point. Start talking, Thomas."

"I don't remember. I was buzzed, man."

"A landmark, then. Was it near the complex entrance?"

"Third floor of the building across from the laundry room. Saw a hot babe carrying a basket of clothes into a laundry room across the street."

Dana's building and floor. Had to be Tim Russell, the neighbor across the hall with ties to The Watering Hole. "Describe the man."

"Just an average white guy with a mustache."

Jon narrowed his eyes. Sounded like Russell, but he had to be sure. "Which apartment?"

"Don't know, man. Can't remember."

He applied more pressure. "Have you helped your friend pick up other women like that?"

Thomas shook his head, sobbing. "I only helped with the one girl."

"How long ago, Thomas?"

"Three weeks maybe."

Had to be Julie. Time frame fit and he was almost positive the fuzzy picture was of an unconscious Julie. "Which construction site?"

"Some shopping center in Wilson County. I didn't pay much attention."

Jon's eyes narrowed. "Why not? What were you doing?"

"I was in the back of the van with the girl. Gage told me to keep an eye on her."

Jon could smell the lie wafting from Thomas's lips. "Don't lie to me, Thomas. Did you touch her?" Her clothes had been intact from what he could see on the grainy picture, but that didn't mean Thomas hadn't taken the opportunity to cop a feel or do something worse and re-dress her.

"No."

Another change in the pressure.

"Okay! Yeah, so I peeked. She was a looker."

"Last time, Thomas. Did you touch her?"

126

"A little. Wasn't much time, man. I didn't hurt her. I swear."

"Think hard, Thomas. Who else do you know from Sartelli Construction?"

CHAPTER ELEVEN

Brenna booted up Eli's laptop, typed in his password and waited for the programs to load while listening to his low-voiced murmur in the next room. As long as Eli was occupied, she could spend some time surfing the Internet for references to Scarlett's Beauties. Eli's warnings to stay out of that part of the research still rang in her ears. But some small piece of information might be the key to finding Dana and freeing her. Brenna rocked at researched. She had to be good at it for her historical romances. Nothing ticked readers off more than catching factual errors in fiction.

Once the programs loaded, she clicked on an icon tucked in the corner of the screen. An icon for Fortress? The security group Eli and Jon freelanced for? Brenna leaned close to study the options on the screen and chose what looked like an information database.

The cursor blinked in a dialog box beside the search button. She hesitated a minute, eavesdropped on what she could hear of her bodyguard's conversation until satisfied Eli would be a few minutes more, then typed in the name of the human trafficking organization.

Within seconds, information flooded the screen. Brenna read as fast as she dared, eyes widening with each new level of data revealed. Nausea bubbled at the atrocities the victims suffered, the degradation inflicted on the innocent. How could more than 20,000 people a year in the United States be taken by human traffickers and no one seem to care?

"What are you reading, sugar?"

"A nightmare."

"What kind?"

"A tragedy, one with women and children being sold, some by their own families, into a hopeless existence. Did you know Scarlett's Beauties is a high-end business? They only deal in special requests for sleaze-bag clients. Highest bidder gets the prize." Bitterness laced her voice. A tragic existence that might swallow Dana in the next few hours.

"You're not surfing the Internet with my standard browser, are you?"

She tore her gaze from the screen. "I clicked on the Fortress website and tapped into their database. I should say I'm sorry for breaking my promise and searching a secured site, but I won't. I'm not sorry. I'm mad. How can they get away with this? Why isn't the news media squawking about this instead of global warming or a third-world disaster? Aren't people's lives more important than the environment? How many commercials do we see all the time on television about animal abuse? What about people abuse? This is inhumane."

"You don't have to convince me, Brenna."

Something in his voice, a conviction, sorrow, registered through her fury and caught her attention. "Why not? What do you know about this?"

"More than I ever wanted to. More than I can live with some days." He held out his hand. "Log off the computer and we'll talk."

Although reluctant to stop her research, Brenna complied with Eli's request. She allowed him to lead her to the living room couch. She turned sideways, one leg bent on the cushion, her back resting against the arm of the couch so she could observe his facial expressions. Tough to watch this hurting man. She suspected his story would be both painful and personal, an idea supported by Eli leaving the room encased in darkness broken only by one lamp's soft glow at its lowest three-way setting.

"I won't be able to tell you everything you want to know, Brenna. A lot of it is confidential, an op while I was a SEAL."

"Your operation involved Scarlett's Beauties?"

"Yes, though it wouldn't matter if it were this group or any of the many others that prey on humans." He stopped speaking for a minute, his hand clenching into a fist.

Brenna's heart squeezed, almost prompting her to give him an out, but she needed all the information available. She hated to cause him more pain or resurrect difficult memories. Brenna reminded herself that this man was an elite warrior, one trained in deadly combat, a lethal weapon himself. This wouldn't be the first or last difficult task he ever performed. And if this group was as determined to survive and thrive as she suspected, more ugly things lay ahead in their quest to free Dana.

"A few years ago, a dignitary's daughter was snatched from her home overseas. My team and I were deployed on a mission to rescue the girl. Intel told us she was being held in a compound about three miles inland."

Brenna's throat tightened. She remembered this kidnapping since it sparked a storyline in one of her historical novels. It was an ambassador's sixteen-year-old daughter. Her stomach lurched. The kidnapping didn't end well, so she had changed the ending to suit the romance she was writing. And Eli had been involved in the rescue attempt? What horrors had he and his team been exposed to on that operation?

"The father contacted an old friend, one connected to the military. The father was told to go along with the demands. The Scarlett Group contacted him with instructions for delivery of the ransom. He followed them to the letter, Brenna. Even had the money transferred to a Swiss bank account ahead of the deadline."

Eli leaned forward, forearms resting on his thighs, hands clasped between his knees. "No one was supposed to know about the mission. We arrived in the middle of the night. Took a few minutes to get the team and equipment into position. We reached the compound around three a.m., the time most people's biorhythms are low. The goal was to get in and out with the girl before the enemy knew we were there. Same objectives as most of our missions.

"We didn't encounter any resistance. No guards, no booby-traps, nothing, and that was unusual. We knew something was wrong, but without further intel or a change in mission instructions, we followed orders and proceeded to the compound."

"What happened?" Brenna whispered.

"We were too late. The kidnappers had killed the girl and several other women and children before our boots hit the ground. It was such a blood bath several members of the team resigned after that failed op."

"What about you?"

"Jon and I were the first to walk away. We had already realized we were slowing down. Special forces work is for young men in top form. Jon and I were reaching the end of our time on active missions and neither one of us wanted to ride a desk for the rest of our careers. That last op helped us make the decision to walk away while we still could with our sanity intact."

Brenna couldn't imagine the nightmarish end to Eli's last mission. Didn't want too, either. Unfortunate for her, a vivid imagination was prerequisite to writing fiction. Brenna's overactive story generator supplied graphic details her logical side wanted to suppress. "There's no way you walked out of that compound without scars, Eli. They might not be visible, but I know they exist. How can you sleep at night with that burned into your memory?"

Eli gave a mirthless laugh. "Oh, I sleep every night, sugar, even if it is only four hours. It's the faces of every one of those women and children that populate my dreams, the same rush to rescue them before the kidnappers slit their throats. And, no surprise, I always fail to arrive in time to stop the slaughter of the innocents. And when I can't sleep, there is always The Duke."

"The Duke? You mean John Wayne?"

"My sisters keep me well supplied with movies where the good guys win out in the end." Eli grinned at her. His eyes remained bleak, haunted. "Can't beat a good John Wayne film."

"After what you went through, they give you war movies?"

"Westerns most of the time. It's probably Dad's idea, but it sure wins hands down over any chick flick the girls would have bought me. I know that might be a great disappointment to you, sugar, but I just can't handle crying into my hankie."

"Was your father in the military as well?"

"Sort of."

Brenna frowned. "How can you sort of be in the military? Was he in the National Guard?"

"Nope. Dad was a jarhead. Career."

Brenna grinned. "Jarhead? That's the Marines, isn't it?"

"Oh, yeah. Dad was Recon. Special forces. He hoped I would follow in his footsteps." Eli chuckled. "He carried on like I'd committed some heinous crime by joining the Navy, but I knew he was proud of me for serving in the military. He didn't care what branch though he trash talked the Navy any chance he got."

"What did he say when you resigned from the SEALs?"

"Nothing except he loved me and would stand behind me whatever I did. He understood, Brenna. Dad saw things just as bad when he served, things he couldn't talk about and still had flashbacks of years later."

Brenna studied Eli's face in the dim light as she thought back through their conversation since they left the kitchen. Was the conversation meant as a warning, that despite all he and Jon could do, they still might not be able to save her sister? "Why did you tell me this story? Are you afraid we might be too late this time, too?"

"You have to be prepared for the worst while hoping for the best possible outcome. This girl on our last SEAL mission never had a chance despite her father following the Scarlett Group's instructions. They weren't after the money, but they took it and probably spent every dollar with smiles on their faces. The father was a human rights activist, one who focused on human trafficking. He was calling a lot of public attention to their organization, the kind of attention that scares off potential clients. He was cutting into their profits."

"So they killed his daughter to get him to back off?"

"Along with a warning that his wife would be next, then his son. These people play for keeps, Brenna."

"But why take Dana? We're not wealthy. We don't have parents alive to pay ransom. We're not activists of any kind. We both lead quiet lives that don't cross paths with human traffickers." She paused. "Is it possible Dana was just in the wrong place at the wrong time?"

Eli shrugged. "Maybe. It's also possible that Sartelli Construction is involved in this somehow. There are too many connections back to Sartelli not to consider he and his goons know something if they don't run the whole trafficking operation."

A buzzing noise interrupted the silence following Eli's last statement. He reached into his pocket and pulled out his cell. "Talk to me."

Brenna noted the transformation on Eli's face as he listened, a shifting from curious to dangerous in the space of seconds.

"Where are you?" Eli glanced at his watch. "I'll meet you in 15 minutes." He ended the conversation and turned to Brenna. "Are you up for a field trip?"

"Why are we back here?" Brenna asked.

Eli parked in front of Dana's apartment building and shut off his engine. "Jon got a tip that someone in this building might be involved in Julie's kidnapping."

"Do I want to know how he came by this information?"

He climbed out of the car and stood on the asphalt. "It's best if you don't."

"Why did I know you were going to say that? Oh, right. It's because I hear that statement from you about Jon a lot."

Scanning the area, he closed the driver's door and circled the hood to meet Brenna on the sidewalk. A cricket chorus was in full voice as they ascended the stairs to Dana's apartment. He unlocked the door and motioned for Brenna to wait. After checking each room, Eli returned to the landing and ushered her inside.

"I assume Detective Taylor released the crime scene?" Brenna frowned up at Eli. "He did give us permission to return, right? I don't have the money to bail myself out of jail right now. And if you try to include your bail on an itemized bill, you're going to have a fight on your hands."

Amusement zipped through Eli's body. "I'm hurt, sugar. Do you think I would skirt the law to achieve my own ends?"

"The question I should have asked was how long after the police left did you wait to return."

He grinned. Man, he loved a spunky woman with a quick, sharp sense of humor. All the women his mother tried to set him up with were the perfect impersonations of June Cleaver, something he admired in his mom, but not in a potential date or mate. Beautiful, true, but they were aiming for a position as arm candy with their personalities checked at the door.

They all but drooled on him when they found out he'd been a SEAL. What was it with women and their fascination with men in uniforms? Several cop friends also complained about the phenomenon as well. Some relayed stories about simple traffic stops turning into trips to the Criminal Justice Center when women tried to buy their way out of a traffic ticket by exposing skin and offering services. Eli mentally shrugged. At least he didn't have to worry about that problem with Brenna. She hadn't demonstrated any hesitation speaking her mind or calling his hand on things when she believed they were flat out wrong or questionable.

A sharp rap on the front door interrupted his thoughts. He let Jon in the apartment. His BUD/S partner carried a small black bag in his left hand. Dressed in all black, Jon seemed to absorb light like a black hole. Wasn't just his clothing. Eli's eyes narrowed. Something had happened and he'd just bet Brenna would be better off not knowing about it. "He's at work?"

"Yeah. Called and confirmed."

"Let's move. The search might take a while." Eli turned, lifted a hand and stroked the back of Brenna's neck. The softness and warmth of her skin distracted him for a few seconds. He yanked his attention back to the business at hand. "Stay in this apartment, sugar. Don't open the door for anyone except me, Jon or Cal."

"Where are you going?"

Eli wanted one more kiss from Brenna's perfect pink mouth. You never know. They might run into trouble on their fishing expedition. At least that's what he tried to convince himself as he brushed his lips across hers in a light caress. Eli lifted his head, withheld the sigh wanting to escape at the touch of her soft lips, and angled his head toward the door in silent direction to Jon. He eased the door open a crack, checked for people in the walkway and slipped across the hall.

Eli followed and stood behind Jon, blocking anyone's view of his partner picking Tim Russell's lock. Within seconds, a satisfying snick reached his ears. "Alarm?" he whispered.

"None registered," came the almost soundless reply.

Didn't mean Russell hadn't installed one, but it wasn't likely given that this was an apartment complex with maintenance people and contracted pest control workers traipsing in and out of residences on a regular basis. Not something he could live with. It was one of the many reasons he'd bought a house.

Not seeing or hearing residents close, Eli said, "Go." He knew without looking that Jon had his Sig P226 in hand before he crossed the threshold. Eli slipped his own weapon free and followed his partner into the gloomy interior of the apartment.

They moved through the rooms, the two men confirming it was empty before meeting in the living room.

"Wish my cheap boss would spring for NVGs," Jon murmured.

Eli grinned. Yeah, night vision goggles would be nice, even though they couldn't read anything with them on. "Maybe we can liberate a pair from Fortress."

"On pain of death, sure. Maddox takes it personally when inventory disappears. I wouldn't want on that man's bad side. I'll search the bedrooms. You start in here."

"Roger that."

Eli tugged on gloves and palmed a small flashlight with black tape over the end which allowed a pinprick of light to shine through. A quick perusal of the bookcase in the corner revealed their man's reading taste ran to horror and sports along with two years of skin magazines stacked on one end. Not surprising if he had connections to Scarlett Group.

Next, he searched the entertainment center. Timmy boy had excellent taste in electronics. Large flat screen television, a newer model from the looks of it. Top of the line entertainment system along with a Blu-Ray player and Bose speakers. Didn't believe in skimping on his video game collection, either. Eli leaned closer to read the video covers and choked back laughter. So, he fancied himself a video warrior? All of the games featured the military— Marines, Army, Navy, and black ops stuff. From what he'd observed about Russell earlier, the military would have a lot of work to do whipping the man into shape. Hmm. Maybe he could tap into that fascination for all things military when he and Jon confronted Russell later.

Finished with his search of the small living room, Eli moved into the kitchen and found the typical frozen food preferences of bachelors and an up-to-date supply of lunchmeat and bread. Eli had to hand it to the man. At least he kept up with expiration dates on his food, unlike Eli's own tendency to use the sniff test. If it smelled okay, it was edible. His mother cleaned out the contents of his refrigerator every couple weeks. According to her, it was a wonder he survived without several trips a month to the hospital with food poisoning. Aside from food, Timmy hadn't secreted anything interesting in his appliances.

"Eli."

Jon's almost toneless whisper brought him to the second bedroom. He found his partner sitting in a pitch-black room lit by a computer screen. "Well, well. So our boy is literate enough to use a computer. He spends most of his time with video games, skin magazines, and a few horror books."

Jon grunted. "Take a look at this."

Eli bent to get a clearer look at the screen. "Huh. His bank records. How did you crack his password so fast?"

"He wrote the password down and left it under the mouse pad."

"And here I was about to bow down and kiss the feet of the master code cracker. I'm disappointed, bud. Some of us don't have photographic memories, so help me out. What am I supposed to notice?"

"Russell made cash deposits of $9,500 the day after Julie disappeared and the day after Dana disappeared."

Fury boiled in Eli's gut. Russell paid for his expensive electronic toys by targeting women for human trafficking. But why focus on Dana? He considered the possibility of revenge. Dana made no secret of her reluctance to start any kind of relationship with Russell. Maybe the man didn't take rejection well. Seemed a little over the top to sell the offender off to the highest bidder.

Brenna's theory about Dana being in the wrong place at the wrong time made the most sense. Otherwise, why didn't Russell move on Dana sooner? Why wait all this time before selling her to the Scarlett Group?

"Any other deposits in that amount?"

A few taps on the keyboard. "Six others in the last four months."

"Make a copy for us to take and examine closer. Cal might be interested in an anonymous tip about those deposits and the dates."

"Already on my flash drive."

"Anything else interesting on his computer?"

"Several emails with throw away addresses. Nothing incriminating unless you know to look for dates and phrases. I already downloaded those as well."

"I assume he won't know we've been snooping through his digital trash?"

"What do you think?"

Eli laughed softly. Russell wouldn't have a clue either of them had been in his apartment and computer unless they wanted him to know. Nobody covered tracks as well as Jon Smith. He was the master of stealth and invisibility in cyberspace. And just about anywhere else he wanted to go. He'd hate to meet his BUD/S mate in a dark alley. Not that he'd admit it to Jon, but Eli figured his friend could put him down in under two minutes. He'd get some licks in, but he'd go down just the same.

"You want to wait for him here or take him down at work?"

Jon turned off the computer and screen before replying. "Is there a dark alley behind The Watering Hole?"

"What self-respecting bar doesn't have one? As the bartender/manager of that joint, I doubt he lowers himself enough to take out the trash."

"Should. He fits in with the rest of the garbage." Anger and disgust sounded in Jon's voice.

"Cal and company would be obligated to show us the wrong side of the cell doors if Russell presses charges. And he'll be inclined to do just that when his face meets the brick wall a few times." And kissed the pavement, not to mention broken ribs and nose.

Jon grabbed his bag and stood. "He'll talk and there won't be a mark on him. At least not to the naked eye. Greater chance of someone spotting us there."

Eli shrugged. "So, we wait."

Brenna paced the floor of Dana's apartment. Eli had slipped through the door hours before and told her to get comfortable, that he and Jon would be a while. They were waiting for Tim to get in from work to confront him with what they'd found.

The aggravating private investigator and his partner refused to share what they learned in Tim's place or let her wait with them. Brenna scowled. She could have waited with them. She knew how to be quiet for hours on end. She did it all the time when she was in the zone of her story and writing.

She ran her hands through her hair and twisted on her heel one more time. Brenna could handle whatever Eli and Jon did to Tim. She didn't care if they ripped off the man's fingernails or hung him up by his thumbs. If he knew where Dana was or if he had been involved as Eli and Jon suspected, Brenna wouldn't complain over any method they used. Then again, maybe it was a good idea for the guys to question Tim without her around. What she didn't see she couldn't testify about. Deniability. She knew a few good lawyers. The guys probably had great ones at their disposal considering their chosen career. Brenna suspected Fortress had high-priced lawyers on retainer for all their operatives.

She frowned. Maybe chosen wasn't the right word to apply to the men across the hall. After all, with Eli and Jon's skills, what other type of career could utilize their knowledge besides law enforcement or military, whether U.S. government backed or private?

She turned for another circuit around the apartment when her attention shifted to Dana's bedroom. Did the guy who broke into the apartment leave the computer intact? Brenna hadn't heard Eli or Detective Taylor say anything about Dana's computer being vandalized. Now, if the police had just left it alone, she would be in business. She needed to work on something, anything, or the endless waiting would drive her insane.

Brenna changed direction and hurried to Dana's bedroom. As soon as she walked through the doorway, the scent of her sister's favorite body lotion brought tears to Brenna's eyes. The clean, fresh aroma of vanilla always reminded her of Dana. She missed her, feared what unspeakable horrors her sister endured.

She pulled out her phone and glanced at the countdown. Her hand trembled. Thirty-six hours left. When would the kidnappers contact her again? She figured it would have to be soon.

Swiping at the tears trickling down her cheeks, Brenna's gaze darted to the computer sitting on the desk in a corner of the bedroom. No visible damage. She yanked the chair back, slid into the seat and turned on the machine.

While waiting for the computer to boot up, Brenna scanned Dana's room for changes since her visit two months earlier. A few more romances littered the bookshelf, including Brenna's latest release. A framed picture of her and Dana together. Brenna tilted her head. She didn't remember that picture being taken.

She got up from the chair and walked to the dresser to examine the photograph closer. They were in a restaurant. Qdoba from the look of the décor. Who had taken a picture of them together at Qdoba the last time she'd been in town to see Dana? And the picture hadn't been snapped with her knowledge.

Brenna's eyes narrowed. Dana's friend, Grace Peters, had been at the restaurant that day for lunch, too. Maybe she took the picture and gave her sister a copy. Huh. Nice thing to do, although it bordered on invasion of privacy. At least her fans usually asked permission before snapping a shot of her with their cameras.

She glanced at the screen. The cursor was waiting for her to enter the password. Brenna keyed in the letters and numbers she and Dana had devised for both their computers. Neither of them had any other family. Dana's mother had died of leukemia after her birth. By the time Dana had turned two, her father had married Brenna's mother. Since both Brenna's parents and Dana's were gone, it seemed prudent to make access to information easier if anything happened to either of the stepsisters.

With a silent apology to her sister for invading her privacy, Brenna clicked on the emails and began reading. She waded through and deleted all the spam that had flooded the inbox in the last couple weeks. How did so many pharmaceutical companies, legitimate or not, get private email addresses? Didn't these folks have anything better to do than push their wonder drugs on the public? Brenna skipped the emails from her and concentrated on the rest.

She scanned several emails forwarded from Sartelli Construction. Most of them concerned event dates and times connected with the work Dana had been doing for Elena Sartelli. The rest of the emails discussed the kind of mundane details sprouted by construction business, the kind of details that would drive Brenna into a coma from boredom. She shuddered. How did Dana stand dealing with those dry details?

Her sister had expressed the same disdain for the details in Brenna's books. While she lived for in-depth research and valued mining gold nuggets of obscure knowledge for her novels, Dana used history books as a sleep aid. Her sweet sister had barely passed each history course in school. Brenna had lost count of how many nights she stayed up way past their bedtime to help Dana study for a test. No matter how much they studied together or tried different study techniques, Dana's mind didn't retain many historical dates or names.

She clicked on a message that had been sent one day before Dana's disappearance. She scanned the message, her eyes widening the further down the screen she read. The message was unsigned. If she didn't know better, Brenna would say their stepfather, Ross Harrison, had written the email. But wasn't he still in jail? Could he send a message from behind bars? She knew some prisoners were allowed computer privileges, but weren't the incoming and outgoing emails monitored?

Brenna's cell phone vibrated. She jumped, heart leaping into her throat. Brenna dug her phone out and scanned the message. *Midnight. Come alone or she goes to the highest bidder.* An address followed, one Brenna didn't recognize.

She blew out a breath. Great. More cloak and dagger stuff in the middle of the night. And she could guess what Eli's response would be when he learned about the meeting.

CHAPTER TWELVE

Dana sat up on her cot, listened to the sounds growing louder outside her door. A girl crying, begging to go home. The echo of flesh against flesh. A slap? A sharp command from a male. She scowled at the door. Ape man. She could be a hundred years old and would still recognize his hated voice. But who was the girl? Her voice sounded like it belonged to a young girl. Maybe a teenager.

Something about the voice seemed familiar, but Dana couldn't place it. Maybe the combination of drugs and weird acoustics in this cement prison. She eased off the cot, felt her way around the walls of her pitch-black cell, and pressed her ear to the crack between the door and the frame. "Come on, sweetheart," she whispered. "Say something else."

As if the teen heard her near silent plea, the girl said, "Please, just send my mom a message. She'll give you anything you ask for to get me back."

Dana gasped. Julie Lynch. She knew it was her young friend. How did Ape man get Julie? She raised her fist and pounded on the door. "Hey, Ape man. Open the door. I need to go to the bathroom."

Ape man's meaty fist slammed against the door, making the door rattle. "Keep your mouth shut or I'll tape it closed."

"I really need to go. Right now."

Another cry from Julie. "Dana?" She started screaming. "Help me, Dana. Please." Then her voice was muffled as if a hand clamped over her mouth.

Dana worked the doorknob desperately despite knowing it was locked. "Come on. Open the door. I already know who the girl is with you in the hall. Let me see Julie for a minute."

She listened, prayed Ape man would listen to reason. What difference did it make if she and Julie spent a couple minutes together? It's not like they would be able to escape since Dana was so weak from the small amount of food and water she consumed. The drugs they kept pumping into her system didn't help. She didn't stand a chance of escaping.

One minute was all she needed to encourage the petrified teen, maybe help her stay calm. If Julie panicked, Ape man and his friends might hurt her. She couldn't live with herself if she didn't at least try to help.

A moment later, a key sounded in the lock. Dana moved back, unsure if Ape man would grant her request or backhand her for causing trouble again. Her thug captor shoved open the door and threw the teenager to the floor at Dana's feet. Dana caught a glimpse of the girl's jeans and t-shirt before the door closed with a hard clang. A click locked them into the darkness.

Dana knelt beside Julie and gathered the weeping girl into her arms. "Julie, are you okay? Did they hurt you?" She waited for her sobs to subside, anxious to find out whether Julie's treatment by Ape man and Skyscraper was similar to her own experience.

"They didn't really hurt me. Some weird doctor guy made me strip. Said it was to prove I was healthy. I don't understand any of this, Dana. Why won't they let me go home? Do they want money? If it's money, Mom will sell everything we own to get me back. All they have to do is ask her for it."

Although glad her captors hadn't hurt the girl, Dana didn't dare tell the teenager what she suspected, that it wouldn't matter how much money Ms. Lynch scraped together. These people weren't interested in a ransom. She hugged the girl tighter. "What happened, Julie? How did you end up here?"

"I'm not sure. I've been thinking about it for days, but I don't remember much. I got a message from Grace to meet you at your apartment, but you weren't home."

A sharp spear of pain stole Dana's breath. Grace? Could her friend be involved in all of this with these people? It couldn't be true. What possible motive would Grace have to betray her and Julie? She forced herself to be honest. Not a betrayal. If Grace was involved, she had sold out both her and Julie. But why? Dana had never crossed Grace on anything more important than shoe styles, certainly nothing vital enough to destroy a friend's life over.

"Your neighbor across the hall said you were running late and you wanted me to wait with him. That's the last thing I remember." Julie paused. "How long have I been here? Do you know?"

"About three weeks."

"Three weeks? My mom must be insane with worry."

"Chad is, too."

Julie moaned. "I miss him so much. I just want one more chance to tell him how much I love him. We talked about getting married in a few years. Dana, I want that life with him and my mom. We've got to get out of here. But I don't think I can run. I'm so tired all the time. They keep giving me shots. I'm scared. What if they get us hooked on something?"

Dana feared getting hooked on some kind of narcotic was the least of their worries. Kicking any habit wouldn't be fun, but she would take that any day over what she suspected was in store for both of them.

And she knew exactly how Julie felt about missing Chad. Somehow, her near-silent private investigator friend, Jon, had wormed his way into her heart. She and Jon hadn't gone on a date, only phone conversations, notes, and a few of late-night cups of coffee. He might not think of her as anything more than just a friend who agreed to keep an eye on her boss. Except he did buy her the cell phone, said he'd added her to his plan. He always took her calls, no matter the time. Never seemed in a hurry to end the conversation, either.

And who said she was ready for a date? Dana swallowed against the bile building in her throat. After what Ross had done to her when she was sixteen, Dana didn't know if she really trusted any man. Yet Jon had eased his way under the barriers she erected against the rest of the men who showed interest in her. Jon had his own issues to deal with, ones she suspected were linked to his career in the military and his black ops work. Maybe his fight with his own demons made her more comfortable with him. Whatever the reason, she knew he had started to melt the ice around her heart. And like Julie's wish with Chad, Dana wanted to have a chance at a relationship with Jon. She couldn't give up and lose the one good thing in her life besides Brenna.

"I'm scared, too, Julie. I don't know how much longer Ape man will leave you in here with me, so I want you to listen. I never sent you or Grace a message to meet at my place. I was out of town on an errand for Mr. Sartelli the day you disappeared. I'm not positive, but I think I've been here over a week myself. That means my sister, Brenna, knows something is wrong. I know she's looking for me. And my friends Jon and Eli are looking, too. They're private investigators, Julie. They won't give up until they find us. You have to hold on, okay?"

"Who are these people? Why won't they let us go?"

Dana closed her eyes, glad for the darkness so Julie couldn't see her expression. She refused to tell the teen suspicions she hadn't been able to verify yet. No point terrorizing her further with things that might not be true, suspicions that horrified her in the few waking minutes she was allowed before being forced to accept another shot. "I'm not sure. These bozos aren't chatty."

Julie giggled.

Dana's lips curved upward. "I want you to remember something, Julie. Don't give up hope, no matter what happens."

"Mom will get them money if they give her enough time."

Dana didn't share the truth she did know. The last time she had talked to Ms. Lynch, no ransom demand had been made for Julie's safe return. And unless she missed her guess, there wouldn't be one. Fury flared in her gut. Was it possible Grace had targeted Julie? The girl was young and beautiful, perfect for a human trafficking operation.

But where did that leave her? Dana wasn't exactly a teen anymore. She wasn't the right age or body type. Dana didn't consider herself particularly attractive so why would human traffickers want her?

She shoved aside that troubling thought and rubbed Julie's back. "Sweetheart, I'm not sure what they want, but I want you to promise me something."

"Not to give up? Yeah, I promise."

"That's good. I'm glad to hear that. Since we're not sure if these thugs are after money and I don't know when they'll let me see you again, I also want you to promise me that no matter what, you will do whatever it takes to survive."

Julie froze. "Why did you say that? What do you mean?"

A key rattled in the lock.

"Promise me, Julie. No matter what happens, survive."

"I'm so scared," the teen whispered. She clung harder to Dana. "But I swear, I won't give up. I will survive."

"No matter what it takes. Say it."

The door swung open. Ape man grabbed Julie's arm and yanked the girl to her feet. "Whatever it takes, Dana. I promise."

Ape man dragged Julie out into the hall and slammed the door shut.

The key sounded in the lock and Dana was left alone in the darkness.

Eli jumped to his feet and motioned Jon to take the other side of the door. Within seconds of Tim crossing the threshold, his back hit the wall, the muzzle of Eli's gun shoved under his chin. Jon shut and locked the door after a quick survey of the hall.

"Who are you? What do you want?" Tim swallowed hard, his involuntary muscle movement shifting the position of Eli's weapon.

"I've been hearing some disturbing intel about you, Tim. You lied to me. You do know where Dana is, don't you?"

"Wolfe?" Tim struggled against Eli's hold to no avail. "Are you crazy? Get out of here before I call the cops."

"Oh, you won't call the cops, Tim. If you do, you'll have to explain about the $9,500 that's been deposited in your account every time a teenage girl disappears around here after crossing paths with a scum bag like you."

Tim's movements stilled. "You're nuts. I don't know what you're talking about."

The scent of fear rose to Eli's nostrils. He chuckled. "No, no, Timmy boy. You don't want to play dumb. I'll quit playing good cop and go straight to the bad cop." Eli shoved his weapon harder.

"Okay, okay," Tim said, his voice sounding choked.

He eased back a little on the weapon's position, waited for Tim's coughing fit to end. "You're involved in Dana's disappearance up to your eyeballs, Timmy."

"No, you've got it wrong, Wolfe. I swear."

"Which part is wrong, Timmy?"

"What? Are you an imbecile? All of it is wrong."

Jon slipped to Tim's side, grabbed his hand and twisted the wrist. Eli clamped his hand over Tim's mouth. A muffled groan escaped. At this time of night, people were sleeping. Sounds carried. Unusual sounds drew attention and the cops, neither of which Eli wanted at the moment. He didn't relish the lengthy explanations to Cal, not to mention the heated lectures delivered while he and Jon scowled from the wrong side of the bars.

"I don't think my friend likes you much, Timmy," Eli murmured into the man's ear. "Just a few more pounds of pressure and your wrist will snap like a twig. You better start talking, bud, or I'll walk out and let my friend persuade you to talk. And trust me, he knows ways to hurt you without leaving marks, but forces you to tell every secret you've ever known within minutes."

More twisting pressure from Jon.

Another moan from Tim.

Eli lifted his hand from the man's mouth.

"No more, please."

Even in the dim lighting, Eli could make out the sheen of sweat glistening on Tim's face. If the guy wasn't such a sleaze and involved in Dana's disappearance, Eli might feel sorry for him. As it was, Tim was lucky Eli still had a conscience.

"Start talking, Timmy, or I walk and leave you to my friend."

"I didn't know they took Dana until it was too late."

A wave of fury washed over him. Tim had known, but done nothing to find Dana. Even an anonymous tip to the cops might have helped them find her. Now, the trail was stone cold and he feared Dana wouldn't be able to get free on her own. "Wow. Wouldn't want you for my friend. Real friends pull your bacon out of the fire instead of leaving you to be the enemy's main course."

From the corner of his eye, Eli noted the subtle but telling shift in Jon's hold on their quarry. Tim drew in a breath to yell, but Eli clamped his hand again over the man's mouth, stifling the noise. He glanced at his partner. His eyebrows rose. Jon's face was a mask of pure rage. "Ease off," he whispered. Another minute of Tim's pathetic moans, then silence except for the man's harsh breathing.

"Keep talking," Eli prompted. "Who are 'they'?"

"I don't know who they are."

"Last chance," Jon whispered. Eli wondered if he would be able to keep his partner from killing Tim before they got all the information they needed. If he'd known how emotionally invested Jon was in the hunt for Dana, he would have insisted his partner stay with Brenna. Eli didn't have the same skill for interrogation as Jon, but he could get the job done just the same. Might take him longer, though, and they didn't have time for an extended question-and-answer session.

"Okay, okay." Tim licked his lips. "I'm supposed to watch for young women that fit a certain profile. You know, pretty, curvy, preferably alone, but never with more than one or two friends. I'm supposed to spike their drinks. That's it."

"These girls weren't supposed to be in your bar or any other, Timmy. Bet most of them were underage."

"How am I supposed to know that? I'm not an expert in spotting fake IDs."

"And you think that makes what you did acceptable?" Eli leaned closer, pressed his gun harder. "Didn't take an expert to notice the girls are jail bait. But the real problem is you are a predator, Timmy. What are you giving them? Rohypnol?"

"Yeah. Easy to get on the street."

Jon scowled, his eyes narrowing.

"Who do you call after you spot and drug the girls?"

"I don't know who it is. I don't even talk to them. Just send a text message. Within minutes, a van arrives to pick up the girls."

Jon patted Tim down with his free hand. He reached into Tim's shirt pocket, yanked out his phone and stuffed it into his own pocket.

Tim opened his mouth to protest, noticed Jon's expression, and clamped his lips shut again without uttering a sound. Eli's lip curled. Smart prey knew when the predator had them in sight and Jon had a bead on old Tim. If the bar manager knew Jon's background, he would be terrified. Eli counted himself lucky Jon considered him a friend. Even the idea of Jon targeting him through the sniper scope sent a sheen of cold sweat cascading down his back. When Jon Smith took a shot, he rarely missed. "Do you toss the girls in the van by yourself or does the driver get out and help?"

Tim closed his eyes. "Driver helps."

"Describe him."

"Dude's really tall, man. Maybe Middle Eastern or something. Skin's kind of dark, but it's hard to see at night, especially in the alley. It doesn't have the best lighting. Keep telling the owner he needs to do something about that."

"Yeah, we'll be sure to pass on your suggestion to him." Jon glared at him. "You won't be in a position to talk to him any time soon."

Tim shuddered and turned his pleading gaze back to Eli. "Hey, Wolfe, I'm cooperating. Give me a break here."

"Like you gave those girls? Do you know what those men do with the girls, Timmy?" Eli waited, knowing his answer would determine how painful the next few minutes would be for him.

"I figured they partied a little. You know how teenage girls are these days."

Eli's stomach turned. "Can't say that I do. I don't spend time with jail bait. But that's not what happens to these girls, Timmy. They disappear for good." He leaned in until he could almost see the fear in the man's eyes. "Someone is selling them, Timmy."

Tim's jaw dropped. "Selling them? What are you talking about?"

"Human trafficking, Tim. The people you work for sell these women to the highest bidder. And now they have Dana."

"No. That can't be true."

Jon turned his head and stared at Eli.

No words passed between them. They weren't necessary. Eli sighed. Oh, man. This could get ugly. And he knew Jon was protecting him with deniability, not that Cal would buy Eli's innocence. "No marks," Eli muttered.

"No promises."

Eli released his hold on Tim and stepped back. Immediately his partner assumed control of him, twisting his arm high behind his back and shoving him face first into the wall. Eli left the apartment without a backward glance.

"Where is she, Russell?" Jon murmured.

"I don't know."

"You must have had some contact besides just a text message. Even you aren't stupid enough to answer a text from a number you didn't recognize. Could have been a cop for all you knew."

"I . . ." Tim licked his lips again. "I can't. You don't understand."

"Make me understand. Fast. Do you know your employers have a countdown clock running on Dana? They are going to sell her to the highest bidder in thirty-one hours."

"I didn't know until it was too late. They had already taken her before I realized she was in danger."

"And you think that excuses you? What did you think they would do with her, Russell?" This guy could not have been that stupid. He may have tried to lie to himself, but Jon didn't believe he bought into his own fiction.

Tim remained mute.

"Last chance to do this the painless way," Jon whispered. "In one minute, I start using more persuasive techniques, the kind guaranteed to get answers in the fastest way possible. If you're cooperative, you might survive the next few minutes. And trust me, I will enjoy hurting you for what you did to Dana. I won't lose a wink of sleep if you don't make it out of this apartment alive."

To make his point, Jon slammed his fist into Russell's kidney. The man sank to his knees without a sound. Jon knew from firsthand experience excruciating pain had stolen any breath from Russell and the possibility of noise which might bring the cops.

When Russell finally dragged in a wheezing breath, Jon grabbed hold of his hair, yanked back his head and held his razor-sharp knife against the man's throat. The blade bit into the skin enough to have Russell freezing in place. "How did they first make contact with you?"

"A guy came to the bar where I was working in Atlanta a couple of years ago. Asked if I wanted to make some extra cash. I was behind on some payments, so I agreed to call if a pretty girl showed up who might suit their needs."

"Same deal in every city you've worked in since then?"

"Yeah."

"The guy have a name?"

Russell snorted. "You should know better than that."

"Description?"

"Won't do you any good. The guy turned up dead a few weeks after I moved here."

Jon tightened his grip on Russell's hair. "Description?"

"White. Mid-twenties, maybe. Six foot. Carrot-colored hair."

"Distinguishing marks so I'll know when I've identified the right carrot-topped dead man."

"Some kind of dagger tattooed on his left hand. The tip dripped blood."

Jon's eyes narrowed. The dripping blood off the dagger tip was the symbol associated with the Scarlett Group. In fact, the rescued women and children who had been sold by Scarlett's Beauties each had that particular tattoo somewhere on their bodies. A mark of ownership or identification. The thought of someone marking Dana with that tattoo made him want to vent his rage on whoever might be responsible for marring her satin skin.

"Where do they take the girls, Russell?"

"I don't know."

Jon yanked harder on the hair in his fist and pressed the blade of the knife a little deeper.

"Ow! Hey, I'm cooperating. Aren't I talking to you?"

"You aren't talking enough. And I bet no one would miss your miserable hide if I let this knife do the job it's designed to do."

"Okay, okay. Look, I don't know where they take the girls, honest. But I do know there's some doctor in Murfreesboro who works with them sometimes. Checks out the girls, you know?"

"And you didn't think that was strange? Kind of overkill for a simple roll in the hay, isn't it?" Fury roiled in Jon's gut. It took every ounce of control he possessed to stay his hand from slicing through the vulnerable sweat-slick flesh of Russell's throat. If finding Dana didn't take top priority, he might let that knife slip. Jon scowled. "If you want to live another five minutes, you better have a name or location more specific than Murfreesboro."

"Wilson. I heard the doctor's name was Wilson. That's all I know. I swear." The pitch of Russell's voice betrayed his utter terror.

Although aggravated with the tiny amount of information he'd learned, Jon believed Russell told him the truth. He eased the knife away from the man's throat and yanked his head back at a more painful angle, wrapped his arm around the neck and began tightening his hold, a hold one designed to cut off blood flow to the brain and render him unconscious or kill him if he tightened enough. So tempting. "If Dana is injured in any way while she's in the hands of your friends, I will come back and find you. You don't know the meaning of pain yet, Russell, but you will wish you had never been born before I'm through with you."

When the man slumped, unconscious, Jon dropped him to the floor and left the apartment as silently as he'd entered.

CHAPTER THIRTEEN

"No way. I won't allow it, Brenna."

Yeah, that was pretty much the reaction Brenna had expected. A wry smile curved her lips. Good to know she still understood enough of the male psyche to predict Eli's response. And who did he think he was to allow her to do anything? The last time she let a man help her out of a difficult situation, Ross the Rat had taken advantage of her baby sister. Not this time, even if the man was Eli Wolfe. "Nice to know you care. You, however, are not my father or my boyfriend."

Eli frowned.

"Dana is the only family I have left in this world. I'll do whatever it takes to free her from the Scarlett Group."

Eli jammed his hands through his hair, paced the kitchen. "Sugar, this is a trap. You do understand that, right? These people are terrorists. They aren't going to hand over Dana once they get her recording. She and the deliverer are dead once they get their hands on it. Your sister has been in their hands for two weeks. They can't have kept her blindfolded this whole time." He stopped in front of Brenna and cupped her face between his hands.

"Do you understand what I'm saying here? She can identify at least some of her kidnappers. If she's released, Dana will be able to connect employees to the Scarlett Group. That means they can be tracked through these people. They can't allow her to live."

"What do you expect me to do, Eli? I won't let her die if it's in my power to prevent it."

"Baby, I wasn't suggesting that at all. You aren't equipped to handle this kind of situation. Let me handle it with Jon and our counter-terrorist team. This is exactly the type of op we deal with on a regular basis. You can trust us. The Scarlett Group won't know we're there until it's too late for them to mount an assault against us. I promise you, we'll get Dana to safety and then they will pay. When we asked her to keep track of Sartelli, she became ours. We protect our own."

Brenna stepped back. "No. The Scarlett Group is expecting me and, as drop-dead handsome as you are, you can't disguise yourself as a 30-year-old romance writer. They know what I look like, Eli. I won't take the chance with Dana's life."

"So you're willing to gamble with your own life?"

"I owe her this chance at freedom."

"Do you honestly believe Dana would want you to risk your own safety to secure hers? She loves you too much, Brenna."

"And I love her too much to leave her in their hands when it's within my ability to free her or at least try. I owe her. She stayed in that house with Ross so I wouldn't give up on my dreams. She sacrificed her own happiness for me. I'm not leaving her in Scarlett Group's hands without doing my part to get her free." Brenna dropped onto a stool at the breakfast bar. "You're wasting your breath. I won't change my mind about this. Don't you see, Eli? You're my ace in the hole."

"How do you figure that?" His mouth curved into a frown, one deep enough to hint how frustrating the whole conversation had turned out to be for him.

"I'm beginning to know what you are capable of, what this group you work with on the side can do, but the Scarlett Group doesn't. They think you and Jon are two-bit gumshoes, not the elite counter-terrorist operatives I suspect you are."

The apartment door opened and Jon closed it behind him. He paused in the doorway, looking first from Eli to Brenna and back. The tension Brenna felt in the room must have communicated itself to Jon because he said, "Do I need to come back in a couple minutes?"

"Stay," Brenna said, her throat tight. "Eli and I won't come to an agreement in two minutes. Maybe you can talk some sense into your partner." She hated that she'd disappointed Eli. Somewhere over the hours of their growing friendship, what he thought of her began to matter. A great deal. The wounded former Navy SEAL was beginning to look a lot like the person she'd always dreamed of finding for a mate.

Jon's eyebrows rose. "Sounds like heaven, but very unlikely."

"Makes you a lot smarter than our client." Eli folded his arms across his massive chest. "Brenna got a text from the kidnappers. They want her to deliver Dana's recording to some warehouse off Nolensville Road in Little Mexico. At midnight, no less. Do you see the same problem I do?"

Brenna told Jon the address and waited for his response, not sure if he would take Eli's side or her own. She hadn't missed his flushed face when he'd heard the news about Dana. Considering Dana shut down any man's interest and kept them at a safe distance, she wondered if maybe her sister felt something a lot stronger for Jon. All the other men who hit on her Brenna had heard about. But she never mentioned Jon. Was there something between

Dana and Jon, something her sister was reluctant to discuss, maybe not wanting to vocalize the situation for fear she would jinx it?

Dana had discussed at great length every man she had frozen out. Her sister worried that her feelings would remain in a deep freeze the rest of her life, but what if Jon had melted her fear of chancing a relationship? Maybe Jon was the right man for her, the one with enough patience and love to overcome her sister's fears and well-founded concerns. Tears stung Brenna's eyes. From what she had seen of Jon Smith so far, Dana could do a lot worse than a man whose feelings ran so deep he would risk his life to rescue her. Of that, Brenna had no doubt. Jon would take a bullet in a heartbeat if it would get Dana away from the Scarlett Group. Her beautiful sister deserved a chance at happiness and she planned to do everything in her power to help Dana get that chance.

Her gaze shifted to a still agitated Eli, his hair mussed. He had almost taken a bullet to protect her, had the bandage to prove it, and would put his life on the line as well to get Dana back. Eli seemed cut from the same steel mold as Jon. What were the chances of two men of such sterling character and necessary expertise being in the right place at the right time? Brenna sighed. Slim. Which made the men's appearance in their lives even more of a miracle than she first realized.

Or a mistake. What if she had trusted the wrong people?

"Dangerous," Jon said. "It's a trap."

"Finally. Another voice of reason." Eli swung around to pin Brenna with his glare. "Jon agrees with me. It's a trap, one designed to permanently rid Scarlett Group of two problems."

"If they don't kill you outright, we could lose you as well, Brenna." Jon peeled black gloves off his hands. "They would still get their hands on the evidence which could end their business and capture you, too. A double bonus for the terrorists—the evidence plus two beautiful women to sell to the highest bidder."

Nausea boiled in her stomach. The possibility of some psycho buying her on the open market as if procuring a side of beef made her want to vomit. "That's why I have you and Eli. To make sure the bad guys don't get away with the recording and either girl."

"As good as we are, sugar, we can't guarantee something won't go wrong." Eli closed the distance between them and pulled her into his arms. "Are you willing to put your freedom on the line, your life? What if we lose you in the human trafficking market?"

Brenna burrowed deeper into Eli's arms, her ear pressed tight over his pounding heart. "Can't you tag me or something? Track me somehow? Just in case."

Eli grunted as if kicked. "You're not a cow or a horse, Brenna. No tagging. Sure, we can plant a tracker on you. But what if we're not in time? It could take hours or days, more time than you might have. Too much time. What if they want to sample the goods before they sell you? What if they decide you caused them too much trouble, put a gun to your head and pull the trigger? What if we can't track you fast enough and the battery on the tracker dies? It's too risky, baby. Don't ask that of me." He leaned close to her ear. "Not after what I told you about our last mission. It would gut me if anything happened to you."

Brenna's lips brushed his jaw with a gentle kiss. "So, don't let them take me."

Eli tightened his arms. "It's not that simple."

Jon dropped his gloves on the dining table. "Is Dana's computer up?"

"Yes." She inclined her head toward the back bedroom. "I was checking her emails."

"Anything of interest?" Eli asked her.

"A message that might be from Ross. I don't see how since he's still in jail." At least she thought Ross the Rat was still in jail. He might have been granted early release for good behavior. Her lip curled. She doubted her stepfather's friend, Police Chief Frank Carter, would bother to get in touch with them if Ross had been released. Carter wouldn't spit on either her or Dana if they were on fire. The man believed Ross the Rat innocent of any wrong doing. In his opinion, the juvenile delinquent 16-year-old had set up an innocent Ross Harrison. The good-old-boy club reigned supreme in the chief's corner of the world.

Jon strode down the hallway out of sight, clenched fists the only sign of his struggle for control. Brenna returned to her stool at the breakfast bar, fatigued from being awake all night. She must be wrong about the message. Maybe she was so tired she was becoming loopy, going in circles just like her thoughts.

Eli's warm, solid hands massaged the tight muscles of her shoulders. With almost uncanny accuracy, he targeted and untangled the knots. She sighed as her muscles began relaxing for the first time in days. Maybe since Dana had first called her weeks ago. "I'll give you a month to stop. Wait, I take it back. That's much too soon. Two months."

He chuckled and continued his search-and-destroy mission. "You don't know if the message is from Ross?"

"Not positive, but it sounds like him. Same drivel he's always spouted since the day he was arrested."

"What did the email say?"

His hot breath on her neck sent a shiver racing across her body. "He says he loves Dana and can't understand why she rejected him, that he's willing to forgive her and take her back. If she continues to reject him, there'll be a price to pay." Brenna's head leaned back against Eli's chest.

Eli's hands stilled. "Think it might be from Russell instead of your stepfather?"

She closed her eyes for a moment, considered the suggestion. "It's possible, I suppose." The idea didn't sound right. Neighbor Tim seemed very confident of his chances of success with Dana. Overconfident, arrogant twit. Why would he resort to threats?

Another possibility surfaced, one sure to make Eli unhappy. Brenna opened her eyes and scanned the room. They were still alone. She might not get another opportunity to talk to Eli without his partner. "What about Jon? Could he have sent Dana the message?"

His silence drew her gaze to his face. "Eli?"

He shook his head. "No."

"Put your emotions on ice and think, Eli. It's obvious he has feelings for Dana, but she never mentioned Jon to me."

"She didn't mention me, either, did she? This isn't just gut feeling, though that is part of it. I know Jon, Brenna. He would as soon slit his own throat before he would ever harm Dana or any other woman for that matter. You don't understand, sugar. Jon's mom was the victim of an abusive husband. Jon's father beat her and him on a regular basis. His childhood was filled with trips to the emergency room. I don't know how many broken bones he had. His father was a mean drunk. Eventually he died in a drunk driving accident. Jon says it was the best day in his mother's life."

She considered his statements for a moment before twisting in his arms to face him. "What if you're wrong? What if Dana rejected him like she has all the other men who showed interest in her since Ross molested her? Is it possible Jon hurt her without meaning to? Maybe her rejection triggered some kind of violent reaction and this whole thing with the postcards and text messages is a hoax to cover his trail."

Eli's lips quirked upward. "Been reading too many thrillers at night, sugar? Sounds like a plot to a James Patterson novel. If Jon had ever hurt Dana, either by

163

accident or deliberate intent, he'd own up to it and take the consequences like a man. A SEAL would never behave otherwise. That's who he is before anything else, a SEAL."

"What about PTSD?"

Eli stilled under her hands. "What about it?"

"Could he be suffering from PTSD, maybe hurt Dana and not realize what he had done?"

"You might as well call in the cops now and turn me in along with Jon and every other military vet. Many of us deal with the realities of war long after we leave military service. A lot of employers won't hire us because they're afraid we'll wig out on them and shoot the place up." Eli's gaze studied her face. "Are you afraid of me, too?"

Tears stung Brenna eyes. The last thing she wanted to do was hurt Eli or Jon for that matter, but she needed to chase any possible lead, no matter how painful. She hadn't realized seeking the truth might hurt her or Eli so much. How could her reasoning be so circular? Not even minutes ago she wondered if she was wrong to trust Eli and Jon. Yet when he confronted her, she couldn't name him or Jon as evil. "Never. I trust you with my life, Eli. I already have." She lifted a trembling hand and brushed aside the stray lock of hair clinging to the bandage on his forehead. "You have the injury to prove it." A tear escaped and trailed down her cheek.

"And I trust Jon with my life." He caught the tear with his forefinger, his dark gaze on her face. "Do you really believe the tale you're spinning, sugar?"

"I don't know what to believe anymore," she whispered. Everywhere she turned, lies and deception seemed the rule of the day. How could she trust anyone? She didn't understand the intense feelings growing inside her for Eli, was afraid to truly believe in the emotions flaring wildly out of control in a matter of days. She didn't know Eli or Jon, much less Dana's boss. If she trusted the wrong person, Dana could pay with her life.

He sighed and trailed a fingertip down her cheek, traced the trail of tears now flowing down her face. "If I find out he was responsible, I'll take him out myself. You can believe that."

His quiet words of utter conviction sent a shiver down Brenna's spine. Deep in her heart, she knew Eli meant every word. But would it be enough?

Jon strode back into the kitchen, a sheaf of papers in his hand. "Suit up, Wolfe. Time to roll."

"Why are we racing down Interstate 24 before the sun comes up?" Eli checked the rearview mirror, expected to see flashing lights any time behind his Camaro. The THP loved to patrol the I-24 corridor between Nashville and Murfreesboro. He didn't relish a fine from Tennessee law enforcement or a stint behind bars for reckless endangerment. "By the way, if I get a speeding ticket, you're paying."

"If you go any faster, I'll need a barf bag," Brenna muttered from the back, her fingers clutching Eli's seat.

Eli reached over his shoulder and patted her hand. Her doubts about him still rankled. She was the only woman who had caused the slightest stir of interest in months, yet she didn't fully trust him, half expecting him to be a PTSD head case. Couldn't say that he blamed her. Maybe she wouldn't be so doubtful about him if he hadn't spilled his guts about not being able to sleep most nights without ghosts from the past visiting him in his dreams. He hated his leftover issues from the military, but he couldn't change it. Time was helping some, creating a much needed distance. Talking to his dad, he knew he'd never be totally free of the ghosts.

He also hated to bring Brenna with them for whatever mission Jon had in mind, but he hated even more to leave her to her own devices. She needed protection and asking Cal to be on guard duty meant an explanation his friend was better off without. Eli figured the bozo who attacked Brenna was still in the area and might make another try for her and Dana's recording, not to mention the fact his sweet romance writer had a penchant for trouble with a capital T. He wouldn't put it past her to go out investigating on her own, even at this ungodly hour.

He shook his head. Even his thought processes were convoluted this early in the morning before a cup of coffee, especially since he'd been up all night searching Russell's place and questioning the less than cooperative bar manager. Where was a Starbucks when he needed one? Any other time, he passed coffee shops on every street corner.

"Russell volunteered the name of a doctor who might be persuaded to share some information."

Eli's eyebrows lifted. "Volunteered, huh? Should I worry about a visit from Cal in the near future?"

"Russell has a scratch. He's probably had worse paper cuts."

He grinned. Jon knew a lot of ways to make a man tell every secret he knew from childhood on. For that matter, so did he. Jon, however, seemed to take great pleasure in his work when it involved righting a wrong to an innocent woman. "Who is the doctor?"

"Guy named Sam Wilson. Russell claims he checks the girls for health issues."

"Health issues?" Brenna echoed. "You mean he checks them for diseases?"

"That's right."

"But that's . . . ." Brenna stopped.

"Inhumane? Cruel? Sounds too much like buying a horse or cattle? A necessary assurance for the buyer?" Jon glanced over his shoulder at her. "Yes, Brenna. All of the above."

"But he's a doctor. He's sworn to protect human life, not make sure the girls are fit for a life of virtual slavery."

"Doesn't make him any more inhumane than the rest of the garbage involved in Scarlett's Beauties," Eli said. Noticing a Starbucks sign, he flipped on his turn signal and exited the interstate. His stomach rumbled in anticipation of the bracing brew. He prayed the caffeine did its job.

"Pit stop already?" Jon sent him a wry grin. "Told you to take care of business before we left home, son."

Eli chuckled. "Sorry, Dad. We need coffee before interrogating the villain. I image Brenna does, too."

"Make it the largest cinnamon latte they have," Brenna said.

He and Jon exchanged horrified glances, but said nothing. He had never met a latte he liked. Plain Joe for him and the rest of his black ops buddies. Eli pulled into the drive thru and placed their orders. Within minutes, he cruised down the entrance ramp, once again headed for Murfreesboro, sipping steaming black coffee.

By the time the sun crested the horizon, Eli parked in front of Sam Wilson's large Georgian-style home. Also in the drive sat a late-model Mercedes SUV and a Hummer. Guess the Scarlett Group's payoff money came in handy. His lip curled. The physician's gravy train was about to derail. "How do you want to play this?" he asked his partner. "Does the man have a family?"

"Wife named Catrina and two little girls, ages six and nine."

"Does the wife work?" Brenna asked. "Maybe the kids are at daycare already."

Jon shook his head. "No record of her working recently. Seems she's been happy to be a stay-at-home mom since her first daughter was born."

"We don't want to frighten those kids," Eli said, weighing their options. The idea of scaring them made his stomach twist into a knot. He glanced into the backseat. "Do you have a recent picture of Dana?"

Brenna dug through her purse for her wallet, removed a 3 x 5 picture from a plastic protector and handed it to him.

He and Jon checked their weapons and got out of the car. Brenna scrambled from the backseat onto the concrete drive. "Stay behind me, sugar. The man's got a lot to lose in this game."

"I thought you weren't going to scare the little girls." She stared at the P226 in his hand. "That's not a normal part of a doctor's black bag."

Jon grinned. "We have a medic on our black ops team who would disagree with you. He never goes anywhere without one of those. Says he feels underdressed if one of these babies isn't within reach."

Eli grabbed a lightweight jacket and pulled it on over his black t-shirt and jeans. He slid the weapon into his shoulder holster. "Better?"

Brenna nodded at Jon. "What about him?"

"We'll make sure the kids don't see his gun." Eli led her up the walkway to the porch. "One of us needs a weapon ready, Brenna. We don't know how Wilson will react when we confront him. I can tell you it won't be good. Question is how bad will it get and will it attract enough attention to bring the police?"

He climbed the stairs and pressed the doorbell. Eli motioned Brenna to stand behind him while Jon took position on the other side of the door frame, out of sight unless one of the Wilsons came out of the house.

A beautiful Latino woman opened the door and smiled. "Yes, can I help you?"

For a moment, Eli regretted the necessity of tearing her world apart. Then he remembered the terror Dana endured. The regret vanished. "Mrs. Wilson?"

"Do I know you?" Puzzlement showed on her face.

"No, ma'am. I need to speak with your husband."

"He's getting ready to leave for the hospital. He has rounds in a few minutes. Can't you make an appointment with his office?"

Eli shook his head. "I won't take much of his time, Mrs. Wilson, but this is a matter of life or death."

Catrina Wilson frowned, her concern evident. "I'll get him. Would you like to come in?"

"No, ma'am. I'll wait out here for him." Squealing laughter sounded from another room. Eli smiled, the noise reminding him of Christmas mornings with his nieces and nephews. "I don't want to disturb your family."

"He'll be right out."

A couple of minutes passed before heavier footsteps heralded the doctor's approach. A middle-aged man, medium build, unremarkable brown hair and eyes stepped into view. "My wife said you have some kind of emergency. What's going on?"

How had Wilson managed to capture the beautiful Catrina? He didn't seem the type to garner the interest of such an exotic beauty. "Step outside with me, Dr. Wilson. I don't want to disturb your wife or your daughters." He slid his jacket aside enough so the good doctor got a look at the weapon at his shoulder.

Wilson paled. "Please, don't hurt my family. I'll give you anything you want."

"Sweetheart, is everything okay?" Catrina Wilson said, a few feet behind her husband.

"I only want information, Doc," Eli said softly. "I would hate to scare your wife and daughters." His tone left no doubt that despite his words, he would do just that if the doctor didn't cooperate. Dana's safety was at stake.

Sweat beaded on Wilson's forehead, his eyes trained on the gun at Eli's shoulder. "Everything's fine, honey. I'll just be a minute."

"You promised the girls a pillow fight before you leave for the hospital."

"Catrina, please." His voice cracked. "Go take care of the girls."

"This won't take long, Mrs. Wilson," Eli said. With a firm grip on the lapels of the doctor's jacket, he drew Wilson out onto the porch. He nodded his thanks to the uncertain woman and closed the door. They couldn't do what they needed with a delicate audience and they didn't want her calling the police before they obtained information to help them find Dana before the clock ticked down to zero.

As soon at the door shut, Eli covered the peephole with one hand and crowded the doctor against his front door. The man's eyes widened when he noticed Jon and his gun to his left, boxing him in place.

"What do you want?"

"Not what, Doc. Who. I want Dana Cole."

The doctor shook his head. "I don't know anyone named Dana Cole."

"Wrong answer, Dr. Wilson," Jon said, his voice a deep, angry growl. He stepped close enough that the physician pressed his back tighter against the door. No place to hide from Jon Smith. "If you want to keep those beautiful little girls healthy, come up with a better answer."

"No, please. I'm telling you the truth. I don't have a patient with that name."

"She's not a patient." Eli showed Wilson Dana's picture. "I know you recognize her, Doc. For the sake of your wife and daughters, you want to rethink your answer."

The physician's eyes closed for a moment. When he opened them again, resignation and fear warred for dominance in his gaze. "You don't understand. They'll kill my family."

"Yeah? They aren't here, but my friend has a weapon pointed at your gut. Trust me, Doc, he's very good with it. Maybe you should think about which danger is more immediate. How did you get involved with the Scarlett Group?"

"Bad luck. I was in the wrong place at the wrong time. I left the hospital late one night. A van pulled up to the emergency room entrance. The driver asked if I was a doctor. I thought he might have a relative or friend inside who needed emergency assistance. I went closer. The passenger grabbed me and stuffed me in the back with a gun in my face. He tied a blindfold over my eyes until we reached some farmhouse out in the country."

"Why did they grab you?" Jon asked.

"One of the girls had a bad cut that was infected."

"How was she injured or did you even bother to find out?"

"Of course I asked. Do you think I'm heartless?"

"You don't want me to answer that question, Doc." Jon smiled, more a baring of his teeth since it lacked any warmth.

Wilson swallowed hard. "One of them put a gun to my head, so I quit asking. I had one goal. Survival. I did what I could for the girl, kept my head down and prayed they wouldn't kill me before the night was over."

"It's obvious you survived. Why didn't you call the cops?"

"And tell them what? I didn't know where they took me. How could I help them find this girl again? Besides, they took my wallet while I worked on the girl. Do you understand what that means?" Wilson's voice fell to a whisper. "They know where I live. They know about Catrina and the girls."

"You sure?" Eli asked, dragged the doctor's attention back to him.

"Money is wired to my bank account every month. I haven't spent a penny of their blood money, but they also send pictures to my personal email account. Recent pictures of my daughters along with the going price for girls that age. I didn't have a choice. I have to protect my family and I didn't know what else to do."

A white van drove past the house at a snail's pace. Jon watched the vehicle until it turned the corner. He glanced at Eli, his expression granite.

Eli's stomach knotted. Great. Jon suspected something was off about that van. Maybe more trouble had followed Brenna, but he didn't spot a tail earlier. He wanted to believe he or Jon would have noticed a vehicle, considering his quick, unexpected stop at Starbucks. No one had followed them off the interstate. That early in the morning with so little traffic, trailing headlights attracted attention.

If this vehicle belonged to someone in the Scarlett Group, he and Jon had just brought more problems to Wilson's doorstep, the kind that could land more innocents on the auction block or in the morgue. Not something Eli wanted to add to his nightmares.

In his head, Eli heard the ticking clock eroding Dana's safety margin. "We might be able to protect your family, Doc. First, what do you know about Dana? When did you see her?"

"Two days ago."

Behind Eli, Brenna gasped. "Where? Is she okay?"

Startled, Wilson peered past Eli's shoulder. "Who are you?"

Eli tensed, wondered if Brenna would remember his instructions not to mention names. If he contacted the right people, Wilson wouldn't be a threat to Eli's security or his team. However, people in the witness protection program often created problems for themselves by refusing to change their habits. Eli couldn't see the man not continuing to practice medicine and doubted if either of the Wilson's would be willing to give up all ties to their families. If Wilson fell into the wrong hands, the less he knew about Eli and Jon, the safer it would be for them and their team.

"I'm looking for Dana, too."

Eli's muscles lost some of their tension. Smart girl. He should have known Brenna would keep her wits about her. "Stay focused, Doc."

"Ms. Cole was fine when I saw her."

"She won't be for long," Jon said. "Scarlett Group has a countdown clock running on her. We have a little more than 24 hours to find her. You want us to protect your wife and daughters. We're willing to do that. For a price. Dana. Will you help us find her?"

"I want my family's safety guaranteed."

"No such thing as a guarantee in this business," Eli said. "We'll do the best we can. We know people who are the best at protection. They can be here within the hour, but we need something from you first. Where is Dana?"

CHAPTER FOURTEEN

Brenna's heart pounded against her chest wall. Adrenaline flooded her system. Were they finally getting the break they needed to find Dana? She prayed they'd find her sister before anything more happened, something from which Dana might not recover. Just thinking of the horrors Dana might be going through made Brenna's stomach lurch.

"I don't know," Wilson said.

Blind fury roiled in her gut. Was the little weasel holding out on them? Why? Money? She pressed her lips into a tight line. For a few seconds, she contemplated asking Jon to make Wilson talk by any means necessary. She knew SEALs were quite capable of getting whatever information they needed. Maybe she should turn the guys loose and return to the car.

Her eyes narrowed. Then again, maybe not. Dana was her sister. Nobody loved Dana as much as she did. "How can you not know where she is?" Brenna pushed past Eli to confront the physician. "You said you saw her two days ago."

"I told you the truth. I did see her, but I didn't see where she was being held. I'm still blindfolded every time they take me to check the girls."

"You're lying." Hands clenched, she beat on his chest until a steel band wrapped around her waist and lifted her away from her target. "No." Brenna fought against the restraining arm, determined to force the information out of the cowering doctor if he wouldn't tell them voluntarily. It didn't matter to her if he refused to talk from fear or lack of conscience. "Let me go. I have to make him talk. He knows where she is."

Eli clamped a hand over her mouth and carried her squirming body around the side of the house. In some distant corner of her mind, Brenna realized she was making such a scene, they'd be lucky if some neighbor didn't call the police to help the doctor and cart off the deranged woman on Wilson's doorstep.

A moment later, Brenna found her back against the Wilson's brick wall, Eli's hand still pressed over her mouth, his face inches from hers, dark eyes blazing with fury. She fought harder. She had to get free.

"Stop it, Brenna." His hard body pressed against hers and forced her into absolute stillness. "Are you hearing me?"

Lips pressed into a tight line, jaw clenched, she nodded, alert. She needed a small opening, a distraction of any kind. Nosy neighbor or dog, anything to give her a chance to return to her target. Wilson knew more than he was saying. Dana's life hung in the balance. Nothing stood a chance of getting in her way, not even her drop-dead gorgeous Navy SEAL.

"Listen up, sugar girl. If you don't get a grip right now, we will spend the next several hours in a police station instead of tracking your sister. We need every minute and lead available, even lousy ones like the doc might give us. We won't get anything from him if he thinks you're a straight-jacket candidate or he's afraid you'll rip his face off and hurt his family."

Eli's intensity, his words, penetrated the red fog clouding her mind. The blinding rage sweeping through her moments before dissipated, left shock in its wake. Good grief. What had she been thinking, attacking the doctor that way? Maybe she was crazy. That was the only logical explanation available for trying to outsmart and outmuscle a SEAL. Make that two SEALs. She closed her eyes and let her head fall back against the brick, panting from exertion. Guess the fact that Eli hadn't hurt her showed the measure of his control. She hadn't been thinking at all, simply feeling. All the pent up fear and frustration had exploded and created a firestorm out of her control. And here she'd been concerned about Eli's PTSD issues. Looked like she was the one that needed help.

"I'm going to lift my hand from your mouth. So help me, if you start screeching again, I'll kiss you until you shut up and the neighbors assume we're in a heavy-duty make-out session in broad daylight. Am I making myself clear?"

Brenna's eyelids sprang upward. She tried to smile, couldn't because of his tight grip. Eli must have seen the smile in her eyes or realized the tension in her body had vanished. He eased the pressure on her mouth until he lifted his hand clear and slipped it beneath her hair, cradling the back of her neck.

"Are you okay now?" he murmured.

She nodded. "I'm sorry."

Eli tugged her into his arms, squeezed her tight. "You scared me but good, baby."

Scared him? Her loss of control still made her stomach want to lose the cinnamon latte all over the yard. "Bet I scared the doctor as well. Think he'll talk to us now? What if I scared off our best lead to Dana?"

He pressed a kiss to the top of her head. "Let's hope Jon gave him a plausible excuse and convinced him to talk." Eli cupped her chin and lifted her gaze to his. "Can you hold it together? If not, I'll have Jon question him while you and I walk around the neighborhood."

"I'm fine. Let's see what he knows." Brenna placed a light kiss on his lips and walked toward the front of the house.

Within two strides, Eli caught up with her and nestled her hand in his. "Remember, sugar, any more theatrics and I'll tell the good doctor you skipped your meds the past few days."

Lips curving upward, Brenna glanced at him. Despite the light tone, his expression dispelled any notion he was joking. "I promise. No theatrics. There won't be any need to call the guys in white coats to haul me off."

They rounded the corner to find the doctor talking with Jon, still standing on the porch. Wilson eyed her as if expecting another outburst. Brenna's cheeks burned. How embarrassing. She sighed. A great emotion to include in the next manuscript. Too bad the experience was so personal.

Jon turned toward them. "The doc might be of some help after all."

Eli's hand tightened around hers as they climbed the stairs again. "Anything you can do to help us find Dana we won't forget. We'll owe you a favor, Doc. Anytime, anyplace."

"Does that include protecting my family from these animals?"

"That one's on us," Jon said. He pulled out a business card and handed it to Wilson.

Brenna's eyes widened. He was giving the doctor his name? What if the Scarlett Group found the doctor and the card?

Wilson read the card, then raised a puzzled gaze. "This only has a phone number. How do I know who to ask for?"

"It's a private number, a company that we do freelance work for. Tell whoever answers the phone that you are cashing in a favor and give them the code shown under the number. That code is assigned to me. They'll know what to do. I'll give them your name so you will be listed in a secured database. Within minutes, I'll be notified you called. We'll get to you ourselves or send someone to help."

"Please, Dr. Wilson," Brenna said. "Will you help us?"

He put the card into his wallet. "I don't know where the girls are, but I think the place where they are being held is somewhere in Rutherford County."

Jon stiffened. "Girls? They have more than one right now?"

"One more, a teenager. Blond." Wilson grimaced. "She keeps begging me to call her mother."

Eli and Jon exchanged a look.

Brenna noticed the glance between the two men and bit back the acidic words threatening to spew from her mouth despite her promise to Eli. The doctor must be talking about Julie. Unless the human traffickers had kidnapped another young girl. She bit down on her lower lip, hoping that wasn't the case. No one deserved to be treated like cattle, especially a teenage girl with her whole life ahead of her.

"Rutherford County's a big place, Doc. We need more information to help us narrow it down," Eli said. "Did they drive on the interstate, back roads, unpaved roads, what?"

"Interstate, then paved side streets. No stop lights once we were off the interstate." He paused. "Look, I can't swear to this, but I think it's somewhere between Murfreesboro and Christiana. It doesn't take a long time to get from the Medical Center to the place where they keep the girls."

Tires squealed close by.

Jon glanced over his shoulder. "Inside, now."

Brenna caught a glimpse of a white van barreling down the street before Eli threw open the front door and shoved her and Dr. Wilson inside.

Eli ran through the hallway toward the kitchen where he heard the girls and Catrina Wilson. He burst into the room. Elena was on her knees in front of the girls, wiping their faces with a cloth. "Get down on the ground."

She remained kneeling, frozen in place with a shocked expression on her face.

Not having time for niceties, Eli shoved her to the floor in front of the refrigerator, grabbed the screaming girls, and rolled with them in his arms until he covered them with his body.

"Don't hurt my babies, please!" Catrina tried to get up.

"Stay down."

Rapid semi-automatic gunfire shattered the morning stillness and the living room windows. Glasses on the kitchen table exploded. Orange juice spilled onto the floor. Catrina screamed and crawled closer to her crying daughters and Eli.

Return fire erupted from the front of the house followed by silence.

"My husband. Where's my husband?" Catrina's terror-filled gaze searched Eli's. "I have to go to him."

"Wait, Catrina. Just for a minute." He crawled off the girls and pushed them into Catrina's arms. "Keep them right here. Don't move until I come back for you." Eli didn't know if Wilson had been hit or, God forbid, Brenna. Catrina Wilson and her daughters shouldn't have to deal with further trauma. He didn't worry about Jon. His tough teammate could fend for himself.

With a need bordering on panic to know if Brenna was injured, Eli moved into a crouch. He pulled his gun from the holster and shifted toward the living room. "Jon?" he called.

"Doorway. We're clear for now. Cops are on their way."

He ran to the living room, shoved his weapon into the holster, and lifted Brenna to her feet. "You okay, baby?" He scanned her body, prayed he wouldn't find an injury, whether from the shooter or from him throwing her to the ground. At her nod and seeing no visible injuries, he tugged her into his arms. He rubbed her back, holding her as shudders of fear wracked her body and he struggled to regulate his own breathing and heart rhythm. Yeah, wouldn't his SEAL buddies hoot and holler if they could see him now. They claimed he'd had ice running through his veins on missions. Not the case today.

Jon helped the shaken physician rise.

"Catrina?" he croaked. "My girls?"

"They're fine," Eli said. "Do you have a basement?"

Wilson nodded.

"Take your family down to the basement and keep them there until the police arrive." Jon grabbed Wilson's arm as he moved past. "Doc, don't try to run with your family. If you do, Scarlett Group will find and kill all of you. We'll provide protection if the police can't or won't do it."

"I promise." Wilson hurried to the kitchen.

"It was Scarlett's thugs?" Eli asked.

"Yeah. Wilson recognized the van."

A cold knot formed in his belly. If Scarlett's thugs recognized him or Jon, they might move Dana to another location. He scanned his partner's frustrated expression. Eli suspected he'd come to the same conclusion. It didn't matter where they moved Dana. He and Jon wouldn't stop searching until they found and freed her. He prayed the Scarlett Group didn't kill her before then.

Brenna burrowed closer to his chest. Eli pulled her tighter against his body. Once again, he'd almost lost her to these bozos. One step slower and he would have been holding a lifeless body instead of her warm, scared one. Another ghost to populate his already haunted nightmares. Never, he vowed. No matter what it took. He wasn't losing her. "Did you get a plate?"

"Oh, yeah." Jon's lips curled. "Call Cal. He'll want to be here even if this is out of his jurisdiction."

Eli loosened his grip on Brenna and grabbed his cell phone. When Cal growled a greeting, he gave Cal a run-down of the situation and the address. He ended the call to a symphony of police sirens and screeching tires. He brushed his lips against Brenna's for a moment. "Don't volunteer any information, sugar. Tell them what happened here, nothing else. We don't want to mention Scarlett Group or Dana. There is a slim possibility this isn't connected to our investigation."

Although he didn't believe that, Eli also didn't think it necessary to tell everything they knew and be tied up in endless questions based on simple speculation. Good, probable speculation, but speculation nonetheless. They had no proof. Yet. They'd get it.

"Why not? Do you think they are on the take or something?"

"No, but the more we share with them, the longer the interview process will take. We're running out of time and we can't afford to have our faces plastered all over the media. Neither can Dana. If the Scarlett Group thinks we've gone to the cops for help, they'll move her or kill her and cut their losses, pull up stakes and start again somewhere else. The bottom line is Dana will be lost in their human trafficking system or dumped in a hole six feet deep."

Brenna sat at Dana's breakfast bar once again and glared over the rim of her coffee mug at the stubborn SEAL cooking a mountain of scrambled eggs at the stove. "I'm not hungry, Eli. And even if I was, I couldn't eat that many eggs in a week much less in one meal."

"This is not just for you. You do need protein, though. You haven't eaten in too many hours. Adrenaline and stress zap the appetite, but your body needs fuel to keep functioning or it shuts down at the wrong time."

"The voice of experience again?"

"Oh, yeah. Trust me, sugar. Coffee can only take you so far."

She sipped the hot, bracing brew and grimaced. Jon's idea of coffee blazed a trail of fire all the way to her stomach. Thick and strong enough to keep her awake through eternity, Brenna decided milk or cream might make it more palatable. Another sip, another shudder. Nope. Ugh. Eli and Jon must have steel-lined stomachs.

"You don't want to keep drinking Jon's coffee without food in your stomach."

Despite Eli echoing her own conclusion, Brenna scowled at his back. "You could have warned me earlier."

"Don't spill it on anything you want to keep. Peels paint right off whatever it touches."

Brenna's mug hit the counter with a thud. "Something tells me you're not kidding."

Eli chuckled, tossed her a twinkling glance, turned off the burner and slid the skillet of steaming eggs to the side. He opened cabinet doors until he found plates for the three of them. "Toast?"

Why not? Toasted bread slathered with butter and orange marmalade sounded good. Maybe the smell of cooking eggs awakened her taste buds. "Sure." She padded to the refrigerator and peered into the interior for her favorite spread and butter. Holding the items in her hands, Brenna nudged the door closed with her hip. "Hand me a small plate."

She warmed the butter in the microwave before placing it and the marmalade on the table next to a heaping platter of scrambled eggs cooked to perfection. "Where did you learn to cook like this?"

"Mom made sure all the Wolfe kids mastered the basics of cooking. Can't say I have gourmet skills, but I get by." He grinned. "It came in handy when Jon and I were in the Navy."

"When did you have time to cook? I know the military feeds their soldiers."

Jon walked into the dining area and seated himself next to the wall which left the space across from Brenna for Eli. "SEALs are deployed for months. The rest of the time we're on training maneuvers. Believe me, we enjoyed cooking for ourselves whenever possible. Sea rations and food on the naval base was like typical cafeteria food."

"Short on taste?"

"Knew you were a smart woman." He winked at her. Warmth heated her cheeks at his teasing. No wonder Dana didn't share her feelings about Jon. So many different sides to that quiet SEAL.

"Find anything from the Internet search?" Eli asked.

The teasing light left his eyes, replaced by a glint of what Brenna suspected was anger. "Ross Harrison is out of jail. Paroled early for good behavior." Jon piled eggs and toast on his plate. "He's also overdue to check in with his parole officer."

Brenna dropped a fork with a clatter onto her plate. "He's missing?" Her skin crawled, almost as if Ross the Rat was in the room, staring at her with his arctic blue eyes.

"Seems so." Jon rose and refilled his coffee mug. "Should have checked in June 15 and his boss at the mine hasn't seen him, either. Your good friend the police chief isn't talking to anyone about Harrison."

She chewed and swallowed a bite of eggs that now tasted as appealing as cooked cardboard. "They're friends. Carter thinks Dana lied about what happened with Ross. He believes my sister went after Ross, not the other way around. How else was a normal, healthy adult male supposed to respond to a blatant invitation from a beautiful female? Didn't matter if she was underage. She knew what she wanted and went after it. Poor Ross never stood a chance."

Jon growled.

"I agree," Brenna said. "I doubt Frank Carter would tell me if he knew where Ross went. According to him, Dana and I were out to get Mom's money and house back from our stepfather because she left those to him in her will."

Eli frowned. "Why didn't your mother leave the money and house to you and Dana?"

"Neither of us wanted the house and Mom left us money in a trust. Dana spent her part of the money on college."

His eyebrows rose. "Sounds like a sizeable trust fund."

"I wish that were true." It certainly would have made things a lot easier. Not only had Brenna written short contemporary romances under a pseudonym to help pay the school bill, she also contributed a few columns to the local newspaper, neither of which paid much. "Dana attended a community college in Wise."

"Is your part of the money still in trust?"

Brenna smiled. "I'm spending my part of the trust to help Dana pay for the apartment and her groceries. She doesn't know that and you and Jon can't tell her. My sister thinks I earn decent money as a published author."

"You don't?"

She laughed. "If I did, Pound, Virginia would be a distant speck in my rearview mirror. I can write anywhere and email the manuscript to my agent. When I make enough to support myself in a bigger city, I'll leave Pound and never look back. Too many bad memories in that town I'd love to leave behind. Doubt anyone would miss me either."

Jon dropped back into his chair, coffee mug in hand, thoughtful expression on his face. "Would Carter protect Harrison from any inquiries, including one from the parole officer?"

"Very possible if he believed Ross's offense was mild. Carter made Dana's life miserable while Ross rotted in jail. That's why I encouraged her to get out of Virginia as soon as she graduated." She shot Jon a wry smile. "I didn't tell anybody where Dana moved. I thought she would be safer here."

"What happened to Dana is not your fault." Jon pinned her with his dark gaze. "The innocent get hurt all the time, Brenna. You ought to know. You're caught in the same web of violence that captured Dana. Don't concern yourself with Harrison. If we don't catch up with him beforehand, we'll find him after we free Dana. He'll pay for what he did to her. I promise you that. He'll regret touching her."

They finished the rest of their meal in silence.

Brenna had to admit she felt better after eating. Eli understood how the human body responded to situations like this. The sound of chimes from her cell phone caught her attention. The kidnappers calling or maybe Dana if she broke free? Brenna raced to her purse and dug out her phone. She frowned, puzzled at the number, one she didn't recognize. "Hello?"

"Brenna, it's Grace. I learned some information, but I can't talk here at work."

"Where can we meet you?"

"We? Who's coming with you?"

"Eli Wolfe." Silence greeted Brenna's statement. Her hand tightened around the phone. "That's okay, isn't it?" It had to be all right. She doubted Eli would let her go anywhere without either him or Jon after what happened at the Wilson home a few short hours ago.

She glanced up. Eli leaned one shoulder against the wall, watched her with an intent gaze.

185

"I suppose. Look, I'm going to the Sartelli estate in another hour. Why don't you meet me there?"

"Hold on, Grace." Brenna placed her hand over the phone's speaker. "Can we meet Grace at the Sartelli estate in one hour? She says she has some information but can't talk to us at work."

"Ask her if the gate guard will let us in without compromising her job or does she want us to meet her on a side street nearby?"

"Grace, will the guard let us in without causing you problems? We can meet you on a side street if you prefer."

"The guard is a friend. He won't sell me out. Drive to the back of the house. I have flowers to deliver for the Sartelli party this evening. See you in an hour."

Eli straightened from the wall. "What did she say?"

"The guard's a friend and we should drive to the back of the house."

"Huh. Sartelli probably won't be home at that time. I'd say there's little chance of crossing paths with him, although I think we should talk to him today. I still think Sartelli is involved in Dana's disappearance. I don't want Grace in jeopardy, though. Maybe we can catch him at work while Grace is out. We should go see him right after we leave the Sartelli place."

"He's not like the other men you and Jon persuaded to spill what they knew. Sartelli has his own NFL-sized bodyguard who carries a big gun. How can we make him talk?"

He grinned. "Charm, baby. How can he resist me?"

Eli flipped on his right turn signal and headed up the steep Sartelli drive to the gate. A guard in a familiar Thompson security uniform approached the driver's side of the car, clipboard in hand, a semi-automatic holstered at his waist.

He gritted his teeth, hoped Grace had left their names with the guard. Eli knew the owner of Thompson Security. Jason Thompson hired ex-military along with a few former mercenaries, none susceptible to the famous Wolfe charm. He made a mental note to call Jason after they found Dana. His friend might be interested in some of Sartelli's rumored activities.

The guard motioned for Eli to lower his window. "Can I help you, sir?"

"Eli Wolfe and Brenna Mason to see Grace Peters."

"Yes, sir. Ms. Peters just arrived. She's waiting for you at the back of the house." The man returned to the guard shack and released the lock on the gate.

Eli drove through the open wrought-iron arms and up the long drive, then circled behind the house. Grace's Lexus was parked near the separate garage, hatch still open. Two large floral arrangements were in the back. He parked behind her vehicle and climbed from his Camaro, scanned the area as he opened the passenger door for Brenna.

Imaginary needles pricked the nape of his neck. He didn't see anything out of the ordinary, but he'd learned never to discount those needles. Something wasn't right, but what?

"Is anything wrong?" Brenna asked.

"Not sure, sugar," he said, his gaze quartering their surroundings again. "Stay here for a minute." He unlocked his trunk and retrieved his Go bag, wondered if he was overreacting. Eli knelt beside Brenna, dumped his bag on the car floorboard by her feet, and unzipped it.

"What's going on, Eli?"

"A bad feeling. We're hedging our bets." Something he'd learned while in the military. Hope for the best, prepare for the worst, and always have another plan ready. Marine Corp buddies had taught him that two is one; one is none. Intending to do better than that, he rummaged in the bag and pulled out three tiny skin-colored patches. A small inconvenience if he was wrong, a life saver if he was right. "Take your shoe off, sugar."

Eli peeled one of the small tags and pressed it to the arch of her foot. He slid her foot back into her shoe. "Stand up for me." He rose and stepped back, the other two tags adhering to his finger. "Do you trust me, Brenna?"

She nodded, her eyes wide, glittering with uncertainty.

He hated knowing he had put that look in her gorgeous eyes. She deserved so much better than the hand she'd been dealt in this whole situation. Brenna rated safety and security, a lifetime of love and care, something he'd like to be the one to give her if she'd let him. Yeah, he'd been sideswiped by his feelings. She mattered to him on a level deeper than any other woman had in his life. "Someone is watching us. I don't know where he is, but I feel him just the same." He bent until his mouth brushed against her ear. "You have one tracking tag on the bottom of your foot. I need to put two more on you. The only way to do this without him realizing I'm placing trackers on you is to kiss you."

Her mouth brushed his neck. He felt a smile curve her trembling lips. "Tough duty, but you can handle it," she whispered.

"I'm going to put one tag behind your ear." He hesitated, unsure of her reaction to his next statement. "I need to place the other one on the lower part of your back, baby. Are you okay with that?"

"Shut up and kiss me, Wolfe."

"Yes, ma'am," he murmured. He slid his hands into Brenna's hair, angled his head and pressed his mouth to hers. Keeping the kiss light and playful, Eli nibbled at her lips. He carefully nipped, then licked away the sting, but focused most of his attention on positioning the tag. Once it was in place, he lifted his mouth a scant inch from hers. "Remember the kiss we shared at the airport?"

"Oh, yes," she whispered. "Best kiss of my life."

He chuckled. "Good to know. Same for me. I need a repeat performance, sugar." He grinned. "Will you share your gum with me this time?"

Brenna lifted her arms and wrapped them around his neck. "Depends. Do you like Spearmint?"

His gaze dropped to her kiss-reddened lips. "I need a sample before I decide." Eli wrapped his arms around her and took her mouth with a hunger that surprised him. This was supposed to be for their watcher's benefit, but Brenna snared Eli in a trap of his own making. While one small corner of his mind remained alert to their surroundings, he reveled in a kiss hot enough to sear his senses.

He believed he could control the fire Brenna stirred until he realized seconds or maybe minutes later he was on the verge of forgetting their audience. He jerked his attention back where it belonged. Eli's hands tightened on Brenna's waist, warning her of his intentions. She squeezed his neck before loosening her hold a little. Stay focused, Wolfe. Something told him that might be the hardest part of his task. The gorgeous writer in his arms distracted him like no other woman had in his life.

Eli changed the angle of his kiss and pressed Brenna between the still open car door and the Camaro's frame, hoping it appeared to observers that he was losing control of his emotions, very close to the truth. He also figured the car would block most of his hand movement from the watcher's line of sight. The thought of some thug looking at Brenna's bare skin had his muscles hardening, readying to defend the woman in his arms.

He slid his hands around to her back and beneath her shirt at her trim waist. As soon as his fingers touched her warm flesh, a shudder wracked his body. How could Brenna's skin be so soft beneath his hands? Much as he wanted to stroke the living satin a few moments longer, he didn't dare. Eli forced himself to concentrate on slipping the last tag from his finger to the small of Brenna's back.

With a last lingering caress, he moved his hands back to her waist, broke the kiss, returned to her lips and stole a few more light caresses, then stared down into her beautiful face.

Brenna smiled at him, her eyes sparkling. "So what do you think about my gum?"

"Spearmint is my second favorite flavor."

"Hmm. What's your first?"

"You."

"Eli, Brenna." Grace stepped onto the gray flagstone patio and waved. "Will you bring those flower arrangements into the house for me?"

"No problem. We'll bring them inside in a minute." After Grace returned to the house, Eli's gaze shifted back to Brenna. "Talk to me for a minute or two, sugar."

Concern shimmered in her gaze. "Is something else wrong?"

"Couple of things. One, I want to give the adhesive a little longer to set."

"And the other?"

His lips twitched. Embarrassed to admit the truth, he still forced himself to suck it up and be honest with her. "Baby, your kiss almost set me on fire. I don't think I can walk anywhere just yet."

Brenna's cheeks flushed. "The feeling's mutual."

Eli cupped her face with both hands, as if contemplating a renewal of their kiss. "If something happens and we are separated, don't touch the tags, not even to check if they are still in place. You don't know who is watching or if a camera will capture the movement."

The color drained from Brenna's face. "Do you think the Scarlett Group will try to take me here?"

"I don't think so, but I'm not taking a chance. You mean too much to me not to use any tool at my disposal to secure your safety." Eli dropped his hands and urged Brenna to move ahead of him toward Grace's SUV. He lifted the largest arrangement while Brenna grabbed the smaller one. After shutting the hatchback, he followed her into the Sartelli kitchen, a symphony of Italian tile floors, black marble countertops, and gourmet cookware. No food aromas greeted him. The Sartellis must be having their party catered. Can't say that surprised him. He couldn't picture Elena Sartelli slaving away in the kitchen, preparing for a party.

"Thank you so much for bringing those inside." Grace sighed. "I've been running errands all day, helping Mrs. Sartelli prepare for tonight. Dana was supposed to do this and Mrs. Sartelli has been frazzled the whole day."

"Is Mrs. Sartelli here? I have a few questions I want to ask her." Eli asked.

Grace shook her head. "She had an appointment to have her hair styled for tonight. She won't return until 5:00, in time to dress for the party."

Yeah, should have figured that for himself. Guess he'd have to catch Elena tomorrow to ask her about Dana and Julie.

"Where should we put these arrangements?" Brenna asked. "I don't know about the one Eli is carrying, but this one is heavy."

"Oh, I'm sorry, Brenna. Yours goes in the dining room." Grace pointed to the other side of the kitchen. "Straight down that hall and take a right. You can't miss it. Eli, take yours to the front entrance. Follow Brenna down the hallway, but keep going until you see the front door. There's a large circular glass table in the middle of the entranceway ready for the arrangement. Come back in here when you're finished. I'll have glasses of cold Coke for you and we can talk."

After dropping off the arrangements and retracing their steps down the hall, Eli and Brenna seated themselves at the kitchen table.

Grace brought their drinks and sat across from them. "I can't tell you how much I appreciate you meeting me like this."

"You told Brenna you were afraid to talk at work. Was Sartelli in the office?" Eli sipped his carbonated drink. Man, the icy Coke hit the spot on such a scorching day. He drank almost the entire glass before he realized it.

"Sartelli had meetings scheduled all day. He's been grousing the whole week about Mrs. Sartelli's lousy timing for this party. He has several construction bids out and some negotiations for others around Davidson County. He's been a real grouch today."

"Are they celebrating a special occasion?" Brenna asked, sipping her own beverage. "Oh, wait, isn't this the engagement party for Maria?"

"That's right. Mrs. Sartelli and Mrs. Martin have been planning this party for several weeks." Grace smiled. "They spared no expense. Only the best for their children." She described the vast amounts of food and drinks to be served and the latest speculation on the location of the upcoming Christmas wedding and honeymoon.

Somewhere in the lengthy descriptions, Eli realized his vision had become blurry. He blinked. No difference. He frowned. Was he that tired? He had to admit, a nap sounded good about now. Maybe another glass of Coke or coffee. Yeah, coffee. Caffeine. That's what he needed. Hardly able to keep his eyes open, Eli tried standing, but toppled to the floor, coordination nonexistent.

From somewhere far off, he heard Grace call his name and laugh. Why was she laughing?

He had to get off the floor. Brenna was in danger. Eli rolled to his side and couldn't move further. He grasped at tendrils of thought winding like ribbons through his mind. What was wrong with him? Was he finally losing his mind?

Eli's eyes were so heavy. He fought to keep them open, lost. Had to be drugged. God help him, he'd failed to protect the love of his life. His last coherent thought— Brenna.

Brenna watched in horror as Eli fell to the floor. She jumped to her feet and almost hit the floor herself with the first step. Grasping the edge of the table, she forced her body to move around the table toward Eli, ignored Grace's maniacal laughter. Why wouldn't she shut up and help Eli? The room tilted although she knew that wasn't possible.

The floor was flat, despite her perception telling her otherwise. Crawl. She could crawl to Eli, tilting floor or not. After a few seconds, Brenna's hand received the message her brain sent to let go of the table.

She dropped to the floor, her gaze fixed on Eli's prone body, determined to reach him. Her arm extended as if in slow motion. Brenna grasped Eli's shoulder and rolled him to his back. He groaned. Her hand slipped. She bit her lip, used the pain to focus for a few precious seconds. Had to try again. Eli. She edged closer, closer.

Someone was sobbing. Who was crying? Brenna tasted salt on her lips. Realized she was crying. No more tears. So tired. She just wanted to sleep for a minute.

She shook her head. Get to Eli. Then nap. With the last of her strength, Brenna crawled the remaining inches to Eli. Had to protect him somehow. More tears. Too tired. She sprawled across his chest and collapsed. Her eyes drifted shut.

CHAPTER FIFTEEN

"Eli. Wake up, buddy. I need your help."

Eli frowned, batted at the hard hand shaking him from sleep. Still so tired. Couldn't have slept more than a couple hours to be this wiped out. What was Cal doing in his apartment this early in the morning anyway? His friend usually called before barging in with food. Another scowl. Whatever Cal had brought smelled more like rubbing alcohol than food.

He wanted to slide back into oblivion. Later. Eli would talk to his friend later. He settled deeper into the pillow.

"Come on, Eli. Fight the drug. I need help to find your girl."

His girl? Eli groaned. Who was Cal talking about? What girl?

"That's right, Eli. Wake up and look at me." The same hard hand tapped his cheek. "Open your eyes, sleeping beauty."

Eli forced his eyes open to slits. Bright lights almost blinded him. He squeezed his eyes shut again. "Lights," he croaked. Why had Cal turned on every light in his bedroom? He tried to throw his arm over his eyes and block the light, but someone grabbed his wrist and held it still.

"What did he say?" another man asked.

Cal brought someone else to his place? Eli hoped he'd gone to bed wearing sleep shorts.

"The lights are bothering him."

Footsteps, then blessed relief as the light disappeared. Eli opened his eyes again, searched for Cal and noticed his surroundings. Not his bedroom, that was for sure. It smelled medicinal. He blinked. A hospital? How did he end up here?

"Eli? Are you with me?" Cal stepped into Eli's line of sight. "Hey, buddy. About time you woke from your nap." He held up a glass with a straw in it. "Drink this. You've got to be thirsty."

Eli eyed the cup, sudden suspicion forming in his gut. A thought flashed through his mind too fast for him to grasp. Something to do with a drink. He scowled. His brain worked as though wrapped in multiple layers of cotton.

"It's okay." Cal moved the cup closer and positioned the straw at mouth level. "This is just water. You have to flush that crap from your system."

What crap? He wondered at his own reluctance to drink the water. Cal was his friend, an occasional fellow teammate on the Zoo Crew. The cop could be trusted. Eli accepted the straw and drank. He was so thirsty and the water tasted amazing.

Outside the room, a ruckus erupted in the hall. "Sir, you can't barge in there."

"Watch me."

A small smile settled on his lips. Jon.

The door flew open. "How is he?" Jon crossed the room in three strides.

"He's going to be fine," Cal said. "The doctor already pumped fluids through him with an IV and gave him something to counteract the drug."

Drug? He'd been drugged? That was important. More thoughts raced through Eli's mind at the speed of lightning, but he couldn't grasp any one of them long enough to understand the threads. Why couldn't he think?

"Eli, do you remember what happened?"

He hesitated, thought back. "I remember driving, kissing Brenna." Eli sat bolt upright. "Brenna!" Adrenaline dumped into his system. "Jon, she's . . ." The sentence was gone before he could finish it. Frustrated, he stared at his friend.

"She's what, Eli?"

"I can't remember. Why can't I remember?" He swallowed hard. What was wrong with him? Some kind of latent memory problem stemming from his SEAL duty or his black ops work? Was he losing his sanity after all?

"You've got to remember," Jon said, his gaze intent. "Brenna's missing."

Eli flung the sheet from his body and swung his legs over the side of the bed. "We have to find her. I can't lose her, Jon."

"Eli, wait." Cal grabbed his arm and held on. "Where are you going?"

"I . . ." His memory blanked again. He gritted his teeth. What had Cal said? Drugged. He'd been drugged. "Who drugged me? What did they give me?"

"Rohypnol."

Eli stopped struggling against Cal's restraining hand. "The date rape drug? That's the same garbage the Scarlett Group uses on their victims." He grasped Cal's shirt in a white-knuckled grip. "Who? Who did this to me?"

"I was hoping you could tell me, but I have a good idea."

"Who?" Eli snapped.

"Grace Peters."

"Grace?" Stunned, Eli released Cal and dropped his hand to the bed. He grimaced at the stabbing pain from the

IV needle. "Why would she drug me? She was trying to help us find Dana." Wasn't she? But if she had been trying to help, why drug him? Had she drugged Brenna as well?

"She has to be involved with the Scarlett Group," Jon said.

Eli forced himself to reason beyond the drug haze and sense of failure. Please, God, not again. He couldn't fail Brenna, too. He didn't think he'd ever get over the guilt if he lost Brenna. "No way Grace could lift Brenna into a vehicle without help. She's also not capable of dragging an unconscious woman." He refused to let the word "dead" past his lips, let alone think it.

"Who said anything about them dragging Brenna away?" Cal said.

Eli grabbed Cal's shirt and yanked him close to his face. "Don't go there, Taylor. Brenna wasn't part of this. She didn't set me up and she sure didn't drug me."

"How do you know that?" Cal stared at him, his gaze cold. "You can't remember anything. Maybe Brenna and Grace worked together."

"Why?" He twisted Cal's shirt to the point of ripping the fabric. No way. He refused to believe Brenna would hurt him like that.

"You wouldn't let up. You and Jon are determined to find Dana. Maybe Brenna has been playing us all for fools, pretending to search for her sister. What if she didn't want you and Jon to find her? What if Brenna was the one who sold Dana to the Scarlett Group? It's obvious from what happened this morning in Murfreesboro that you and Jon are making the Scarlett Group uncomfortable. Maybe Brenna asked Grace to slip the drug into your soft drink. You're lucky they didn't shoot you when you were unconscious."

Soft drink. Eli twisted and turned those words in his mind. Yes, a Coke. Grace gave him a Coke. Satisfaction swirled in his gut. Grace gave Brenna one as well. But

197

Dana's so-called friend hadn't drunk anything. "You're wrong about Brenna."

"Prove it, because from where I stand, she's a suspect. I've already asked for a complete background check on her, including her bank accounts. Might be interesting to see if she's had any sizable deposits made to her account in the last month. I'd love to find out she has an account in the Cayman Islands. I think she's dirty, Eli, and she conned you."

"Grace gave me a Coke and one to Brenna, but Grace didn't drink anything."

"Proves nothing, my friend. You were unconscious, remember? Maybe only your Coke was drugged. Brenna could have downed her whole drink without any ill effects."

"No." Stitches popped at the seams of Cal's shirt "That's not true."

"How do you know it's not? Talk it out, Eli," Cal prompted. "Convince me."

"Because . . ." Eli closed his eyes. A memory floated at the edge of his awareness. What was it? A vague memory, almost like a dream, of a woman crying, calling his name, touching him. Brenna. He knew that touch. Her weight collapsing across his chest, the sweet smell of her shampoo. Vague impressions. Brenna begging someone, maybe Grace and her accomplice, to leave him alone, not to kill him, her words mushy as if drunk. A man's voice, then blackness until he woke to Cal's ugly mug.

He opened his eyes and glared at Cal. "She was drugged as well."

"How do you know?"

"She collapsed on top of me. I remember her begging someone not to kill me, her words slurred." His eyes misted. "She tried to protect me." He wished she had begged Grace or the man to take her with her. At least when he recovered, he might have been able to help get her free. Now he'd have to do this the hard way and pray the traffickers didn't rape or sell Brenna or worse, kill her, before he found her. And he would find her, no matter how long the search lasted. He would never give up until he located her or, he swallowed hard, her body.

"From who? Grace, someone else?"

Eli thought hard, his gut tightening into a knot. "I heard a man talking to Grace."

"Sartelli?" Jon asked.

"I don't think so." Eli released his grip on Cal's shirt a second time. "We were in the Sartelli kitchen, but I don't think he was home. I don't remember seeing him."

Jon snorted. "You sure wouldn't have sat down to share a Coke with Sartelli, Eli."

"I found your Go bag on the floorboard of your car," Cal said. "Do you remember why you had it out of your trunk?"

Another memory zipped across his mind too fast to grasp. Something about kissing and Spearmint gum. Brenna in his arms. His hands under her shirt? Heat burned his cheeks. Why would he have his hands on her skin? Eli jerked his head around to pin Jon with his gaze. "Tags."

His friend raced from the room. Knowing Jon, his laptop was locked in the trunk of his car.

"You tagged her with your tracking devices?" Cal sat beside him on the edge of the hospital bed. "What made you do that? Think, Eli."

Aggravation welled in him as his memories skated away. "I can't remember anything except kissing Brenna and Spearmint gum."

"Must have been some kiss," Cal said.

Another angry scowl at his friend which resulted in a grin on the cop's smirking face. "How did I get here?"

"The Sartelli chef found you on the kitchen floor when she returned from the grocery store. She called for an ambulance and Metro PD. The responding officer recognized you and notified me."

"How did Grace get Brenna out of the estate? The gate guard would have noticed an unconscious woman in the front seat."

"According to the gate log, Grace left ten minutes before the chef returned. The guard thought it a little odd for her to leave you and Brenna inside the estate, but he didn't have a chance to investigate. The estate security system showed a breach at the back of the property. The guard found signs of an attempt to scale the fence."

Eli sighed. "The man I heard probably tripped a sensor. Doesn't Sartelli have security cameras? Can't imagine Jason Thompson leaving a hole in the security grid."

"The camera covering that part of the fence showed nothing. Someone hacked into the computer because the camera recording was time stamped for yesterday."

"So it showed nothing but blue skies and trees."

"You got it."

Jon rushed through the door, computer case in hand. He unzipped the bag, flipped up the lid and turned on his laptop.

"Where are my clothes?" Eli asked Cal.

"Bagged and tagged as evidence. I brought your clothes from the Go bag." He nodded at the chair beside the bed.

Eli grabbed his jeans and pulled them on, grateful the hospital staff hadn't stripped his underwear although going commando wouldn't have stopped him. Nothing would keep him in this place with Brenna's life in danger. Jon's fingers flew over the laptop keyboard, clicked in rapid rhythm.

"Eli, you can't leave the hospital." Cal grabbed his arm, hindering Eli from buttoning his jeans. "The doctor said you took a heavy dose of that drug."

"If the Scarlett Group had your girlfriend, would you lay in a hospital bed and sleep?" He yanked his arm free and reached behind him to untie the hospital-issued gown. "Find a nurse to unhook this IV in the next two minutes or I'll yank it out myself."

A sharp look at his statement, then, "She means that much to you?"

Eli narrowed his eyes.

Muttering about idiots who don't listen to medical professionals, Cal stalked from the room.

He tugged socks on his feet and slipped into the running shoes he kept in his bag. "Anything?"

"Yep. Hold on." More keystrokes. "5539 Paintsville Pike, outside Murfreesboro." Jon growled.

Heart pounding, Eli jumped to his feet. "What?"

"We have to hurry. That's Sartelli's mother-in-law's place." A tortured expression flitted through Jon's eyes. "Sartelli had a private airstrip put in a few years ago."

"Cal!" Eli glanced at the clock. Six o'clock. He'd been out of it for four hours and Nashville traffic would be at a standstill this time of the night. How much longer would Grace remain at the old lady's place? What if they had discovered the tracking tags and left them at the house, but took Brenna somewhere else?

His stomach threatened to hurl the water he'd drunk to the room's farthest corner. He'd never find Brenna before they hurt her. She had trusted him to protect her and find Dana. What if he failed, again?

Cal hit the room at a dead run, a male nurse at his heels. "Did you find her?" he asked Jon, pulling out his cell phone.

Jon turned his computer screen so Cal could read the information.

While Cal called the Rutherford County Sheriff's department, asking for deputies to assist, the nurse removed

Eli's IV. Eli watched the procedure, mentally urging the man to hurry. He feared he might already be too late.

A key rattled in the lock and bright light blinded Dana. She squinted against the glare. Skyscraper. Better than Ape man. Another bathroom break?

"Let's go." He grabbed her arm and hustled her into the hall.

"Wait. Where are we going?" Right. Like he'd tell her after weeks of silence. Still weak and wrapped in brain fog from the last injection, Dana stumbled against her captor. With a vile curse, he threw her over his shoulder and ran down the hall past the bathroom.

The black-and-white floor tiles sped by at a gut-churning pace. She moaned. If Skyscraper didn't stop bouncing her stomach against his shoulder, she'd leave more than bread crumbs behind. Not in any condition to defend herself against possible repercussions from him, Dana doggedly fought the nausea and prayed for a quick end to their journey.

Skyscraper raced up two flights of stairs and threw open a door.

Dana breathed deep. Fresh air. For the first time in days, she dragged in breaths of hot, humid Tennessee air. She smiled. No doubt about where she was now. No other place on earth like it. Turning her head to the side, Dana forced her eyelids up. Had to be late afternoon or early evening from the amount of daylight left. The sun's rays bathed her face in heat, a welcome change from weeks of air conditioned captivity. Needed sun glasses. Dana squinted against the unaccustomed glare.

She had to figure out where they were holding her, find a way to escape. She almost laughed at her crazy thoughts. Sure, and after escaping she'd jog to the nearest town and call the cops. She doubted her ability to walk two feet on her own much less escape Skyscraper and Ape man and their friends.

Still, she had to try if they left her an opening. But what about Julie? Guilt pricked her conscience. She couldn't leave the terrified teenager in the hands of these creeps.

"What's the hurry?" Dana scowled at the slurred words coming out of her mouth. What had these clowns shot her up with?

"Shut up."

He ran up an incline and onto a slab of concrete. Dana frowned. A driveway? No, they couldn't move her. How would Jon and Eli find her? She started to struggle, realized after a few seconds that she was only exhausting herself. Skyscraper didn't seem to notice her movements. "Please, don't do this. Let me go."

"Open the door," Skyscraper called to someone.

"No." Dana found herself off the shoulder and face to face with her angry guard.

"Give me any more trouble, I'll shut you up without a shot of happy juice. Got it?"

The expression on his face told the story. Skyscraper meant what he said. She tried to swallow, couldn't. Whatever drug he'd given her left her mouth feeling as if she hadn't drunk water in days. "Yes."

Ape man stepped into her line of vision, smirking. "Too bad, baby." His gaze stripped Dana bare of the scrubs the doctor had given her to wear. "I wanted a taste of your sweetness."

She shuddered, revulsion crawling through her body at the idea of his hands and mouth anywhere on her.

Skyscraper shoved her toward the waiting white van. "Inside."

Dana fell against the rear bumper, her ribcage and arms taking the brunt of the hit. Pain stole her breath and the ability to move.

Cursing, Ape man grabbed her around the waist and threw her into the darkened interior of the vehicle. Dana caught a glimpse of Julie. The teen didn't move, even when she sprawled on top of the girl's legs. The door slammed shut and total darkness enclosed her. Seconds later, the engine cranked and the van began to move.

On hands and knees, she crawled to Julie's shoulder. "Julie. Hey, you okay?" she whispered. A moan, then nothing. Dana shook her. If she could get Julie to help with an escape attempt, they might have a chance. "Come on, wake up." No response.

Despair sapped Dana's small store of energy. She couldn't leave her young friend in the hands of these animals. "Julie. Come on, baby. You have to wake up." She shook her friend harder, then switched to tapping her cheeks.

Finally, Julie stirred and came awake with a gasp.

"You're okay, Julie. It's Dana."

"Where are we?" Her words sounded mushy.

"In the back of a van. That's why there isn't any light."

"Are we going home? Did they call Mom?"

Dana hated to dash her hopes. "I don't think so. Skyscraper and Ape man didn't say anything about letting us go home." She refused to say what she suspected the outcome of this move might be—either being sold or killed. She fought back a sudden surge of tears. This was so unfair for both of them. Julie deserved a life doing what she'd dreamed in medicine and Dana wanted a chance with Jon. Looked like neither of them would see their dreams become a reality.

Julie started crying. "But, Dana, how will Mom and Chad find me? They can't move me."

Dana pulled the girl into her arms and rocked her, swaying with the motion of the van. "Calm down, Julie. We have to think, come up with a plan." Yeah, tough words when she could barely string sentences together. She beat down the urge to quit. She must find a way to free Julie, if nothing else. But how? The girl seemed to be in worse shape than Dana. Probably a result of being in Skyscraper's hands for a week longer. What if Ape man killed Julie because she was so much worse off? Resolve hardened in Dana. No. She couldn't let that happen.

"What can we do? These guys are so strong and I can't stand by myself any longer."

Dana stroked her hair. "I don't know, but I'll think of something."

The police siren screaming overhead added teeth to the already vicious headache pounding inside Eli's skull. He drank more water from the liter bottle his nurse had shoved into his hand right before he checked himself out of the hospital in true Wolfe fashion. He'd run without waiting for permission from the doctor. One corner of his mouth curved upward. Well, okay, he had walked out, his friends on either side ready to catch him before Eli hit the floor. The definition of a true friend in his book. He'd made it to Cal's SUV before collapsing into the front seat.

Eli glanced at the speedometer. He wanted to yell at his teammate to step on it, but at 120 miles per hour, Cal had pushed the gas pedal to the floor. Eli's jaw clenched. He needed to go faster.

Cal's cell rang. He grabbed the cell and tossed it to Eli. "You answer it. I'm kind of busy here." He muttered curses under his breath when another civilian driver pulled to the left instead of to the right in response to his siren. With a quick glance in the rearview mirror, Cal whipped the vehicle into the right lane and raced past the driver.

Eli flipped open Cal's phone. "Yeah?"

"Detective Taylor?"

"This is Wolfe, his partner." Cal shot him a glare. Eli just grinned. He had to tell the guy something believable, didn't he?

"This is Crocker, a deputy with the Rutherford County Sheriff's office. We're five minutes from the residence and airstrip. The Tennessee Highway Patrol is on alert, but no signs yet of the suspect's white van or Lexus SUV on the interstate."

"Copy that. We're exiting the interstate now." Eli clamped his hand on the overhead grip to keep his balance as Cal used top-notch combat driving skills to maneuver around vehicles and swung his SUV to the right. "Park some of your guys on that tarmac. Do not let any plane off the ground. We believe hostages may be on board."

"We'll do our best."

"Who was it?" Cal asked, again weaving in and out of traffic.

"Crocker with the Sheriff's office. They're five minutes out."

Cal glanced at the clock and swore.

"Yeah," Eli said. "I know." Fear formed a ball of ice in his belly. The chances of finding the women before the plane took off hovered between a sliver and absolute zero. "Jon?" He glanced over his shoulder at his partner.

Jon's gaze remained on the screen "Still no movement."

Eli tried to convince himself that was a good thing, but his gut knew better than to swallow that lie. "If they get off the ground?"

His face hardened. "We'll find them."

Eli twisted around in his seat, his hand in a death grip around the phone. They had to get to the airstrip before that plane left the ground. He swallowed hard. If it hadn't already left the ground. *Hold on, baby.*

Brenna glanced around at her surroundings, zip ties biting into her wrists. Thick carpeting, plush seats, a large screen television. More luxurious than other planes she had ridden in. "Wow. A posh prison. Should I feel privileged?"

"Shut up." Grace gestured with the gun for her to sit. "You won't make many more smart remarks. I have something very special in mind for you." She laughed. "Guaranteed to break you of that annoying habit."

Goosebumps surged across Brenna's skin. Any surprise Grace had in mind likely meant humiliation and pain. How had Dana misjudged this woman? The answer was obvious. Her sister had serious trust issues, but with men. She doubted Dana ever considered Grace might have ulterior motives.

Not that Brenna could claim great insight into the human psyche on her own behalf. Her misplaced trust in Grace had brought Eli into this crazy woman's path. Tears stung her eyes. He had to survive the drug Grace dumped in his drink. She wouldn't believe otherwise. To survive SEAL missions all over the globe only to be killed by poison at the hands of this woman? No. She wouldn't believe it.

Brenna resisted the urge to scratch the skin around the tracking tags. She'd neglected to mention how adhesives always caused a skin rash, figured the tags wouldn't be in place long enough to cause problems. If the tags did their job, she'd gladly slap lotion on the itchy places. Her lips curved upward. Or let Eli apply the lotion. He wouldn't mind the job.

"Why are you involved with the Scarlett Group? Money? Blackmail? Is Sartelli forcing you to do this?"

"Sartelli has nothing to do with Scarlett Group." Grace frowned and shoved Brenna into a nearby gray seat. "Scarlett is mine. I built it from the ground up."

"Then why were you working for Sartelli?" Brenna pushed herself into a more upright position. "The flesh trade doesn't pay well enough for your lifestyle?"

"Sartelli is nothing but a fool. His wife's money built the company. The only thing he accomplished is expansion into different parts of the country. But those expansions gave me access to more merchandise."

"Merchandise?" Brenna glared at the woman holding a gun pointed at her chest. "Most of them are young teenage girls with their whole lives ahead of them. How would you feel about being merchandise for sale?"

"I used to be 'merchandise for sale' as you phrased it." Grace's eyes glittered. "My mother ran off when I was a baby and left me in my father's care. Dear old dad ran a stable of low-rent hookers. One night, one of his women got sick. He sent me in the woman's place and threatened to beat me if I didn't satisfy his customer. My career blossomed from there."

"So instead of just being a victim of abuse, you became an abuser. Why didn't you call the police or social services when you were a teen and report your father?"

Grace poked Brenna's chest with the gun's barrel. "I became a survivor." She leaned in close enough to whisper, "I built my own empire on what dear old dad taught me along with his johns."

Doors slammed outside the plane and caught Brenna's attention. Eli and Jon?

Grace pivoted and walked to the open door. "Bring them up here," she called. "Hurry. We don't have much time."

Heart slamming against her chest wall, Brenna sat up straighter. A familiar voice cried, "Leave her alone." Dana. She leaped to her feet.

Grace swung the gun back in her direction. "Sit down or I'll tell my men to break Dana's neck."

Brenna dropped to the edge of the seat, gritted her teeth, glaring at the woman who had caused her and Dana so many weeks of misery.

The sound of struggles, a slap, a cry of pain, reached Brenna's ears. Her body vibrated with the need to race for the door and help because she knew Dana was fighting her captors. She listened, prayed for her sister's successful bid for freedom, even if it meant she would be left in the hands of Scarlett Group.

Another slap of flesh hitting flesh. Then silence.

Heavy footsteps thumped on metal stairs outside the door and in stepped the man who dragged her into this nightmare, carrying a still struggling Dana, one hand clamped over her mouth, the other around her waist.

"Dana." Brenna leaped to her feet again, heedless this time of Grace's gun.

Dana stilled. Her gaze searched the plane's interior until she saw Brenna. Her eyes widened. Skyscraper promised. She shouldn't have trusted him. Tears filled her eyes and spilled over, falling in a waterfall of love and regret. She would have been willing to do anything to keep Brenna out of this nightmare. Now, it was too late. They would never let either of them go. And what kind of hope did Julie have to survive this?

Grace thrust a gun inches from her face. "Stop fighting or your sister dies."

Her eyes narrowed. So, it was true. Her so-called friend was a traitor. How could she have been so stupid? Why didn't she see the truth before now? She nodded and made a conscious effort to relax her muscles. Skyscraper released her.

Dana staggered, caught her balance and walked to Brenna on trembling legs. She threw her arms around her sister and hugged her. "I'm so sorry," she whispered. "I begged them to leave you alone."

"Are you okay? Did they hurt you?" Brenna murmured into her ear.

Dana shook her head.

Sirens screamed in the distance and sounded closer by the second.

"Thank God," Brenna whispered. "I think we may have help in a couple of minutes."

"We need to get off the ground," Grace said, her words clipped. "Get the other one in here."

Dana released her grip on her sister and swiveled toward the door. "No, Grace. Leave Julie here."

"Why should I do that? She's worth at least $20,000, more if she's still untouched."

Dana's stomach lurched at the reduction of human life to dollar terms. "You don't need her." She glanced at Brenna. Her sister gave a slight nod, knowing where she was going with this without a verbal explanation. A swell of admiration bloomed in her chest. Her sister had more courage than anyone she knew. Except Jon. She pushed aside the sharp spear of hurt as Dana realized that she might never see him again. "You have both of us. Julie is just a scared kid, and your bozos have kept her so drugged up the last few weeks she's weak, sick."

Grace scowled, turned to glare at Skyscraper. "Is this true?"

He shrugged. "She wouldn't stop begging us to call her mother. She drove us crazy. It was either keep her knocked out or kill her."

The police sirens grew louder by the second. Dana's heart raced. Could this nightmare finally be over? Surely Grace and her thugs realized they didn't stand a chance against the police. Jon's beloved face flashed into her mind, his dark gaze intent. She couldn't wait to see him. Maybe he would hold her for a minute. Or two. A lifetime. Dana blinked back the tears. She would give almost anything to have a chance at building a life with him.

Grace strode to the open doorway, peered out into the deepening twilight and uttered a curse. "Drop her and get in here," she yelled at Ape man.

Panic grew in Dana's gut. The police weren't close enough. Even she could tell that from the sound of the sirens. Her gaze sought Brenna's. The same horror dawned on her face. Their rescuers might not make it in time to stop the plane from taking off. And only God knew where Grace would take them.

Ape man pounded up the stairs at a dead run, reached back, hauled up the stairs and secured the door.

Grace nodded in Dana's direction. "Restrain her. If she resists, kill them both."

CHAPTER SIXTEEN

"There it is." Eli lowered the window on the SUV and listened to the whine of the Lear jet's engine. "She's powering up. Go, Cal."

The SUV leaped forward, joining the other police cars surging onto the tarmac. Fury exploded in Eli's gut as the plane taxied down the runway, gathered speed until the craft lifted off, its wheels missing a patrol car by inches. "No!" Eli slammed his fist on the console.

"Get the registration," Jon snapped.

Eli ripped open his Go bag, yanked out a pair of binoculars. He shoved Brenna to the back of his mind and focused his attention on the plane's tail section. He spat out the registration numbers and twisted in the seat.

Jon was already repeating the information into his cell phone. Eternal seconds later, his partner's face showed satisfaction. He nodded at Eli. "Zane has them. He's tracking, but they are changing call signs like most women change shoes."

Cal's head jerked around for a second. "That's impossible."

Jon gave a mirthless laugh. "He says if he didn't know what to look for, he'd assume it was a glitch in the software."

"Tell him to contact the FAA," Cal said.

"No."

"Why not?"

"Do you really want to know?" Eli asked. "This way you have deniability if anything goes wrong."

Cal scowled over his shoulder before returning his attention to the tarmac. He leaned closer to the windshield, pointed. "What's that?"

Eli focused the binoculars on the mound in the middle of the tarmac behind a white van. He frowned. Clothes? The closer the SUV came to the mound, dread grew greater until he drew in a sharp breath. "It's a woman."

"Who?" Jon asked, his voice tight.

"Not ours." Eli dropped the binoculars into his bag and released his safety belt. "Blond hair."

When Cal slowed enough, Eli and Jon bailed out. Eli ran to the woman while Jon circled the van, weapon up and ready. Blond hair covered her face, her body shuddering with quiet sobs.

Eli dropped to his knees. "Sweetheart, my name is Eli. Can you tell me if you're injured anywhere?"

A soft gasp and a trembling hand reached out. "Help me."

"That's what we're here for." Eli clasped her hand, brushed aside the strands of hair covering her face, and smiled. "Julie, I know a couple people who will be very happy to see your beautiful face."

"How do you know me?"

Cal dropped to one knee beside the girl. He grinned. "Hello, Julie. My name's Cal. I'm with the Nashville police. I've been looking for you for weeks and so has your mother." He pivoted on one foot and asked one of the deputies to call for an ambulance.

Eli squeezed Julie's hand gently. "Sweetheart, I'm a friend of Dana Cole. We've been looking for Dana and her sister, Brenna. Did you see them?"

More tears. "Dana. They forced her onto the plane." She started to shiver despite the lingering heat and humidity.

Jon ran to the SUV and grabbed a blanket from the back.

Once he draped the cover over the girl, Eli sat beside Julie, still holding her hand. "You didn't see Dana's sister?"

"No, but I heard those creeps talking about another woman already on the plane."

His gut clenched. The other woman had to be Brenna. Some of the deputies had already left the tarmac, headed in the direction of the house and surrounding buildings on the chance Brenna was still on the Garibaldi estate, but he knew in his gut that the love of his life was trapped on that plane, scared to death. "Why did they leave you here on the tarmac? Are you injured?" He scanned her body for blood stains, saw nothing. Didn't mean those creeps hadn't hurt her.

"They didn't touch me." She stopped, anguish filling her eyes. "At least I don't think so. They kept me drugged. What if they did something while I was out of it?"

"You're going to be okay, Julie," Cal said. "No one will hurt you now. The doctors at the hospital will take good care of you. Can you tell us why they left you here?"

"They made us ride in a van to the plane. Dana told me to act like I was still unconscious."

"Why?"

"I begged her not to do it, but she wouldn't listen." Julie started sobbing once more.

Eli rubbed his thumb over Julie's knuckles, dragging her attention from the depths of her anguish back to him. "We'll find Dana and free her. We need your help to do that, Julie." He waited for the teen to calm herself enough to answer more questions. "What was Dana's plan?"

"She told them I was too sick, that she could bring them twice as much money. I told her not to do it, that my mom would pay whatever they asked."

Eli's gaze shot to Jon. His friend's eyes glittered in the fading light, face a mask of stone. Julie didn't understand the stakes, but Dana had. She'd figured out what lay in store for her and Julie, and she did the only thing she could to free the teenager. He blinked away the mist gathering in his eyes. Dana Cole had more guts than almost anyone he'd ever met in spite of the fear that must be almost consuming her at her possible future.

"Is that what happened when you reached the plane?"

"I don't know. I tried to be dead weight. Dana fought the tall one, but he slapped her a few times."

Jon's fists clenched so hard his knuckles shone stark white through his skin.

"The other one dragged me out of the van and was taking me to the plane's stairs when some woman yelled at him to drop me and get in the plane."

"Did you see what she looked like?" Cal asked.

Eli stiffened and glared at the detective. Still pursuing his theory of Brenna's guilt? Cal raised an eyebrow at him, dared him to protest the question. He knew it needed answering. Didn't mean he liked the smear on his girl. He'd plant a fist in Cal's face after he rescued Brenna.

"Not really. I couldn't make out her features, just the blond hair. She sort of sounded like Dana's friend Grace." She frowned. "But that doesn't make sense. Why would Grace be on that plane?"

Eli felt like kissing the teen, but figured he'd scare her to death after what she had already been through. Blond hair indicated someone other than Brenna. Julie's tentative identification confirmed Grace's involvement.

"Did you hear any names or where they were headed?"

Julie shook her head. "When can I see my mom?"

An ambulance siren wailed in the distance. "As soon as we load you into the ambulance, I'll call your mother and have her meet you at the hospital." Cal smiled. "This is one phone call I'm looking forward to making."

"Could you . . . ?" Julie stopped, bit her lip.

"What?" Cal prompted. "You can ask me anything. If I can't take care of it, I'll find someone who will."

"Could you go to the hospital with me?" Tears flowed down her cheeks. "I don't want to go by myself."

"You bet." He patted her shoulder. "I don't have jurisdiction in this county, anyway." Cal waved over the approaching ambulance. He dug out his SUV keys and tossed them to Eli. "Take my ride and leave it at the airport. Make them pay, buddy."

"Count on it." Eli lifted Julie's hand to his lips and kissed her fingers. "I'm going after Dana, sweetheart. Anything you need from me before I leave?"

"Just bring her home safe."

Eli squeezed her hand, nodded. "Would you like me to call your boyfriend, Chad?"

"That would be great. I missed him so much."

Yeah, Eli knew how she felt. He missed Brenna so much his heart ached. He rose and stepped back as EMTs raced to the girl's prone form.

In the SUV, Eli turned the key in the ignition and drove off the tarmac. "Time to rock the boat, Jon."

"What do we need?" Brent Maddox asked.

For a moment, Eli's throat closed off with the force of his emotions. Maddox had included himself to head the teams the moment he'd learned what transpired at the airstrip. "Everything." Eli intended to hit the Scarlett Group with a full-scale assault if they couldn't free Brenna and Dana by stealth. As soon as the Zoo Crew knew where to land, Eli and Jon would have two full teams at their backs, ready to take the women with fire power if necessary.

"RPGs?"

"Oh, yeah." Eli weaved through the twilight traffic, lights flashing, siren blaring, pedal to the floor. "This is a pitch black op, Brent. I don't know where that plane is headed, but I'm not handing this mission off to local law enforcement or military." He and Jon had trusted the wrong people the last time they tangled with human traffickers and arrived too late to save any of them. Not going to happen this time, especially not with Brenna's and Dana's lives at stake.

"I understand. If questions arise, I'll handle it. Anything else?"

Eli drew in a ragged breath. "Nothing matters but the safety of the women."

Maddox remained silent a moment. "Like that, is it?"

"Yes." He tossed a quick glance at his partner. His next words might represent his feelings alone, but doubted it. Jon may not have acknowledged to himself how he felt, but the emotions were there all the same. "For both of us."

"We're wheels up in two hours. Need that much time to refuel the bird, load our supplies, and mobilize Teams 1 and 2." Maddox ended the call.

"Two hours," Eli said to Jon. "Are the tags still working?"

"Yeah, but not much longer."

He checked the time. Another hour at most and the batteries would run out. "Which direction is the plane headed?"

"Southwest. No deviation in course."

Eli thought about that for a few minutes. "Mexico?"

"Maybe." Jon looked up from his computer screen. "They have to refuel. That bird doesn't have the tanks to get across the border without refueling."

"And if you were on the run with the law on your tail, you couldn't land at an airport. Grace must know the cops have alerted the FAA and, through them, airport security across the country." Eli tightened his grip on the steering wheel. "Where would you go to refuel?"

"One of Sartelli's other landing strips."

"Do you know where they are?"

"No. I can find them, but it would take longer than we have."

Eli glanced behind him and crossed three lanes of traffic to a chorus of horns and tire squeals. "I know a quicker way to learn the information we need. Call Cal. Find out where Sartelli is right now. Tell him to have the undercover guys look the other way a few minutes. I'm not leaving Sartelli without that information, no matter how I have to get it."

"You two, on your feet."

Brenna rose, still unsteady from the drug and air turbulence. She helped Dana to her feet and, after a shove from Grace, they staggered down the aisle toward the back of the plane. What now?

An NFL-sized man waited in front of a closed door, an ugly glitter in his gaze.

Dana stopped, a shudder wracking her frame, her gaze fixed on the thug at the door. Brenna watched the interchange, a sick feeling in her stomach. Oh, man, had he raped her? But her sister said the kidnappers didn't hurt her. Maybe Dana lied. It wasn't as if the sisters had discussed what happened to Dana in detail. There hadn't been time. Yet. Before too much longer, she would weasel the information from her sister.

He opened the door, grabbed Dana by the arm and shoved her inside the room. Grace prodded Brenna in the back with the gun.

"You're next."

On trembling legs, she walked into the darkened room illuminated by light from the cabin. She froze a few steps beyond the doorway. Her shadow fell across the single piece of furniture in the room. A king-sized bed. Her throat tightened and she wondered if Grace planned to let the thugs entertain themselves at their expense during the hours before they reached their destination.

Dana turned around, her face an impassive mask. "Grace, please, take Brenna back to the cabin. If our friendship meant anything to you, don't let this creep touch her."

He laughed at her. "Scared? You should be."

Brenna's breath caught. "Dana, no."

"Oh, don't be ridiculous," Grace said. "I have something much more special in mind for the two of you. You ladies are going to be a gift for my lover. After he tires of you, he can sell you or kill you. I don't really care which he chooses." Grace nodded to the thug. "Restrain them." She turned away, stopped. "There's no phone. The door is locked from the outside and the room is soundproof. It's pointless to try escaping on this plane anyway. You have nowhere to run."

The thug removed the zip ties, tossed Brenna and Dana on the bed and replaced the plastic restraints with metal handcuffs attached to chains which were fastened to the wall. With deep laughter that sent chills over Brenna's body, he closed and locked the door, leaving them alone in the dark.

She yanked on the chains, tested how much play she had, and scooted close to the middle of the bed. Her foot touched Dana's. She pulled back and thumped her sister's foot with the side of hers.

"Ouch. What was that for?"

"Don't do that again."

"Don't do what?"

"Offer yourself as a sacrifice for me. We fight them together, Dana. If we stick together, we can beat them."

"Are you kidding?" Dana's voice was tinged with anger. "Don't you think I've tried since they took me? I've got bruises on top of bruises, Brenna. Ape man and Skyscraper are too strong and they love hurting women."

Brenna's lips curved at the appropriate monikers her sister had given the two thugs. "You didn't have me with you." Or Eli and Jon. She hoped the tags were doing their job. Resolve stiffened her spine. Even if they didn't, she and Dana would figure out how to get away from Grace and her cronies. "Don't you dare give up. Don't let them win, sis."

"What are we going to do?" A shifting of weight on the mattress and Dana's voice sounded nearer. "I can't run, Brenna. I'll try if we get the chance, but I'm too weak to go far. Ape man and Skyscraper fed me once a day and didn't give me much water. I'll hold you back and both of us will be captured again. You should escape yourself and come back for me with help."

"No." Brenna rolled over. She didn't dare tell Dana about the tracking tags, especially since she had no idea if they worked. She could, however, give her sister some hope. "Can you move closer?"

More shifting and her sister's breath fanned over Brenna's face. "That's as far as I can go."

Brenna dropped the pitch of her voice, worried Grace and company had the place bugged. The idea of someone listening to anything going on in this bedroom made her stomach queasy. "You can't give up, Dana. Eli and Jon will find us."

"Jon? You met him?"

She smiled, a bubble of happiness forming for her sister. Oh, yeah, her sweet sister had it bad and, if Brenna was right, so did Jon. "I met them when I started looking for you."

"Is he okay?"

"Crazy with worry about you."

"Really?" Wonder laced through her word. "Are you sure?"

"Trust me, sis. I know it when I see it. He and Eli knocked heads and kicked in doors searching for you."

"I've missed him so much," Dana whispered.

"Why didn't you tell me about him? I'm surprised you didn't spill the secret about your SEAL."

She remained silent so long Brenna nudged her thigh, reminding Dana that like all good sisters, she wasn't going to accept silence for an answer.

"I was afraid to say it out loud," Dana admitted. "Jon never indicated he felt anything for me beyond friendship and I don't know how to read men well. I never dated anyone after that nightmare with Ross."

"Yeah." Brenna swallowed the knot forming in her throat. "I understand." She nudged her sister's leg again, wanting to divert Dana's attention from Ross the Rat. "Still, you could have told me how drop dead gorgeous that SEAL is." Would Dana take the bait? She got her answer a moment later.

"You think Jon is good looking?" A hint of dismay came through in Dana's voice.

"Oh, he's okay I guess."

"He's better than okay."

Brenna laughed. "Eli Wolfe trumps your SEAL any day, sis."

Dana drew in a ragged breath. "Eli? Oh, Brenna. He's such a great guy. All tough on the outside, but a marshmallow on the inside. Is the interest mutual?"

"I'm pretty sure it goes both ways. You're right, he's an amazing man and so is your Jon. Now, tell me how you got mixed up with the Scarlett Group."

Eli pocketed lock picks and motioned for Jon to go into the outer office low and to the left while he covered the right side. Both men held semi-automatics in their right hands, Ka-Bars with black handles and blades strapped to their legs. A rumble of men's voices drifted from deep in Sartelli's office. Light spilled from the doorway and illuminated Dana's desk.

They edged closer to the interior office, their movements practiced and silent. Uneasiness grew in Eli. This kind of op was the most dangerous. No time to prepare or gather information, including the layout of Sartelli's office.

He and Jon paused to the side of the door. Eli shifted as close to the doorway as possible without stepping into the light. He held himself away from the wall to prevent a rustle of clothing from giving away their presence. He listened to the voices. Sartelli and his thug, Mendoza, for sure, but were there any others present who remained silent? The clock ticking in his head reminded Eli he didn't have time to waste since Sartelli would be uncooperative. He didn't even give serious consideration to questioning Mendoza. He'd met men like him in the field. Even faced with his own mortality, Mendoza wouldn't give information unless Sartelli told him to talk.

"Get me the Mt. Juliet shopping center file, Juan. It should be on Dana's desk. The city council is threatening to renege on the tax incentives."

Eli glanced at Jon, his eyebrow raised. Did Jon want to take on Mendoza? Jon nodded. Eli grinned and positioned himself to guard Jon's back in case someone else exited the office and alerted Sartelli to his unexpected company. He trusted his partner to take down Mendoza, but they had a minute at most before Sartelli or someone else wondered what kept him. They had to do this fast. Jon unsheathed his Ka-Bar.

Mendoza's hulking figure stepped into the outer office. Jon waited until the man lumbered to Dana's desk and bent over to search for the needed file. In seconds, Jon's hand was over Mendoza's mouth, knife blade against his jugular. The thug froze. In an almost toneless whisper, Jon said, "One sound, you die." He glanced at Eli.

Eli raised his weapon, prayed he hadn't missed a third person, and entered the office. Sartelli sat, desk facing the door, head down as he wrote on a yellow legal pad. "Did you find it, Juan?" he asked without raising his head.

He aimed the pistol at Sartelli's massive chest. "Your yard ape is a little busy right now."

Sartelli looked up, scowled. "Wolfe. I trust you have not hurt my former employee."

"Harsh, Marcos. One tiny mistake and he's canned." Eli picked up the sound of a short-lived scuffle in the outer office and muffled ranting from Mendoza. "Hard to find good help these days."

"What do you want, Wolfe?"

"Information and I want it fast."

Sartelli gave a short bark of laughter. "And what makes you think I will supply you with this information? You're nothing but a two-bit private investigator. You have no badge. I don't have to answer any questions."

"Two reasons. First, I won't miss your heart at this range and, trust me, I don't need much incentive to pull the trigger right now. Second, if you don't talk fast, you'll find yourself in jail along with your Scarlett Group cronies. Doubt you'd look good in prison orange, Marcos."

"I don't know what you're talking about. What is Scarlett Group?"

Eli stared hard at the old man, took in his puzzled expression. And his heart sank. He didn't want to believe the old geezer was telling the truth. If he was, chances were excellent that Sartelli wasn't responsible Brenna's and

Dana's kidnapping. He reserved judgment about Joe's death, however.

He sensed Jon enter the office. "You believe him?" he asked without taking his gaze from Sartelli.

"Unfortunately, I do. He can still help with the information."

Sartelli's eyes narrowed. "Why should I help you? Aside from the guns, of course."

"Simple. Your crazy temporary secretary orchestrated Dana's and Brenna's kidnapping, drugged me, and tried to kill Brenna on at least a couple occasions."

"I'm sorry about Dana, but I care nothing about the rest of your problems."

"Oh, you better care, Sartelli. Grace is working with the Scarlett Group, a human trafficking ring, and she's using your company to hide her activities."

"You lie."

"No, Marcos, I'm not."

Sartelli appeared to consider Eli's words, his mouth pressed into a thin line. "You have proof?"

Eli motioned for the construction owner to pick up the phone at his right hand. "Call your mother-in-law. Ask her what's happening in her backyard."

Sartelli scowled.

"Yeah, I know how much the old lady ticks you off, Marcos. After that, call your wife."

"My wife is dressing for our daughter's engagement party, Wolfe. Why should I disturb her?"

Confident his partner had his P226 drawn and aimed, Eli shoved his weapon into his holster and crossed the office in two strides. Fists crushing coat lapels, he yanked Sartelli to his feet and slammed the old man's back against the wall. Sartelli's mouth gaped with shock. "I don't care if your wife is inconvenienced, Marcos. Grace Porter drugged and kidnapped my girlfriend. You might not care about that, but she means a lot more to me than your wife or daughter. Are you catching my meaning here, Marcos?"

"You wouldn't dare harm my family."

"Try me." Eli glowered at Sartelli. "The only thing I care about is rescuing Brenna and Dana."

"I will kill you for this, Wolfe."

"Get in line. There are many others ahead of you." Most of them terrorists who made Sartelli look like a kindergartner pitching a temper tantrum. "Maybe you'd be more interested in helping if you knew Grace took off in your corporate jet."

"What?" Sartelli's voice thundered in the enclosed space. A deep flush surged across his cheeks. "She cannot do that. She has no authority to use my jet."

"Your mother-in-law and the cops will confirm it. There are two plain-clothes cops outside your building. You can ask them."

"I didn't know about any of Grace's activities, I swear."

"I'll put in a good word for you with Metro PD if you give me the information I want." Eli waited. If he pushed too hard, Sartelli would tell him to take a hike. Jon, a whiz with his computer, could get the information they needed, but it would take time Brenna and Dana might not have.

"And if I agree to cooperate, what will you do for me in return?"

Eli stilled. No way could he give Sartelli carte blanche to ask for anything. No telling what the old buzzard would demand in repayment. He glanced at his partner. Jon's mouth curled at the corners. Yeah, Eli agreed. How ironic, them owing Sartelli a favor. He dragged his gaze back to Sartelli. The old man's gleaming eyes almost made Eli break his implied promise until Brenna's beautiful face surfaced in his mind. "Protection for your family. Nothing illegal, Marcos. You call, my team responds within minutes."

Sartelli snorted. "Team? You and Smith? A team is more than two. I can hire two-bit security people like you with one phone call."

"We work for another group on the side with some of the best security people in the world."

"Still not enough, Wolfe."

"What do you want, Sartelli?" Jon asked.

"Drop the investigation into Joe Baker's death."

"Why?" Eli demanded. Drop Joe's investigation? A sick feeling curled through his gut. He and Jon had promised Joe's widow to find out who murdered her husband. If he agreed to drop the investigation, how could he face Louise? He and Jon owed it to their mentor to find his killer.

"Let us say that it upsets my wife." He smiled, teeth flashing in the bright light. "She does not like for my name to be linked to a murder, especially with Maria's wedding only months away."

Eli hesitated. This might be his one chance to find Brenna before the Scarlett Group sold or killed her. But it felt like a betrayal to Joe. How could he drop the investigation and still live with his conscience?

"Eli," Jon said, a warning in his tone.

They were running out of time. He hated the triumphant light in Sartelli's eyes. With a mental apology to his friend and mentor, Eli said, "Done." He would find a way to tell Louise somehow. "I want to know all the places you had runways built."

"Inside and outside of the United States," Jon added.

Sartelli nodded at his computer. "Release me and I will print a list for you."

Eli grinned. "Jon will do it, Marcos. You tell him where to look and what name the deed is filed under. We already know you don't use your own name for many real estate deals." Most were listed in the names of cousins, aunts, and uncles. He tugged Sartelli to a nearby chair, shoved him onto the leather cushion, and pointed his weapon once more at the man's chest.

"So much for your promises," Sartelli spat out.

"I'll keep my word, but I don't trust you. I prefer to leave this building without bullet holes. Makes rescuing my girl kind of difficult if I'm having a bullet removed." Not that he planned to tell Marcos, but he'd completed missions with a bullet or two in his body. Didn't like it. Bullet holes hurt. "Tell Jon what he needs to know."

Fifteen minutes later, he and Jon exited the building and climbed into Cal's SUV. Eli peeled out of the parking lot, swung the vehicle onto the interstate, and turned on the lights and siren. "Learn anything interesting?"

"Our new friend Marcos has airstrips all over the world," Jon said as he woke up his laptop. "A lot of them are in unfriendly areas."

An invisible band tightened around Eli's chest. Sartelli's plane could fly to any one of those strips. He doubted Grace was stupid enough to fly Brenna and Dana somewhere in the U.S. Grace had to assume the cops would plaster her picture over the airwaves nation-wide. "Best guess on their ultimate destination?"

"Probably Mexico. Fewer refueling stops. Less chance of the authorities stopping them. A lot of human trafficking in that area as well."

He frowned. "Most of the trafficking is from Mexico to the U.S, not the other way around."

"Makes Brenna and Dana a unique commodity on the market, doesn't it? If Grace gets them out of the country fast enough, it will be harder to find them in a Mexican province. The Scarlett Group is a powerful, rich organization. Grace has to have bought the loyalty of the local police and military."

"Yeah, the right price buys anything. And with women and young teens sold like a commodity, Scarlett Group is making a ton of money." Eli sighed. "Are we that cynical, Jon?"

"Maybe, but we're also realistic. Everybody has a price. Even us," Jon said, voice quiet.

He glanced at his friend. Gaze locked onto his screen, Jon's jaw was clenched tight. "You sorry we made that deal with Sartelli?"

"Wrong question, Eli."

His eyebrow swept upward. "And the right question is?"

"Could we have done anything else?" Jon's fingers flew over the keys, inputting data from the list he'd printed from Sartelli's computer. "The answer is no. If we used other methods to learn the information we needed, Brenna would pay a heavy price. She might still." His voice grew thick. "Dana has already paid in spades because I didn't realize she was missing soon enough. Whatever horrors she experienced are on my head, Eli. She's already been through so much. That she endures more abuse is my fault."

Eli squeezed Jon's shoulder and returned his hand to the steering wheel. "I'm as much to blame as you are. I asked Dana to help us without keeping tabs on her. I didn't think she was in danger, either." He pressed the gas pedal to the floor. "Are the tags on Brenna still active?"

More keys tapping on the keyboard. "No. Zane is still tracking the call sign."

Eli swallowed hard and prayed Zane didn't lose them.

Half an hour later, he and Jon raced across the tarmac at John C. Tune airport and ran up the steps of the Fortress plane, Go bags slung over their backs.

Brent Maddox, a barrel-chested former SEAL with buzz-cut blond hair, turned and pinned them with a glare. "Almost left you boys behind. You're the last ones to this dance. What took you so long?"

"Had to chisel the information out of granite," Jon replied. "Also handed one of your cards to a possible murderer."

"Nice to know you're bringing us high-class clients, Smith." Maddox folded his arms across his chest. "Where are we heading? The pilot likes to know these things ahead of time."

"Brenna's tags ran out of juice," Eli said. "Last reading was somewhere near the Texas border."

Maddox regarded them in silence. "Mexico?"

"We think so."

"Figures. I wanted to stay out of that hot zone for a while. Guess it's a good thing we loaded enough firepower to take over a small country. We'll need it. Fortress isn't popular in some of those provinces."

"Does Zane still have a lock on the plane?" Jon asked.

"He did five minutes ago." Their boss waved them to their seats. "Belt in. We're wheels up in two minutes. You can change clothes and give me more details after we're airborne."

CHAPTER SEVENTEEN

Brenna awoke with a start. She blinked at the sudden blinding light piercing the darkness of the plane's bedroom. From the size of the backlit figure, she realized Skyscraper had entered the room. What time was it? Felt like she and Dana had been sleeping for hours.

Beside her, Dana's eyelids flew up. "What's going on?" she whispered.

"Get up," Skyscraper said. "If you try to run or fight, I'll knock you out again with the drugs. You'll still end up at the same destination but with a lot of painful bruises my friend will delight in giving you."

"Think I'll skip that part of the program," Brenna said.

"Where are we?" Dana asked Skyscraper.

"Your new home. At least until the boss's boyfriend tires of you." He laughed and strode across the room. Skyscraper unlocked Dana's cuffs and yanked her off the bed. He slipped another pair of flex ties over her wrists, cinching them before pushing her through the doorway to Ape man.

Brenna sat up and raised her hands. Anything to get those painful cuffs off her wrists. With a twist of the key, the metal bracelets fell away. She rubbed her skin, noticed bruises forming already. "Doesn't Grace ran Scarlett Group? Is she really in charge or is her boyfriend?"

Skyscraper gripped Brenna's arm, cinched flex ties over her wrists, and hurried her through the doorway. Legs shaky from hours of disuse, she stumbled down the aisle behind her sister. Brenna paused at the top of the stairs and stared out into the night. The darkness hid landscape features, but the air felt different than Tennessee, sultry and tropical with the faint sound of waves breaking over sand. She drew in a deep breath of sea and brine. Her eyes widened. They were near the ocean? Florida or Texas, maybe?

"Move." Skyscraper yanked her over the threshold. She and Dana exited the plane, their captors half dragging, half carrying them across the tarmac. Frustrated at her continued lack of coordination, Brenna scanned the surroundings for workers or security, anyone she and her sister could beg for help, but the plane had landed on another private airstrip and the people within shouting distance carried guns. She sighed. Scarlett Group employees or people well-paid to look the other way and keep their mouths shut.

Ahead of them, Grace walked toward one of two waiting SUVs, cell phone pressed to her ear. Within minutes, the two vehicles pulled away from the airstrip, Grace in one, Brenna and Dana in the other. Ape man and Skyscraper carried on a conversation in Spanish in the front seat.

"Where are we?" Brenna whispered in her sister's ear.

"I heard some of the other guards speaking in Spanish. Maybe we're on the Gulf Coast."

"No talking." Ape man glowered over the front seat, gun pointed in her direction.

Brenna lapsed into silence. The dark, tinted windows prevented her from identifying any landmarks or noting the turns the driver took to their destination. If she and Dana managed to escape, they wouldn't be able to find their way back to the airstrip. And if by some miracle they returned to the airstrip, how would they get back to Nashville? They had no money or ID. At least some of the airstrip employees were loyal to Grace.

The SUVs rolled to a stop. Skyscraper opened Brenna's door. Ape man grinned at the sisters and waved them out of the vehicle with his gun. A warm ocean breeze blew Brenna's hair around her face and obscured her vision for a minute.

"No. I can't."

Brenna swiveled to face Dana. Her sister's eyes were wide, her face a mask of terror. "What is it?" She glanced around the area, trying to spot what caused Dana's reaction. And she saw the yacht tied to the wooden dock.

"Move." Ape man shoved Dana onto the dock where she stumbled a few steps and froze, her gaze locked on the craft.

Bile rose in Brenna's throat. This would get ugly, fast. "Dana, you can do this."

Grace spun at the commotion, scowling. "What is the problem?"

"She's petrified of water and boats." Brenna moved closer to Grace. "Is there some other transportation we can use?"

Grace snorted. "The compound is on an island. Get her on the boat or we'll do it by whatever means are necessary." She smirked. "I'm sure the men would be happy to make her obey. However, I can't guarantee they'd stop when they got her on board. I've already had many volunteers to train Dana for her new life."

Chills surged down Brenna's spine. She turned to Dana who was already shaking her head. "Sis, you've got to do this. It's a big boat. The ocean is calm. Nothing is going to happen to you or the boat."

"I can't do it. Brenna, you know I can't. I'd rather die than get on that thing."

Brenna licked her lips, fear ramping up several notches. Dana had to get on that boat under her own power or these thugs might really hurt her, maybe kill her. She'd only seen her sister in a full-blown panic attack one other time. She hadn't been able to calm her. "Dana, please. You have to try. We'll do this together. I'll be right beside you every step. I promise I won't leave your side." She leaned close and whispered to her sister, "Please, Dana, try for Jon. It will kill him if something happens to you. He'll blame himself." She would too, although Jon's feelings about the matter probably meant more than Brenna's since her sister had a soft spot for the tough SEAL.

Dana bit her lower lip and took a small step forward. And another.

Brenna smiled. "That's it, Dana."

One agonizing step at a time, her sister fought against the phobia almost paralyzing her. Dana stopped at the edge of the dock, her body quaking, breathing erratic, sweat beading on her forehead.

"I'm so proud of you," Brenna whispered. "I know you can do this. You're stronger than you give yourself credit for. You can beat this."

A ghost of a smile touched Dana's lips. "Yeah? I'm not on board yet."

"Enough, already. I want to go home." Grace climbed on the boat. "Get her on board or one of my men will do it and they won't coddle her like you are."

Ape man grinned. "I'll take care of her. Be all my pleasure."

"Get on the boat, Dana," Brenna said. "Do you want me to go first?"

Her sister glanced at Ape man and shook her head. "I don't want him touching me."

"I'll be right behind you. I promise."

Dana reached for the yacht's ladder. A swell raised the boat. Lines creaked and groaned under the strain. She backed away, head shaking.

Ape man swept past Brenna and grabbed Dana from behind.

"No." Dana fought against his hold, desperation making her flail in a wild attempt to free herself. "Let me go."

Afraid the thug might injure Dana, Brenna rushed to help until Skyscraper shoved her to her knees, a gun pressed to her temple. "Dana, stop."

Dana's foot connected with Ape man's thigh. Yelling curses, he dropped Dana, yanked her around to face him, and backhanded her. The sound of his hand striking her sister's cheek echoed on the breeze. Dana fell against a wooden post and slumped to the dock.

"Take her inside." Grace climbed the ladder and disappeared.

Ape man slung Dana over his shoulder, climbed aboard, and carried her down into the boat's cabin. Skyscraper jerked Brenna to her feet. "Let's go. Give me any trouble, you'll get the same treatment. Move."

Brenna scaled the ladder and boarded the boat. She followed Ape man, anxious to check on her sister. Had the blow knocked Dana unconscious or was she more seriously hurt? Brenna blinked away stinging tears. How would she get Dana free from Grace and her cronies if she was injured? And if Dana was uninjured, she still had to think of a way to transport them off the island using transportation that didn't involve a boat.

Even if she could pilot a boat, she couldn't force her sister on board, control her hysterics, and navigate through unknown waters back to their starting point. If Eli and Jon didn't find them soon, Brenna believed they would be lost in Scarlett Group's system. What were the chances she and Dana would be allowed to stay together? Zip.

Skyscraper guided her toward the back of the cabin to a bedroom. Ape man bent over Dana, his hands raising the scrub shirt.

"Get your hands off her," Brenna said. She yanked her arm free, hurried to the bedside, and inserted her body between Dana and the thug.

Ape man smirked. "Soon, the boss's boyfriend will tire of you." His glittering gaze swept over Brenna. "Perhaps he will give you to me. I would take great pleasure in training you." He licked his lips. "Or maybe I'll keep you for myself."

Eli leaned closer to Jon's laptop. "Who's that?" The screen showed a man in his late forties, one his sisters would declare attractive.

"Ross Harrison."

Had to admire his partner's tenacity in searching for the man who abused Dana. And it was a good way to utilize the time while following Sartelli's plane across the country. "Have you located him?"

"He's off the grid. Has been since he was released from jail."

Eli frowned. "Does he come from money?" Independent wealth would explain Harrison's disappearance without leaving financial footprints.

"Not according to the IRS. I think old Ross has an offshore account."

"Or he's dead." There were ways to get rid of bodies. He and Jon knew many methods.

Jon considered that a moment, shook his head. "We aren't that lucky. Every person I contacted thinks Ross is a saint wrongfully convicted."

"So no one else had a motive to kill him."

"No obvious reason."

Maddox dropped into the seat facing them. "Zane called. The Gulfstream landed a short time ago in

Guadalupe, Mexico. I got in touch with a friend who lives down there, a former CIA operative. He confirmed the plane landed at a private airstrip owned by Sartelli."

Eli straightened, his gut churning. The Chihuahua government wasn't fond of Fortress Security. If his team was captured, the state officials would gladly house them behind bars for years. Of course, they wouldn't live long enough to worry about the accommodations. The government would see to that. Rental thugs were cheap in that whole country. "Did he see the women?"

"Not directly. He greased an informant's palm with enough cash to start a new life somewhere out of Scarlett Group's reach. The informant saw two white women, both brunettes, one tall, the other smaller."

"Do we know where Grace took them?" Jon asked.

"Scarlett Group has a compound on an island right off the coast. Ortiz says the group's yacht just left the dock."

"How did Grace convince Dana to board the boat?" Eli asked.

Jon shot him a grim glance.

"Problem?" Maddox's gaze shifted from Eli to Jon.

"Dana's terrified of water and boats. She wouldn't board the yacht willingly."

"Huh." Eli's boss blew out a breath. "Not good. There's a storm moving in from the Gulf. We're planning to liberate Scarlett Group's helicopter to airlift the women off the island, but if resistance is too heavy and slows us down, we may be forced to use inflatable boats." He stood. "Boots on the ground in two hours. If you can tear yourselves away from admiring that GQ model, let's plan this op. I've got a lunch date tomorrow I'd rather not miss."

Two hours later, Maddox exited the Lear's cockpit and eyed his teams. "Suit up. Time to rock and roll. Wheels down in ten." Men surged to their feet and started strapping on sniper rifles, AR-15s, Ka-Bars and other knives, back-up pistols, ammunition, flashbangs, grenades, NVGs, bullet-proof vests, radio headsets, and medical kits for each member. The two team medics carried much more extensive medical supplies. With luck, the medics wouldn't have any patients to tend except maybe Brenna and Dana.

Eli adjusted his vest. "Did you check the latest update on the weather?"

"Yeah," Jon said. "Not good."

"Unless that storm slows down, the chopper will be grounded."

"I know."

"Suggestions?" Eli pulled on his headset, the movements automatic. The SEALs had used something similar, but Maddox swore Fortress's communications equipment was better than anything the military used.

"Been thinking about that. Leave Dana to me."

Eli paused. "That's it? You're not going to give me a hint on an alternative plan?"

"No."

He blew out a breath. Great time for his partner to go into silent mode. "Come on, man. Give me a hint. If Brenna's incapacitated, she might not be able to help. You know how Dana is about men touching her. I'm not sure how much she'll trust us after being kidnapped and held hostage for over a week." He leaned close. "We don't know what she's been subjected to, Jon. She might not be able to handle anyone touching her but Brenna. Even your touch might be intolerable."

Jon shot him a glare. "She'll deal. Leave her to me."

Like anyone would try to get between Jon and Dana. Eli's lips twitched. Even he didn't have a death wish, ghosts or no ghosts. The only person who could stop Jon from implementing the plan he'd devised was Dana herself, and that was questionable from what he surmised. If this weren't a life and death situation, it might be fun to watch her drive Jon to distraction. He couldn't think of a man who deserved it more.

Maddox reeled off last minute instructions as the Lear's landing gear touched down on the tarmac. "Remember, silence is the name of the game until we're off that island unless I tell you otherwise. We don't engage unless we have to. Our mission is to retrieve the women and get out before that storm hits. Above all, the women are the priority. We do whatever is necessary to secure their safety. Period." He grinned. "If plans B through Z fail, secure the women and start blowing stuff up. We brought enough fire power and C-4 to overthrow a country."

Laughter broke out up and down the aisle of the plane. As soon as the aircraft taxied to a stop, silence fell in the cabin. Eli and Jon bumped fists and started down the aisle.

Gun up and ready, Eli descended the aircraft's stairs, quartering the tarmac, Jon at his back and to the right. Pleased to note the pilot had stopped in a darkened section of the landing strip, Eli spotted Maddox talking to a bearded man near the forest edge. Must be the former CIA contact, he decided. His boss turned and motioned for him and Jon to approach.

"Tell them what you just told me," Maddox said.

"One of the native kids says something big is going down on that island in the next few days. Rumors about a heavy player coming in day after tomorrow. Big bucks to throw around. Wants something special." Ortiz scowled. "Or rather someone special. He flies in to handpick his next victim. He's into pain, someone else's. According to the scuttlebutt, he likes to hurt women. Once he takes them, no one hears from them again while they're alive. He'll keep them for weeks, sometimes months. When he's finished with them, they show up dead on the side of the road. The women are always riddled with bruises, cuts, burns, lash marks. His preference is American women. He takes great pleasure in breaking them."

Jon growled.

"Not this time," Eli said. "These women are ours. Did your source catch a name?"

The former CIA operative shook his head. "Just that he's from a rich oil family here in Mexico."

"We'll track him down," Maddox said, tone riddled with ice. "With a hobby like that, he won't be hard to find."

Ortiz folded his arms across his chest. "Yeah, so? What are you going to do about him?"

"Do you really want to know?"

He thought a minute. Shook his head.

"You have any assets in the area?"

He snorted. "I'm retired, Maddox. I'm only doing this as a favor to you. Word will get around how I helped out the Americans so I can't stay here any longer. My wife is packing up the necessities right now. I'll leave you, pick her up, and get out of Dodge." He shrugged. "Guess we're finally going home."

"You want a ride to the States?"

"What will it cost me?"

"Information of my choosing. I'll call you when I need it."

"Get my wife and me safely on U.S. soil, and it's a deal. Didn't look forward to outrunning the local law anyway."

Maddox nodded toward the idling transport truck. "That ours?"

"Yeah, such as it is. Not pretty, but it's reliable."

"Good. Get your wife and come back here. Bring your favorite guns with ammo and help protect the plane."

Ortiz chuckled. "Never leave home without them, my friend. Good luck on that island. You're going to need it with that storm blowing in." He jogged off to the black Jeep parked a few yards away, climbed in, and sped off.

Maddox turned and keyed his comm system. "Load up, boys. Time to rock Scarlett Group's foundation."

Brenna wiped her sister's face with a cool, damp cloth, avoiding the bruised, swollen section. Good thing Skyscraper had cut the flex ties off their hands before locking them in the room. "Wake up, Dana. Nap time's over."

Dana moaned, eyelids fluttering. "Go away. Head hurts."

Relief spiraled through Brenna at her sister's cranky words. She'd been terrified that her sister had sustained head injuries requiring medical treatment. She doubted Grace would bother to help Dana. More likely, she would let her sister die. One less complication to deal with. "That's what happens when you tangle with a wooden post." After a beefy thug nails you with a backhand. Stupid jerk.

Dana opened her eyes, her gaze filled with fear and pain. "Where are we?"

"On some island, locked in a bedroom with bars over the windows." This room had some nasty features. The unadorned white walls showcased the large black-draped bed on which Dana lay, wrist and ankle restraints dangling from the four posts. Brenna didn't mention the nauseating array of equipment in the closet and cameras mounted on the walls, two in the bedroom, another in the bathroom. She shuddered. "You were unconscious for hours."

Dana closed her eyes again. "What are we going to do, Bren?"

"We escape and find a way off this rock."

"How? My head hurts so much I feel like throwing up any minute, not to mention my water phobia. I can't swim and I won't get on another boat."

"Nothing a good thump with a rock can't cure."

Dana's eyes popped open on a glare.

Brenna smiled. "Figured that might get a response. One problem at a time, sis. We need to know what or who we're up against. After that, we escape and hide until Eli and Jon track us down." If she could steal a cell phone, she could call Eli. He'd made her memorize his cell phone number before they went to the Sartelli estate. Smart man. His number just might save her and Dana. If they were lucky, his black ops buddies could trace the cell signal and rescue them with a plane or helicopter. Water problem solved.

A key rattled in the lock. Brenna turned, positioned her body between Dana and the door. Her stomach knotted. Grace walked in followed by a man. Brenna ignored the gun in Grace's hand and focused instead on the man. Her eyes widened. She buried the building dismay. Just when she believed things couldn't get worse, in walks Dana's worst nightmare.

He smiled. "Did you miss me, Brenna?"

Brenna stood, ignoring the distressed moan from Dana. "Ross the Rat. So this is where you've been hiding. I know some honest policemen who would love to find out which garbage pit you climbed out of."

"Still mouthy, I see." Ross slid his arm around Grace's waist. "How do you like our playroom?"

Oh, man, way too much information. With her exploration of the room's equipment, Brenna's horrified mind filled in the blanks well and made her want to throw up. "It's as sleazy as you are."

"Sorry you don't like our accommodations, but don't worry. You won't be here long."

Oh, no. Think, Brenna. She had to stall for time. Eli and Jon were coming. She didn't know how they would find her, but they would. Of that she had no doubt. She wanted to make their jobs as easy as possible. And that meant staying in one location. Brenna suspected the tracking tags were dead now. She hoped they had been active long enough for Fortress to get a lock on them. "Planning to kill us so soon, Ross?"

"Not my sweet Dana, just you. Eventually. I've got something very special in mind for you. A buyer who loves American women. He's particularly skilled with knives and whips. Perfect for you." His cold smile sent fear cascading through Brenna's body. "My sweet Dana and I will be spending many hours together once we get rid of you. You always were a wet blanket on our activities."

"Over my dead body," Dana said. "You will never touch me again."

"Ah, you still have fight left in you. Good. Breaking you will be that much sweeter. You'll pay for every day I spent behind bars and beg me to kill you before I'm finished. But I won't take that pleasure for myself. You see, when my friend finishes with Brenna and dumps her body on some deserted roadway, he'll return for you. You're worth more to me alive than dead. I will, however, enjoy making you suffer. I look forward to spending the profit from your sale."

Brenna's gaze fell on the black bulge at Ross's side. The creep still carried his cell phone in the same place. Now to figure a way to steal it and she'd be in business. She and Dana were one phone call away from a rescue.

At that moment, the lights flickered and winked out.

Grace sighed. "A branch must have fallen on the power lines."

"See what's happening. I'll stay with our guests, maybe get some playtime in before you return." Ross said.

Perfect. Brenna stood, ready to launch an attack the minute Grace was out of earshot. Dana couldn't help, thanks to the drugs they'd pumped into her system and her encounter with the wooden post. She hoped Ape man and Skyscraper stayed busy elsewhere. She didn't stand a chance of taking on either one of them.

A flash of light blazed in the distance followed by a deep rumble.

Curses from Grace. "Here. Take the gun." Her footsteps echoed in the hallway along with her rapid-fire orders to an unseen underling.

"What now, Ross?" Brenna asked. "Planning to start the party without your lover? I'm sure Grace would hate to miss all the fun."

His bark of laughter gave her the direction she needed. Ross sounded as if he still stood in the doorway. Good. Fit perfectly with her plan.

"I'm surprised you're anxious to become part of Scarlett Group's world so soon," Ross said. "Could be you're not such a prude after all. Maybe I misjudged you."

Brenna eased to her right, arm extended. A moment later, her hand touched the cool surface of the wall. She inched forward and located the edge of the door. With Ross's nauseating cologne and breaths as guides, she eased in front of the door, gathered her nerve and rushed him. Brenna shoved him toward the door frame.

She heard Ross's head connect. He groaned and slipped to the floor. Brenna expected him to retaliate, but he remained silent and motionless. Praying the blow knocked him out, she dropped to her knees.

"What's going on?" Dana asked.

"Shh." Brenna searched the floor by feel until she bumped against Ross's leg. She smiled. He'd landed on his back. It would have taken some effort to turn the creep over if he fell on his stomach. The less she had to touch him, the better. Plus, she needed to conserve what strength she had to help Dana escape. She confiscated the cell phone, scrambled to her feet, and shoved their only source of communication deep in her pocket. If the power outage lasted long enough, darkness would provide cover for an escape. All they required was a little bit of luck to find their way out of the compound without anyone seeing them. Freedom was so close Brenna could almost taste it.

She took two steps in her sister's direction. A pair of steel-hard arms wrapped around her from behind and a hand clamped over her mouth.

CHAPTER EIGHTEEN

Eli easily thwarted Brenna's frantic movements. Securing her head so his wildcat wouldn't pop him in the mouth, he placed his lips against her ear. "Stop fighting, sugar. It's Eli."

Her tense body stilled, then relaxed. Brenna nuzzled against him, a small sound coming from her throat.

"No sound," he whispered. "Guards are nearby."

She nodded. Eli lifted his hand, turned her in his arms and gathered her close. Relief weakened his knees for an instant. He'd been so afraid they would arrive too late. "Are you hurt?"

"No. A little woozy from the drugs."

With his night vision glasses, Eli noted Jon's silent entrance into the room. His partner closed and locked the door with a soft click.

"Brenna?" Dana whispered, sitting up. "What's happening?"

A quick glance at the man on the floor confirmed he was still out. He grinned. Brenna hadn't left him much of a job. Jon, however, stood still near the bed, afraid to move closer. If he touched Dana without her knowing who it was, she was likely to scream the place down around their ears and bring the guards. "Tell her we're here. Jon is standing next to her."

"Ross is unconscious. He can't touch you," Brenna said, her voice soft. "Dana, don't say anything. Just listen. Eli and Jon are in the room with us."

Dana drew in a sharp breath.

"Reach out your hand, sis. Jon's right beside you."

Through the eerie green light of his enhanced night vision, Eli watched Dana slowly extend her hand, palm up.

Jon shifted closer. "I'm here," he whispered. He touched her hand with his fingertips at first, afraid a strong grip might send her into a panic. He wanted to hold her in his arms, doubted she'd let him. His emotions rioting all over the spectrum, Jon inched closer, moving slow until her fingers wrapped around his hand and tugged.

He swallowed hard, longed to gather her into his arms and never let go. The clock in his head, however, denied the chance for more than a minute or two at most.

Her hand still in his, Jon sat beside Dana, moved his hands to her forearms and let her make the next move. Jon's heart almost leaped out of his chest when she flung herself into his arms. He pulled her close, his throat tight. "I've got you, baby. No one will take you from me, I promise." He placed a soft kiss on her neck. "We'll have to fight our way out of here. Can you run?"

Dana's shaking hand caressed his cheek. "I'll try, but they've kept me drugged."

Fury roared through his gut. They kept her on some crap for almost two weeks? He ticked off the side effects in his mind. Muscle loss, dizziness, weakness. Depending on the drugs they'd shot her up with, withdrawals. He'd been where she was a few months earlier. "It's okay. Don't worry. I'll take care of you." He wouldn't leave her side unless she sent him away. He hoped she didn't. It would take everything he had to let go of her now that he'd found her again. But if she couldn't handle a relationship with him, he'd man up and bury his emotions. Whatever she needed, he would give her.

In his ear piece, Joe Rivers broke the radio silence. "Tangos approaching from the west."

Jon activated his headgear's microphone. "Copy that. We're moving now."

Dana trembled in his arms. "What's wrong?"

"Company." Jon hesitated. After what she'd survived in the past weeks, would his touch be distasteful to her? He hoped not since he'd dreamed for months of holding her in his arms. He swallowed hard. "We need to move fast. I'll have to carry you, baby." Instead of the hesitation or protest he expected, Dana wrapped her arms around his neck. His heart squeezed. No time to check her for injuries. Praying he didn't hurt this brave woman, he lifted her from the bed.

"Time to go, sugar." Eli gave Brenna a hard, brief kiss and stepped in front of her. "Stay behind me. Do exactly what I tell you. If I tell you to drop, do it, no questions or arguments." He opened the door enough to monitor movement in the hallway.

He signaled the others to move out. Eli palmed his P226 and led them down the corridor, away from the approaching danger.

Joe's soft murmur in his ear piece confirmed what his other senses told him. He needed to get the women out of the hallway, fast. The odds of them escaping this part of the compound without encountering resistance were slim and diminished by the second as the tangos learned of their presence.

Footsteps clattered on the stairs ahead of them.

"The room on your left is empty," Joe said.

Eli opened the door to a storeroom, scanned, noted the window on the far wall, and motioned Brenna and Jon inside. He stationed himself deep in the shadows and waited.

How long before the tangos noticed Brenna and Dana were missing? He considered slipping from the room and clearing the area himself, but Maddox's orders echoed in his mind. Retribution was off the table. This was a search and rescue op. No unnecessary risks, no blowing up buildings or enemy combatants unless deemed necessary to protect the lives of the hostages or the Zoo Crew. If the unsanctioned op went unnoticed by the local government, so much the better for all of them. Maddox didn't want a fire fight at the airstrip despite the fact his teams were better armed than most military groups. They couldn't hold out forever with their limited arms supply.

"One tango outside the door," Joe said.

Eli detected the sound of clothing brushing against the door. He unsheathed his Ka-Bar and shifted position. The tango couldn't be allowed to raise an alarm or the death toll would skyrocket. Didn't bother him if Scarlett Group lost a ton of men, but no one was taking Brenna from him again. To his right, Jon urged Dana into the deepest shadows with Brenna by her side, and positioned himself in front of the women, weapon ready.

The knob turned and the door swung open in a slow motion. A gun appeared. Within seconds, Eli neutralized the threat with a palm over the mouth and a knife hilt to the head. He dragged the body into the storeroom, locked the door, and moved him to the far corner. Zip ties around his wrists and ankles, Eli ripped the man's shirt from his body, tore it and made a makeshift gag. Should be enough to keep him from raising the alarm for a short while. After piling boxes in front of the unconscious man so he wouldn't be visible with a cursory inspection, Eli examined the window. No bars and enough room for him and Jon to squeeze through. Excellent. He and Jon were bulked up with the vest and equipment. They'd made it through tighter spots.

This time they didn't have minutes to spare taking off equipment and suiting back up once outside.

"More tangos from the west and east," Joe murmured. "Room to room search. Time to go or you'll have to fight your way out."

Eli's gut tightened. No alarm had been raised, but Grace's men knew the women were gone. Old GQ man himself must have roused sooner than Eli thought he would and spread the word about the escape. "One hostage is mobile, one's not. What's outside this window?" He unlatched the lock.

"Fifty feet of open space followed by jungle. No heat signatures on that side of the compound."

He eased open the window. Salt-scented air poured inside. "I need a diversion in one minute."

"Copy that."

He shrugged out of his pack and knelt beside Brenna, his hand nestling in her hair. "We go out the window, sugar. Grace's people are searching for you." He leaned closer to Dana. "Can you run a short distance, Dana?"

"Watch me."

"Good girl." He stood and keyed his mike. "Still clear, Joe?"

"Affirmative. Diversion in thirty seconds."

Eli leaned out the window, dropped his bag on the ground, and followed feet first. Crouching, he strapped on his pack again, scanned the area. A rumble of thunder in the distance caused him to rip off his NVGs. "Storm moving in, Jon."

"Copy."

"Area clear. Dana first."

A rustle of clothing had Eli shifting to stand beneath the window. Jon maneuvered Dana over the sill and into Eli's extended arms. "Stay on your feet in case we need to run," he whispered as he set her down and positioned her against the wall to his right.

Brenna climbed out, followed by Jon.

"Fifteen seconds," Joe warned.

Jon scooped Dana into his arms and raced for the forest. Eli grabbed Brenna's hand. "Run."

They ran over the rough terrain, leaping over a tree branch blown down in the stiff wind. Brenna stumbled at the edge of the tree line. Eli slid an arm around her waist and urged her to move faster, deeper into cover. At the last second, he tugged Brenna to the ground and covered her body with his, arms wrapped around her head, Jon and Dana in a similar position just ahead of them.

A flashbang lit the night sky. Screams and gunfire shattered the stillness.

Eli jumped to his feet and lifted Brenna. "Go." Jon set off again at a fast clip for Zoo Crew's rendezvous point. They needed to make tracks fast before the tangos located them and proceeded to pick them off. As long as it was just them to cover the women, he and Jon were vulnerable because their attention would be divided.

"That sounded like a bomb," Brenna said.

"Diversion, sugar." The nape of his neck tingled. Gaze quartering the area, Eli urged her in front of him. He keyed his mike. "Jon, Brenna's on your six. Joe, I'm dropping back."

"Copy."

"Follow Jon, Brenna. Don't look back."

She swung around. Lightning illuminated her stunned expression. "What? Why?"

He kissed her hard. "Go. I'll catch up." He melted into the darkness.

Brenna stared into the trees, heart in her throat. She told herself the whipping wind caused the tears stinging her eyes. She knew better. Eli was risking his life to protect her and Dana. Why couldn't someone else take the risk this time? She couldn't lose him now.

"Move, Brenna." Jon turned, Dana nestled in his arms. "You'll endanger Eli more if he's distracted. Right now, he doesn't have to worry about hurting you by accident. He can't have his attention divided. If you care for him at all, do what he told you."

Lips pressed together, she hurried forward. Jon would be forced to protect her if she stayed and that meant a greater risk to Dana. No way would she put Dana's life in even more danger because her heart told her to go back and help a very capable man do a job he was well trained to do. "What can I do to help?"

"Get in front of me. Head for the lights."

Brenna grimaced. And in the meantime, Jon would position himself behind her, in front of the threat Eli had sensed. That was the most logical explanation for Eli's disappearing act. He'd gone back to deal with a threat to their safety.

She plowed through the forest, more lightning crackling overhead. Thunder rumbled. Her hair swirled around her face. She wished they could get out of the trees. Lightning and trees weren't a safe combination. Then again, the trees provided much needed cover for their escape. She shook her head. Couldn't have it both ways. Guess she'd choose cover over storm safety.

She pushed forward, still heading toward the lights as Jon had directed. Was it her imagination or were the trees thinning? The lights looked nearer, too. In the aftermath of a lightning strike, Brenna spotted a clearing through the trees. A few yards from the tree line, Jon stopped her. "Let me check the area first." He set Dana on her feet against a tree. "Don't move. I'll be right back."

Between one breath and the next, Jon was gone. How did he and Eli do that? No sound of any kind. "You okay, sis?" she whispered.

A radiant smile lit Dana's bruised face. "Better than I've been in weeks."

Brenna grinned. "I'll bet. Did you notice Jon's not even breathing hard?"

Heavy footsteps thudded nearby and drew closer by the second. Brenna's pulse raced. Not Eli or Jon. They moved through the night like ghosts, no trace of their passage left behind. She figured their co-workers would slide through the landscape the same way. The pursuer sounded like a rampaging elephant tearing through the forest. No, no, no. Her sister couldn't run. She refused to let her be captured again. That meant protecting her, no matter what. "Hide, Dana."

"Come with me."

"Go." She stepped in front of her sister to shield Dana's movements.

Ape man raced into view. Brenna swallowed hard. Why did it have to be him? She had zero chance against him in a one-on-one confrontation. She glanced around, desperate to find a rock or something to bash him in the head.

He skidded to a stop and raised his arm. A gun glistened in his hand. "Nowhere to run." He smirked. "You're mine. The boss gave you to me."

Hadn't she asked herself if things could get worse? Looked like it had. Two former SEALs as rescuers and neither around when she needed them. What now? Stall until one of the men returned. It was their only hope. She prayed they were close. One shot from Ape man's gun and the meager protection she provided Dana vanished. Ape man couldn't miss at this range. "Can we talk about this?"

"Sure. Get over here or I shoot your sister."

Brenna took one step. "That's not what I had in mind."

"Your friends will die." Ape man grinned. "They're outgunned and outmanned. Guess that's why you're alone."

A black clad arm circled his neck, knife pressing against Ape man's carotid. "Never assume, dude. Drop the gun."

"I'll shoot her before you cut me." Black eyes glittered at Brenna with malicious promise.

Eli forced Ape man's chin higher so his gaze skimmed the top of the trees. "Sugar, hit the dirt."

Without hesitation, Brenna obeyed his order.

"Drop the gun or the last sound you hear will be a sniper's bullet."

"You lie."

"Yeah? Look to your right, idiot."

From the forest, a red dot, rock steady, was aimed at his heart. Ape man froze, eyes wide. Brenna almost felt sorry for the cretin. Almost. He'd terrorized Dana, hurt her and countless other women. A little fear was justified.

Ape man swallowed hard. A trickle of blood rolled down the side of his throat.

Brenna's breath stalled in her lungs. Would he sacrifice his life for a shot at revenge against her? She didn't see how he could aim her direction since Eli had forced his head up. He might get off a lucky shot before Jon killed him.

His hand opened and the gun fell to the ground.

"Kick the gun away." Eli applied more pressure to the man's throat. The gun skidded to the right and disappeared in the depths of a bush. "Listen carefully. This is your only warning. You come after my woman or her sister again, I will kill you."

"Not if I kill you first."

Eli tightened his arm, slowly choking off the man's air supply. "Try it and your entire family will pay. We know they live in Juarez. My sniper friend doesn't miss. Am I clear?" His voice conveyed the promise of swift retribution. After the man nodded, Eli knocked him out, dropped him to the ground, and secured him.

He stepped over the fallen thug and yanked a shaking Brenna to her feet and into his arms. Too close. One flinch by the tango and he might have lost her. "No more close calls, sugar. I don't think my heart can take any more tonight."

Brenna buried her face in his throat.

"Should have let me take him out," Jon said as he retrieved the discarded weapon. "He's going to be a problem."

"A few well-chosen words to the right people and we won't have to worry about him any longer. The Scarlet Group won't appreciate an employee who's friendly with the enemy." Eli kissed Brenna's temple as his ear piece clicked.

"This is one. Go to B. Detonation in five."

Eli's heart sank at Maddox's decision. Not unexpected given the weather conditions, but Dana's fear of water complicated their common-sense choice. Flying a helicopter in this storm risked disaster for the whole team. Didn't mean he liked putting a good woman through one of her worst nightmares. "Jon?"

"I'll handle it. Let's go." He scooped Dana into his arms and set off in the new direction.

"What's wrong?" Brenna asked.

"Change of plans." Eli urged her to keep pace with his partner. They needed to get as far as possible from the helo landing pad.

"Is there a problem?"

Not for a SEAL. "Adjusting for the weather." Eli's ear piece clicked again minutes before they reached their second rendezvous point. "Ten seconds." Ahead of him, Jon laid Dana on the ground and covered her. Eli did the same with Brenna, her head tucked against his shoulder. The stormy sky lit and the ground rumbled. Flames shot into the air as timed explosions rocked the surrounding area.

Eli hauled Brenna up from the ground and urged her into a brisk trot. The explosions would bring the enemy to the area and he wanted as much distance between the landing pad and the women as possible.

"What was that?"

"Helicopter and the landing pad, plus a few buildings. Can't let Scarlett Group keep operating here. One of our tech guys uploaded all their computer info to a server at Fortress. Maybe we'll get lucky and find out who has Kaylee Young."

Brenna remained silent a minute. "Please tell me you have your own air transportation stashed close."

He squeezed her hand. "Sorry, sugar. Even if we did, the storm would ground us. Don't worry. We'll take care of Dana." Even if they had to knock her out, an option they were prepared to use. He didn't want Davenport to administer the drug they had ready. No one knew what Grace's goons had poisoned her with while she'd been held hostage. If they guessed wrong, the new medicine their medic administered could kill Dana.

Jon set Dana beside him and touched his finger to his lips. After she acknowledged his command to remain silent, he signaled Eli to keep an eye on her and slipped into the shadows of the tree line and moved closer to the dock. Scattered gunfire broke out near his destination. So much for a stealthy approach to the second rendezvous point. Looked like the Zoo Crew would have to fight its way off this rock.

Suited him fine. He was in the mood to inflict pain on the thugs who'd hurt Dana. He edged closer, his gaze scanning the scene playing out in front of him. Part of the Zoo Crew exchanged gunfire with the human traffickers. His lip curled. Two tangos fell in quick succession. His teammates were better shots.

He keyed his mike. "One, this is Jon. We're south of B in the tree line with the packages."

"Roger that. Hold position. Team 1 is encountering resistance. Team 2 will approach from the east."

"Copy." Jon made his way back to Eli and the women.

"What's happening?" Dana asked, arms wrapped around her waist. Her body shivered.

He drew her against his chest, rubbing her arms. Another time and place he'd give Dana his shirt, but he needed the dark covering to blend into the shadows. A visible sniper soon became a dead sniper. Jon fought to maintain his focus. He wanted nothing more than to kiss her beautiful trembling mouth until all she thought about was him. That kind of distraction could kill all of them. He needed to get his head back in the game. He had a job to do. All their lives depended on him getting it done. "Teammates are closing on our position."

Dana burrowed closer, her arms wrapping around his waist. "Why?"

"Better protection. Our priority is getting you and Brenna off this rock. Everything else is secondary."

"What about Grace and Ross?"

His heart clenched at the tremor of fear in her voice. He longed to set her aside and hunt down the dirty duo. "If they get in our way, we'll take care of them. Your safety is first."

"And if they come after me again?"

"They'll die." Jon eased back enough to see her face. "Make no mistake, baby. We will take down Scarlett Group. Grace and Harrison will pay for what they did to you and the other women."

Dana leaned against his body as if her strength was giving out. His arms tightened around her. Just another minute and he'd find a place for her to sit until time to move to the rendezvous point.

Six men dressed in black fatigues slipped from the shadows into the small clearing. Team 2 with Davenport, their medic. Eli motioned Doc to Dana.

Jon eased Dana away from him and turned her to the approaching medic. "This is one of our medics, Jake Davenport. Everybody calls him 'Doc.'"

Doc slid his bag to the ground, unzipped it and removed a thin Mylar blanket which he spread on the ground.

"Rest for a minute." Jon eased the shivering woman in his arms to the blanket and knelt beside her.

The medic shook out a second blanket and draped it around Dana's shoulders. "Any injuries, Dana? Even a small cut or open insect bite needs to be treated. An open wound in this tropical climate is a breeding ground for infection."

"A cut on my left calf and scratches on my face and arms."

"She's very weak," Jon said. His hand clenched. "Drugged for almost two weeks."

"Do you know what they gave you?" Davenport asked.

Dana shook her head.

"When was the last time you ate?"

She sent a nervous glance at Jon. "I'm not sure. Maybe the day before they brought us here. They weren't too concerned about feeding me."

A fresh surge of rage rose in Jon's gut. No wonder she was so weak. Coupled with two weeks of drugs, Dana had been lucky not to collapse before now.

"What about fluids?" Davenport continued.

Dana sat up straighter. "Nothing. Brenna and I were afraid to drink water from the tap. We didn't know where Grace had taken us. May I have some water?"

"You bet." The medic dug in his pack and withdrew a bottle of water and a packet of an electrolyte mix he habitually carried on ops. After mixing the two, he handed Dana the bottle. "Just sips, okay? You're dehydrated. If you drink too fast, the water will come right back up."

Dana seized the drink and twisted off the cap. She drank three or four good swallows before recapping the bottle, her hands shaking.

Davenport laid out gauze, bandages, antibiotic cream and antiseptic pads on the blanket. "We need to treat your cuts, Dana. If you're not comfortable with me touching you, Jon can do it." He grinned. "Of course, he won't be as good at it as I am. SEALs are clumsy, you know."

Jon snorted. "As opposed to the effortless grace of a jarhead?" His gaze shifted to Dana. "Your choice, baby."

She shifted closer to Jon, shaking her head. "No, I can't. I'd prefer you do it." She glanced at Davenport. "I'm sorry."

"No problem. I'll leave the supplies and check your sister." He grabbed his packs and crossed the clearing.

"Do you think I hurt his feelings?"

Jon opened an antiseptic pad package. "Nope. He's worked before with female trauma victims. This will sting." He cleaned and treated each visible injury. "Let me check your leg, babe."

Hands shaking, Dana pulled up her pant leg.

Jon ripped open another antiseptic pad. "How did this happen?"

"I don't know," she whispered. "I woke up from one of those drugged sleeps and my leg was hurting."

He paused, his stomach churning. Jon's gaze captured hers. "The Scarlett Group's drug of choice is Rohypnol."

"The date rape drug?"

"That's what they used on Eli and Brenna." The terrorists who captured him months earlier had used Rohypnol plus a number of other drugs on him, some addicting, some not. He shoved the memories back into the mental box he kept them in to deal with later. What he'd been through didn't matter. The only thing that mattered was Dana's wellbeing.

Dana lapsed into silence as Jon continued his ministrations. Once he cleaned the cut and squeezed antibiotic cream into the wound, he covered it with a bandage. Didn't look like she needed stitches, but a doctor could check it when they returned home. He eased down her pant leg.

He looked up at Dana. Tears streamed down her face. No sounds escaped. The silence wrung his heart. He almost preferred sobs to this stoic display and that said something since a woman's tears normally sent him scrambling to the closest exit. Jon sat with his back propped against a tree, pulled her close, and wrapped his arms around her.

"What if they . . ."

His arms tightened. "We'll deal with it together."

"We?"

"You aren't alone anymore, baby. Never again. I'll walk through every step of this with you. As long as you'll allow me, we're a team."

Dana pressed her head against his shoulder, her face against his neck. "I'm guessing you know about my history with Ross. That's in the past, before you knew me. If Grace's thugs assaulted me, would it . . .?" She lapsed into silence.

"Affect how I feel about you?" he asked.

She nodded.

"Whatever they did shames them, Dana. You aren't to blame for anything they might have done to you. People in this line of work are masters at their trade. Nothing will affect how much you mean to me or the role I hope you'll play in my life from now on."

She sat up to look into his eyes. "What role?" Hope shined from her gaze.

"A permanent one. When you're safe and on U.S. soil, we'll talk. I meant what I said. We'll get through this together. I'll stay beside you all the way."

"She looks good." Doc zipped his pack and handed Brenna the same type of electrolyte mixture as he had her sister..

The knot in Eli's stomach unfurled. "Thanks."

"A doctor should still check her." Doc's gaze bored into Eli's.

He nodded at the unspoken concern. No telling what the Scarlett Group thugs had done to Brenna while she was unconscious. Just the possibility one of them raped her or Dana made Eli itch to disobey Maddox's orders. "Vanderbilt is our first stop once we're home."

Davenport squeezed Eli's shoulder and rejoined his team.

"I don't need a doctor, Eli. You heard the man. I'm fine."

He sank down beside Brenna and brushed a strand of hair from her cheek and mouth. His fingers stroked her velvet skin. "Drink your water, sugar."

"You're ignoring what I said."

Eli snagged the bottle, uncapped it and pressed the drink back into her hand. "The drink will help keep you on your feet. And, yes, I am ignoring you. You were unconscious for a few hours. We have to be sure one of the thugs didn't hurt you while you were unaware."

Brenna's gaze darted toward her sister. "They kept her knocked out for almost two weeks, Eli." Her eyes glittered with unshed tears. "What if they raped her? I don't know if she can get through that trauma again."

Eli wrapped his hand around hers. "Dana's strong or she wouldn't have fought her way back from what Ross did to her. You helped her grow into the woman she is now. She has you and me. More important, she has Jon. He'll have her back. He won't let her give up the fight." He pressed the bottle to her lips. "Drink, baby. We move out soon."

She guzzled half the bottle. "What's the plan?"

"Which one?"

"You have more than one?"

"Always. We planned to use Grace's helicopter to transport you and Dana to our plane if we could beat the storm. The front moved in faster than anticipated. Plan B is to use our IBSs to return to the mainland."

"IBSs?"

"Inflatable boats."

Brenna cringed. "A rubber raft? Dana can't do it, Eli. There has to be another way."

Eli shook his head. "She has no choice, sugar."

"What about the yacht?"

"Too slow. We want off the water as soon as possible and these boats move fast. Taking out the helicopter prevents Grace and company from coming after us in the air if they're stupid enough to take off."

Another click in Eli's ear. "Team 2, move out."

He placed a quick, hard kiss on Brenna's soft lips. "Time to get off this rock, sugar."

Team 2's members readied their weapons and fanned out. Eli helped Brenna to her feet and they followed the team into the jungle. Jon, carrying Dana, brought up the rear with Davenport.

The sound of sporadic gunfire from Team 1 peppered the night. He quartered the area, motioning Brenna behind him to add one more layer of protection.

The first drops of rain pelted leaves dancing in the wind. He pushed the pace a little faster, wanting to get the women to the boats before the ground turned into a slippery mud bath.

An AR-7 spit to his left. Eli spun and shoved Brenna behind a house-sized boulder. With his P226, he tracked movement in the dense shrubbery. One of Grace's goons emerged from the foliage. Eli pulled the trigger. One shot, center mass. The tango fell and didn't move.

Eli keyed his mike. "Team 2, one tango slipped in to your left. He's down."

"Copy."

He glanced at Brenna. Her eyes were wide, lower lip caught between her teeth. "You okay, sugar?" Not the best impression to make on a woman who meant everything to him. If she rejected him for the violence, he guessed he'd have to live with it.

"Get us out of here, Eli."

Not an outright rejection. Maybe he had a chance. "Let's move."

They arrived at the rendezvous point minutes later. "One, Team 2 and packages at B."

"Copy. Phase 2 complete. Davenport and Ritter, remain with packages. Head to transport. The rest of Team 2 to my coordinates. Water approach for Phase 3."

Eli glanced at Jon, who shook his head. He keyed his mike. "One, Jon will have to remain with packages."

"Roger that. St. Claire, you're up. Move out."

The rest of his team crossed the sand toward the IBSs. They loaded gear and made ready to launch into the water.

"What's happening?" Brenna asked.

He cupped her beautiful face between his palms. "I have to go. Stay with Jon and Dana, sugar."

"Where are you going?"

"To plant bombs."

Bombs? Brenna grabbed Eli's wrists. "Why does it have to be you?"

"Team 2 is going to aid Team 1 in pinning down reinforcements and keeping them off my back. It's underwater work and that's my area. Jon could do it, but he's been carrying Dana plus his field pack for a couple hours. And if anything happens to him, we don't stand a chance of saving Dana. She doesn't trust any man but him.

We're prepared to knock her out with a shot, but it could kill her if the drug interacts with whatever Grace used."

Great. How could she choose between Dana and Eli? In truth, she didn't have a choice. The man had been a SEAL and this was his world. The best thing she could do was let him do his job without falling into hysterics. If she and Eli had a shot at a relationship once they returned home, she had to accept the risks he took. If she couldn't deal, Brenna would have to walk away. She sighed. That wasn't happening.

She released his wrists and scowled. "You better not have a scratch on you when you come back."

He grinned. "Yes, ma'am." After a quick kiss, he boarded one of the boats.

"Time to go, baby."

Dana fought the nausea boiling in her stomach as she stared at the remaining rubber boat. Her throat constricted. She couldn't get on one of those things. Big, little, storm, no storm. She couldn't do it. The panic attack surged to full throttle. Breath seized in her lungs.

She backed away from the water's edge, shaking her head. "I can't. I can't do this." Dana's escape halted with her back pressed against Jon's hard chest.

His strong hands turned her to face him. "This is the only way. We have to get you to the mainland."

Scalding tears slid down her face. "Hide me somewhere until the storm passes. You can come back and get me with a plane or another helicopter." Wheezing, she struggled against his tight hold.

"I won't leave you here alone. Remember what I told you? We do this together from now on." Jon brushed her lips with his fingertips, a gentle touch that filled her with such longing. "If you stay, I stay."

"Dana, look at me," Doc said. He waited until her gaze focused on his grim face. "If you and Jon stay here, you both die."

"Shut up, Doc," Jon snapped.

"She's got to face the truth. It's a death wish. We don't know how long the storm will last and you'll be outnumbered. They won't stop until you're dead and Dana's back in their hands."

Dana drew in a shuddering breath. She didn't want Jon to die. He mattered. She couldn't live with his death on her conscience. "No. Take him with you. Make him go."

Doc shook his head. "Not going to happen. You know he won't abandon you. He'd kill any one of us who tried to force him to leave without you by his side or in his arms."

"Dana." Brenna squeezed her arm. "You care about Jon. I know you do. Save him."

"How?" She dragged her gaze to Jon's. "I can't turn off the panic attacks. I tried when Grace brought us here." Her hand touched her bruised cheek. "That's when Ape man slapped me and I fell against a wooden post."

"Knew I should have killed that clown." Jon's thumb brushed over her lower lip, light as the touch of a butterfly's wings. "I'll help you get on the boat, but you must trust me."

"Will it hurt?"

He smiled. "Does a kiss hurt?"

"A kiss?" Dana whispered. "A kiss will help me into a raft in the middle of a storm?"

"Not just any kiss, baby." His eyes glittered. "Mine."

Her gaze drifted to his lips, lips she'd dreamed of for so many months. A kiss she feared would never become a reality after Ape man and Skyscraper captured her. She shivered, her scrubs clinging to her body in a cold, wet cocoon.

Jon drew her into his arms, the heat of his body penetrating her chilled skin. His hands skimmed her arms, cupped her face with gentleness. "Trust me," he whispered as his head dipped closer to hers in slow motion. "I would never hurt you. I'd sooner slit my own throat than cause you one moment of pain."

His lips brushed hers, soft, warm, perfect. Dana sighed at the feather-light touch of his tongue on her bottom lip, asking silent permission to deepen the kiss. She melted into his embrace. In a haze, she registered one of his hands moving to her neck. Pressure. Darkness descended.

Eli adjusted his mask, gave a thumbs up to his diving buddy and they slipped into the ocean. Within two minutes, he and Trent St. Claire rounded the point and entered a small harbor where the yacht and two smaller speed boats were anchored. Trent, the diver from Team 1, surged ahead with strong kicks.

Using hand motions to communicate, they attached the bombs on the hulls of the two speed boats first. The faster crafts represented the biggest threat to this phase of their rescue mission. The boats could overtake them in a matter of minutes. Even if something went wrong and they couldn't take out the yacht, the chance of it running down their IBS was nil. The lumbering vessel had the grace and dexterity of a buffalo.

When the last charge was set in place on the first boat, Eli and Trent repeated the process on the second, adhering explosives to the craft's hull in two places. Probably overkill, but he preferred that to a nasty surprise on the open ocean. Grace and her minions would have to wait for the storm to pass before receiving more transport off the island. With luck, the explosions would take out some of the enemy as well. They had rough estimates of the number of enemy combatants. On their home turf, Grace's minions held the advantage. He'd still bet on Fortress. They were well trained, well armed, and ticked off. None of them liked thugs who preyed on women and children.

Minutes later, Team 2 hauled Eli and Trent from the water into the IBS. Eli removed his diving gear and donned his communications headset. "One, Phase 3 complete."

"Copy. Eyes on target?"

He raised his night-vision binoculars and adjusted to bring the boats into focus. "Affirmative." Scanning the area, Eli noticed an empty slip. An extra, he hoped, rather than an indication of a missing boat.

"Hold position. Team 1, fall back."

Eli and his team waited, watching the boats and surrounding area. Finally, Team 1 accounted for and in position, Maddox's voice came through the headset.

"This is One. Execute Phase 4."

"Roger that. Ten seconds." He counted down and flipped the remote switch. The night sky lit up. A surge of satisfaction washed through him. Unless they had missed some other mode of transport, Grace and her people were stranded.

"Teams 1 and 2 to transport."

Rain fell in blinding sheets. Gusting wind churned the ocean surface into a rough ride for the Zoo Crew. They beached the boats, deflated and loaded them into the paneled truck hidden in the tree line. Men and equipment on board, Thomas, Team 1's sniper, drove toward the waiting plane.

Maddox slapped Eli's shoulder. "Nice fireworks."

"Anything from Jon?"

"The women are safely on board the plane. Dana's still out."

His head jerked toward his boss. "Doc had to give her the shot?"

"Nope. Jon took care of Dana himself."

Eli leaned his head against an inside wall, resting while he could. Adrenaline had kept him moving while searching for and retrieving Brenna and her sister. The Rohypnol still lingered in his system, evidenced by the unnatural fatigue slowing him down. One more push and he could sleep on the return trip home, his girl next to him, safe. Ten minutes to the plane, then home, provided nothing delayed their departure. In this province with unfriendly Mexican officials, he took nothing for granted.

Seated next to Eli, Maddox yanked his cell phone from his holder and examined the flashing display. Eli's gut tightened into a knot. The team's emergency alert flashed on the screen, the code sent from the plane's pilot. Brenna.

Maddox keyed his mike. "Thomas, emergency signal from the pilot. Kill the lights. Stop a couple minutes out. We'll go in on foot."

Eli and the rest of the crew geared up and, as soon as the truck stopped, exited in total silence. Maddox signaled the scouts from both teams to do reconnaissance. Within minutes, the two returned.

"Six men armed with AR-7s surrounding the plane. No visual of the inside, sir," King reported.

"Any chance we can take the men down one at a time?"

"No, sir. There are three on each side, facing away from the plane with a well-lit tarmac. We don't stand a chance of approaching either side without detection."

Maddox rubbed his jaw. "We need to know how many are inside the plane." He keyed his mike. "Joe, activate Jon's mike. We need to hear what's happening. If Jon's in the loop, he can help execute a takedown of the tangos."

If he was still alive. A moment later, Brenna's voice filled Eli's ear.

CHAPTER NINETEEN

"What do you want, Grace?" Brenna stood and eyed the four men pointing their big guns at her, Jon and a couple men from his team along with Ortiz and his wife, pressed tight against her husband's back. Doc knelt beside Ritter, working feverishly to stem blood flowing from the fallen man's shoulder.

"You, dead, along with your trouble-making sister." A look of pure hatred formed on Grace's face. "Surrender and maybe I'll let your rescuers live."

Right. Knowing they would track Grace and her goon squad again? Not likely that Grace would keep her word.

Jon shifted beside her. Brenna glanced at him, noting he'd moved into a better position to protect Dana. Oh, yeah, she was developing a serious soft spot for this handsome SEAL. Dana deserved a man that crazy about her. Now, all they had to do was survive so she could enjoy dating and maybe a lifetime with him.

All the weapons tracked his movement with the exception of the one covering Doc. "Move again and you die." Grace scowled at Dana's sleeping form. "What is wrong with her?"

"Why don't you ask your thugs how much Rohypnol and other drugs they pumped into her body?" Jon countered. "Good help isn't cheap and I'm betting you didn't pay a dime more than you had to."

Ross the Rat laughed. "Don't shoot him yet, love. I think he's sweet on Dana. Maybe he should watch while we play with her. We can sell the pair of them to our friend. Might be interesting for him to break them down and kill them."

"It's not smart to bait a tiger, Ross." The guns pointed in Brenna's direction sent trickles of sweat cascading down her back. Once Grace and Ross were in jail, Eli had another job to do—teaching her how to handle a gun. Nothing as large as those. Maybe a nice pink handgun. "Of course, no one could accuse you of being smart. After all, you hooked up with a loser."

Grace backhanded her, throwing Brenna into Jon's side. Jon set her upright, his jaw clenched. Brenna wiped blood from the side of her mouth. "Feel better now?"

Her gaze raked over Brenna. "Perhaps I won't let Eduardo kill you, after all. A feisty American will bring more money. After he finishes with you, I'll put you on the auction block, sell you to the highest bidder." A smirk crossed her face. "If you survive Eduardo's attention, that is. I'll ask him to keep your face untouched. Your body is his to do with as he pleases."

Brenna breathed away nausea at the idea of Eduardo touching her. "So this is about punishing me and Dana for interfering in your business? Why do you care about us? Your business doesn't stay in one place for long anyway and you can relocate under a new identity. Walk away, Grace."

"She's right," Jon said. "If you kill us, my friends will hunt you down and destroy you within the week."

"For some kind of hotshot private eye, you really are stupid. Brenna and Dana were the bait, Smith. Sure, Dana was in the wrong place at the wrong time, nosing into things that weren't her business. But you and Eli are the ones I'm after. You two and your pit bull friend. Once he got his teeth into that girl's disappearance, he wouldn't let go."

"I don't understand," Brenna said. "All Eli and Jon did was look for Dana. I'm the one who begged them to find her."

"You killed Joe Baker, didn't you?" Jon said.

"He should have dropped the investigation. Nobody cared about a teen hooker."

Was she kidding? How heartless could the woman be? "She was somebody's daughter, Grace." Brenna's hands curled into fists. "Where is she now?"

"Somewhere in the Middle East, a place you'll never find her." An ugly smile settled on her lips. "Perhaps you would like to join her. Her owner enjoys sharing his toys, especially when he can watch."

Owner? Brenna's cheeks burned. What kind of people did Grace do business with?

Jon moved forward a half step, easing Brenna behind him. "Look, leave Brenna and Dana here in the plane. You wanted me. I'll go with you right now."

"And what about Eli? I want him as well."

"If you have me, he'll come. Ever try to break a SEAL, Grace? I bet you can't do it."

"Jon, no," Brenna whispered. Was he crazy? If Grace killed him, it would break Dana's heart. And Eli's. He wouldn't rest until he freed his friend or avenged his death. "Don't do this."

He motioned her to silence. "Do we have a deal? You'll leave the women and take me?"

Grace tilted her head, her gaze taking in Jon's hard, muscular body. "A SEAL. You won't fight or try to escape. If you refuse to submit to anything, you die. Same goes for your partner. Might be fun to break the two of you. Our methods are quite effective, perfected over many years. We always succeed." An unholy gleam flickered in her eyes. "If you fight me, I will go after Dana first. Remember that while you're in my tender care, Smith."

Ross straightened from the wall, his eyes narrowed. "I don't like this. He's up to something. Navy SEALs can't be broken, Grace. And two of them together? This is some sort of trap."

Brenna held her breath. The thought had already occurred to her, but Jon showed no reaction to Ross's suspicions. His gaze remained focused on Grace. Brenna didn't doubt he would submit to everything Grace demanded to save Dana. She prayed the rest of his team was close because if Grace disappeared with Jon, it might take days to locate him, days which he might not have based on Grace's reaction to his offer.

"You up to the challenge of taking down a SEAL, Grace?" Jon asked, voice soft. "Or is Harrison the dominant in the Scarlett Group?"

Temper stained her cheeks. "Scarlett is mine." She flicked a glance at two of her goons. "Take him."

"Grace," Ross protested. "You promised me Dana."

"I'll give you a new toy to play with." Grace licked her lips as her men bound Jon's hands. "This one is mine."

Brenna opened her mouth to protest, to stall, anything but let Grace take Jon off the plane. A glare from Jon closed her mouth. She watched, raging inside at her helplessness, as Grace, Ross and the four goons left the plane with Jon.

After steps no longer sounded on the stairs, Doc yanked a gun from his ankle holster. "Get on the floor." He dove for the floor himself and crawled to the open doorway. Ritter drew his own sidearm, held it steady, weapon aimed at the opening. Ortiz motioned his wife to the floor, pulled out a gun and crawled to the doorway beside Doc.

Brenna rolled Dana from the seat to the floor and covered her sister's body with her own. Dana moaned and struggled to get free, her movements feeble. Her eyes sprang open. "Where's Jon?" she asked.

"Shh," Brenna whispered. "Jon's okay. He left for a minute. He'll be back soon." And prayed she had spoken the truth.

Flush on the wet tarmac, Eli sighted the M4 on his target. The cretin to Jon's right prodded him with the barrel of his rifle. Jon made a show of stumbling, drawing the attention of all the goons.

"Wait for my signal," Maddox murmured over the comm system. "We want those yahoos away from the plane. Wouldn't do for a bullet to rip through the cabin."

Eli's finger stroked the trigger. A few more feet.

Over the whipping wind, Grace's voice carried to Zoo Crew. "Let's go. I have what I want for now. The other one will be mine soon as well. And then I will make them pay."

Oh, yeah. One of the snipers had a bullet with her name on it. The tangos surrounding the Crew's plane hurried to join Grace and company at the SUVs.

Maddox's voice filtered through Eli's ear piece. "Go."

In seconds, shots barked into the night from M4s. Tangos dropped to the tarmac, some moaning in pain, others silent. At Maddox's order, Eli and his teammates raced to secure the enemy's weapons. Eli checked pulses, didn't shed any tears when he found none on Grace or Harrison. Unsheathing his Ka-Bar, he sliced through the plastic ties which bound Jon's hands.

A hard hand came down on his shoulder. Maddox squeezed. "We've got it covered out here. You and Jon check on the women."

"Yes, sir." Eli ran up the plane steps and into the cabin.

"Eli." Brenna leaped to her feet and threw herself into his embrace.

"You okay, sugar?" He rocked her, savoring the freedom to hold her in his arms. "Show me your beautiful face, sweetheart." Behind Brenna, Jon sank to the floor beside a weeping Dana and gathered her in his arms. He said nothing, simply rocked her with gentle motion.

Brenna pulled back enough for Eli to get a good look at her swollen mouth. "Doc will check it once we get this bird off the ground. We'll have company from the law before long."

"Hey, what about me?" Ritter complained. "I was shot."

Eli spared him a glance. "Aw, it's just a scratch. Jarheads are wimps."

"Scratch?" Outrage sharpened Ritter's tone. "Bullet went all the way through my shoulder, you stupid frogman."

"Want me to patch you up? I rock at field stitching."

Another scowl from Ritter. "Stay away from me, you butcher. I've got a scar from the last job you did on me."

Brenna grinned. "Sounds like you have a tendency for injuries. Maybe you should think about a safer line of work."

"No can do, babe. I'm an adrenaline junkie. Sitting behind a desk all day would kill me quicker than Eli the Butcher."

Eli slanted a pointed look in Ritter's direction. "Watch it, jarhead. This one is mine."

"Put a lid on it, boys." Maddox strode into the cabin, followed by the rest of the men. "You and your wife okay, Ortiz? Good. Everybody strap in. We need to get off the ground right now. The diversion we arranged for the local law has run its course."

Eli grabbed Brenna's hand. "This way, sugar. You're not going to be more than a couple feet from me for the next 50 years or so."

CHAPTER TWENTY

"Don't, baby." Jon brushed the tears from Dana's cheeks. "You're killing me with the tears. I can't take it, sweetheart."

The panic in his eyes set off a spark of humor. She wouldn't have believed a battle-tough Navy SEAL could panic at a woman's tears if she hadn't witnessed it. "You let her take you. She could have killed you."

"She didn't. It's done."

"Why, Jon? Why didn't you fight? Were there too many?"

He snorted. "If they had been special forces, maybe. Doubt it, though. I couldn't chance you, Brenna, or Ortiz's wife being shot."

"So you handed yourself over to be tortured."

"Seemed the best way to get Grace off the plane."

"And if your friends hadn't been close, you would have let her . . ." She shuddered.

"Small price to pay for your freedom."

"Not to me." Dana frowned and thumped his chest with her fist. "You scared me. Don't let it happen again."

"I'm sorry, baby. I'll try to remember that."

She narrowed her eyes at the dry wit evident in his tone.

The plane leveled out and the cabin lights dimmed. Some of Jon's teammates, scattered in small groups, talked among themselves. Others reclined their seats and settled in to sleep on the ride home. Her sister, sitting beside Eli and wrapped in his arms, was already asleep. A spear of envy pricked her heart. Would she ever get a chance like that with Jon?

Dana turned and studied his beloved features. Fatigue shadowed his gaze, lined his face. "You need to rest."

"So do you."

Her gaze dropped from his. "Maybe later." Dana wrapped her trembling hand around the armrest. She was so tired, but sleeping in a confined space with all these people close sent an icy shower through her body. What if she woke up as she did many nights? Brenna would understand. A plane full of security people might think she was looney.

Jon cupped her face and turned her toward him. "What's wrong? If being this close to me while you sleep makes you uncomfortable, I'll move." A wry smile crossed his mouth. "Got to admit I don't want to, but if that's what you need, I'll do it."

"It's not you." Embarrassment burned her cheeks. Why couldn't she be normal? Yet another reason to regret Ross's role in her life. No more. Jon had told her Grace and Ross would never bother her again. Maybe it made her a bad person, but she didn't regret their deaths because she knew they couldn't hurt anyone else again. "Since they took me, most of the time I wake up screaming. They kept me in a room with no light or windows. Sometimes I was alone. Other times, Ape man was there. I never knew what I would face when I woke."

He leaned forward and brushed a soft kiss to her mouth. "Sounds like PTSD. It's nothing to be ashamed of,

Dana. Even the most hardened vets struggle with the syndrome."

"Including you?"

"Can't tell you how many nights I've woken myself up screaming." He shrugged. "It's why I live in a house instead of an apartment. You need to sleep, baby. You've been living on adrenaline and sheer grit for two weeks. It's time to let go. I'm here. No one will touch you."

"And if I start screaming?"

"I'll wake you. Might take a minute to convince the Zoo Crew I'm not the cause of the screams. So, how are we doing this, Dana? Do I stay or move?"

She pressed a kiss to the center of his palm. "Stay. Hold me," she whispered.

A smile lit his features. "You don't know how long I've wanted to hear those words from your lips. I would love to hold you, sweetheart."

Jon reclined their seats and dragged a light blanket from under his seat to cover them. Dana fell asleep with her ear resting over Jon's heart, surrounded by his arms and scent.

Hours later, she woke when the plane's landing gear locked into place and the aircraft bumped along the landing strip. Jon's arms tightened around her for a moment.

"Sleep well, baby?"

Heat flooded her cheeks at the sweet endearment. She nodded. "Where are we?"

"Home. As soon as we grab our gear, Eli and I are taking you and Brenna to Vanderbilt to be checked out by the doctors."

Dana made a face. More doctors. She hated hospitals. The smells, the food, the perpetually cheerful medical personnel all brought back painful memories, ones she'd rather forget. "I just want to go home." She buried her face in Jon's neck.

"I know. We need to make sure you're okay. You'll be able to handle anything they discover if you know the truth. It's the unknown that gets most people. You are so strong, Dana. You already beat what Harrison put you through once. If you've been assaulted again, we need to know. You have to be treated." He raised her up to look into her face. "Do you understand what I'm saying? We can't take chances with your health. No matter what the doctors tell you, you'll deal. You're not alone this time. We're in this together."

A shaky laugh escaped. "I don't know if I'm as strong as you think."

"I do. If you falter, reach for me. I'll be there beside you."

Jon sounded so confident, she believed him. Until the male doctor walked into the emergency room and approached her. The panic attack struck without warning. Between one heartbeat and the next, her breaths became labored, cold sweat broke out over her body, and her heart raced.

"Ms. Cole?" The doctor appeared startled.

Jon. She needed Jon. She couldn't do this, no matter how strong he believed her to be. She didn't feel safe with this man.

Dana slid off the examination table and raced for the door, yanked it open and ran. The doctor's protests rang in her ears. At the end of the long hallway, Jon and Eli both turned. In seconds, Jon reached her side and gathered her close.

"Talk to me."

She struggled to drag enough air into her lungs to talk. Air. She needed air. "Can't . . . do . . . this."

Jon turned so her back was pressed against the corridor wall. "Look at me, Dana. No one but me." He cupped her face with his palms, thumbs stroking her cheeks. "Breathe with me. Match my rhythm. In. Out. In. Good, baby. Again. Focus on me and breathe."

Dana didn't know how much time passed before she was able to grab a full breath and her heart rate settled to almost normal. "Jon."

"Tell me."

"I don't want him to touch me."

Jon stiffened, muscles tightening under her hands. "Who?"

"The doctor."

He turned his head to the left, found the doctor standing a few feet away, waiting. "I'll take care of it. Stay here." He strode to the doctor, had a short conversation, and returned to pull her into his arms once again. "All set. He's going to send in another doctor, a woman this time."

Dana sagged against him. "Thank you. I'm sorry. He walked into the room and I went into a panic attack with no warning."

He pressed a soft kiss to her lips. "Understandable. Can you walk back to the room or do you want me to carry you?"

"My legs work." Sort of. "Will you stay with me?" She made her feet move toward the examination room. With her legs shaking so much, the corridor seemed ten miles long. Too embarrassing to collapse on the floor at this tough man's feet. Enough already. She raised her chin and stiffened her spine. She could conquer a little walk down a safe hallway. Maybe.

"Planned on it. After the right doctor shows, I'll step into the hall. I'll wait right outside your door. If you need me, just call out. Okay?"

She nodded and led the way into the room. Once again, she was perched on the table when the door opened. This time, the white coat draped an older woman, one with twinkling eyes and a ready smile.

"Ms. Cole? I'm Dr. Anderson. I understand you've had a rough time the last several days."

Jon turned to face her, eyebrow raised.

She smiled, nodded, and shooed him out the door. He gave her a quick kiss and left the room, pulling the door closed behind him.

Dr. Anderson pulled up a stool and sat. "That, my dear, is one very handsome man. Yours, I take it?"

"I hope so. It's kind of new."

"Looks to me like the feelings are mutual. Now, why don't you tell me what's been happening with you?"

The door to the examination room opened. Jon straightened away from the wall to face Dr. Anderson.

"Mr. Smith, would you step in the room, please? Ms. Cole wanted you present when I gave her my findings."

He swallowed hard, pushed past her, and crossed the room to Dana's side. He studied her pale face. Jon cupped her cheek with his hand and dropped a gentle kiss on her trembling lips. He threaded his fingers through hers. "No matter what, we'll deal with it together."

A small smile curved her mouth.

He turned toward the doctor. "How is she, Doc?"

"In remarkable shape considering what she endured. I'm going to admit her overnight for observation and to administer fluids. Ms. Cole is a little dehydrated, has cuts and scrapes. I'm prescribing a round of antibiotics as a precautionary measure since she doesn't know how long those cuts were left untreated in a tropical location. I'm happy to say I found no evidence of sexual assault."

A surge of relief swept Jon's body. Thank God Dana didn't have to deal with the aftermath of another rape.

"If all goes well, I expect Ms. Cole to be discharged tomorrow afternoon."

"Excellent." Jon grinned. "Thank you, Dr. Anderson."

She switched her attention to Dana. "Now, young lady, I expect you to rest tonight. If you can't sleep, I'll leave instructions for the night nurse to administer a light sedative in your IV. If your young man stays with you, I suspect you won't need it."

"Thank you," Dana whispered.

"Be honest with the nursing staff. If you need something, tell them. I'm sure you want out of here soon as possible."

"Yes, ma'am."

"One of the orderlies will be here soon with a wheelchair to transport you to your room. If you have any further medical problems, contact your general practitioner." With a smile, she left the room.

Jon squeezed Dana's hand, drawing her gaze to his face. "You okay?"

She nodded, one tear after another slipping down her face. "I was so scared."

Those tears killed him. He couldn't tolerate his mother's tears either. Guess that made him an official card-carrying wuss.

"Are you going home soon?"

"What do you think?"

Her face flushed. "You're exhausted and probably want to go home and sleep in your own bed."

"Yes."

She nodded, her gaze dropping to the floor, but not before he caught the look of disappointment in her eyes. "I understand. It's okay. I'll be fine."

"Yes, you will be fine because I'm staying to make sure you are."

Her head jerked up. "You're staying?"

"Are you booting me out?"

"I don't have the right to ask you to stay."

He leaned close and kissed her until they both were short of breath. "You have the right, baby. I know where I want this relationship to go, but whether we get there is up to you."

"Where?"

"Home. Family. White picket fence. Two dogs." He smiled. "Everything. When you're ready."

More tears. Dismayed, Jon swiped at the waterworks. Had he misread her feelings? Did she not want the same thing? Maybe she did, but not with him. That would kill him.

"I want that, too."

His eyebrows shot up even as his heart leaped, joy exploding inside. "Then why all the tears?"

"I want those things, but I'm afraid."

"Of?"

She blushed and dropped her gaze to his chest.

"Ah. Sex."

Dana nodded.

He nudged her chin up, waited until she looked into his eyes. "I love you, Dana. Because I love you, I'll wait as long as it takes for you to be comfortable with that part of marriage. Make no mistake, I want to marry you the minute you give me the green light to put a wedding band on your finger. Tomorrow wouldn't be too soon for me. The rest will come with time. I'm in no hurry. We have the rest of our lives." He grinned. "I just want my rings on your finger to warn off all my teammates and any other men who might try to steal you from me."

"I love you, Jon Smith."

Satisfaction swelled in his gut. "Excellent. First stop when you're sprung from this joint is a jewelry store. After that, we'll talk about this fabulous job opening at Wolfe Investigations. There are two partners. One's a hopeless hard case. The other thinks he's a comedian and God's gift to women. Interested?"

"Depends."

"On?"

"Will I be required to kiss the comedian?"

Jon scowled. "Not if he wants to live."

Dana laughed. "Deal. I've always had a soft spot for hard cases anyway."

Brenna woke with a gasp and lurched upward. Beneath her, the bed crackled. Her gaze darted around the darkened interior. Voices murmured outside the door. Where was she? A rustle of clothes clued her in to someone else's presence nearby.

"You're safe, sugar." A familiar masculine form crawled onto the bed beside her and tugged her into his arms. His sleep-roughened voice sent a curl of warmth rising through her body.

A woman could definitely get used to waking up to that growling voice in her ear every morning. Brenna relaxed against his chest and kissed him. "Thank you for saving my sister," she whispered.

"Uh, I saved you as well. Do I get a reward for that?"

She shared another kiss.

"I took out Harrison," Eli murmured.

Brenna pressed him backward onto her hospital pillow. His hands cupped her face as the kiss changed from soft and sweet to blistering hot. Lack of air forced her lips from his.

"Have mercy, sugar. If a nurse catches me, she'll toss me out on my backside."

She chuckled. "What time is it?"

"Just after four o'clock in the morning."

She caught her breath. "Did you go home?"

"You're kidding, right? I just got you back. No way am I leaving you."

"Sweetheart, you have to get some sleep. The doctor said you needed to rest, that your body was still flushing that drug out of your system."

Eli said nothing for a moment. "You called me 'sweetheart.'"

"I did?"

"Did you mean it? Cause here's the thing, sugar. You turned my world upside down. I've never been so scared in my life as when I realized Scarlett Group had taken you. I was afraid I wouldn't have the chance to tell you how much I love you."

"Oh, Eli." Tears filled her eyes. Her handsome Navy SEAL loved her enough that he was laying his heart on the line without having a clue she felt the same way about him.. An act of courage from the man staring at her with a wary gaze.

"We haven't known each other long. If it's too soon for you to know how you feel about me, I'll wait. Just know you own my heart, Brenna. I want to marry you and someday watch you rock my children."

She laid her hand over his mouth, stemming the tidal wave of words. "Eli, you don't have to wait."

"I don't?"

"I'm a romance writer, my love. Happy endings are my stock in trade. Without you in my life, I wouldn't have a happy ending because I love you, too, Eli. And, yes, I will marry you."

"Soon?"

"The sooner, the better."

A few kisses later, Brenna curled against Eli's side. "How's Dana?"

He pressed a kiss to her forehead. "She's fine, sugar. Jon's with her. In fact, I'd say she's better than fine. It seems my business partner finally wised up and asked Dana to marry him and offered her a job at Wolfe Investigations."

"Are you serious?"

"Yes, ma'am. Jon is planning a trip to a jewelry store as soon as she's released. Seems some members of the

Fortress team have designs on his woman. To keep from ending up in jail for murder, he's buying the biggest diamond he can find."

"Oh, Eli. I couldn't have asked for a better man for my sister. She loves him so much."

"Yeah, I got that. Feeling's mutual." He stopped, sighed. "You should be released this morning. You up to a drive to Missouri?"

Brenna studied his face in the dim morning light. The shadows dimming the sparkle in his eyes told her all she needed to know about the trip. Eli needed to tell Joe Baker's widow about Grace and the Scarlett Group. "We need to tell Dana first and stop at a big box store."

"A big box store?"

She smiled. "I need a new laptop. I have a book to write so I can go on my honeymoon."

"Write fast, sugar. Write fast."

ABOUT THE AUTHOR

Rebecca Deel is a preacher's kid with a black belt in karate. She teaches business classes at a private four-year college in Nashville, Tennessee. She plays the piano at church, writes freelance articles, and runs interference for the family Westies. She's been married to her amazing husband for more than 20 years and is the proud mom of two grown sons. She delivers monthly devotions to the women's group at her church and conducts seminars in personal safety, money management, and writing. Her articles have been published in *ONE Magazine*, *Contact*, and *Co-Laborer*, and she was profiled in the June 2010 Williamson edition of *Nashville Christian Family* magazine. Rebecca completed her Doctor of Arts degree in Economics and wears her favorite Dallas Cowboys sweatshirt when life turns ugly.

For more information on Rebecca . . .
Sign up for Rebecca's newsletter: http://eepurl.com/_B6w9
Visit Rebecca's website: www.rebeccadeelbooks.com

Made in the USA
Columbia, SC
28 October 2020

23621136R00176